Dear Diary,

Every day it seems t[...]*hospital grows larger. S*[...]*when I come up to the child care centre just to avoid the crush and any prying questions about our little mystery baby. The police are no closer to knowing who her parents are, but at least the little one is safe and loved. Shana brings her into Round the Clock almost every day, and even the other children make such a fuss over her.*

I ran into Seth Nannery today. What a job he has. His first few weeks as the head of hospital PR, and this disaster lands in his lap. Poor Seth. He's such a great guy, but he does look harried these days. And it seems the press is taking a little too much interest in Seth's personal life, although I can't say I blame them.

It struck me that something was up when I saw him with Jill Jamison the other day. Turns out JJ, as the public knows the famous model, and Seth were friends back in their university days. The way they were looking at each other, I'd bet my next pay cheque those two were a lot more than friends.

Staff at the hospital and Round the Clock adore Jill—she's been so generous to all of us. And we do our best to respect her privacy and keep the fact that she has a son a secret from those bloodthirsty newshounds.

But if my hunch is right and an old romance is heating up between her and Seth, Jill will need more than her usual stash of crazy wigs and oversize shades to keep it a secret.

Till tomorrow,

Alexandra

LESLIE KELLY

is a stay-at-home mother of three who says she started
writing as a creative outlet after one too many games of
Snakes and Ladders. Since the publication of her first
book in 1999, she's gained a reputation for writing hot
and funny books.

Forrester Square

LEGACIES . LIES . LOVE .

LESLIE KELLY
THE ONE THAT GOT AWAY

SILHOUETTE®

*First published in Great Britain 2005
Silhouette Books, Eton House, 18-24 Paradise Road,
Richmond, Surrey TW9 1SR*

© Harlequin Books S.A. 2003

*Special thanks and acknowledgement are given to Leslie Kelly for
her contribution to the FORRESTER SQUARE series.*

ISBN 0 373 61282 6

142-0205

*Printed and bound in Spain
by Litografia Rosés S.A., Barcelona*

Dear Reader,

I've always enjoyed working on connected books with other authors. So when I was offered the chance to participate in this special continuity project I was thrilled. The idea of creating one piece of a large, sixteen-book story appealed to me, a jigsaw puzzle lover. And the chance to work with some very talented authors was the icing on the cake.

I was so fortunate to get to write exactly the kind of story I most enjoy—snappy, sexy, playful and a little bit naughty. Seth is my kind of sexy, gamma guy hero. He was also my first hero who's been struck by that ticking biological clock, and I loved turning this sexy PR guru into father material. As for Jill, well, who wouldn't want to create a slightly goofy supermodel heroine, surrounded by hunky male nurses, a mischievous son and a big, drooly dog?

Their story was lots of fun. I hope you agree, and I hope you find *The One That Got Away* a worthy addition to the exciting and unique FORRESTER SQUARE continuity series.

Happy reading,

Leslie Kelly

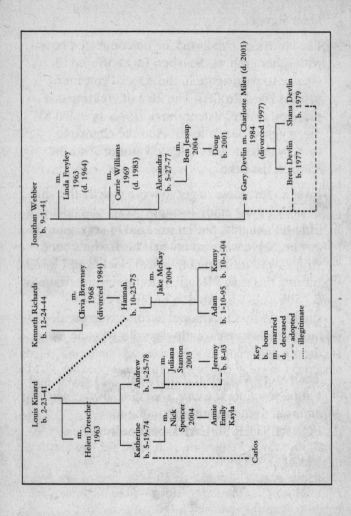

PROLOGUE

October, 1993

SEX, JILL JAMISON decided one perfect autumn afternoon, had definitely been worth the wait.

Curling closer to Seth Nannery, the guy who'd stolen her heart with his sexy, dimpled grin two years ago in freshman lit, and her virginity a few minutes ago in her narrow dorm room bed, she finally understood what all the fuss was about. Making love for the first time was the best birthday present she'd ever get.

"You okay, birthday girl?" He trailed his fingers across her bare back in a gentle, deliberate caress.

Nodding, she nibbled the smooth skin of his neck, remembering how he'd felt on top of her just moments before. His lean young body, the sweet way he'd kissed her, his tenderness in being so very careful not to hurt her, and the way he'd said her name over and over again at the end.

"I've *never* had a better day. Even with everything else we've done." And they'd done a lot since they'd started dating, both hungry for each other but wanting to wait to go all the way. "I still wasn't prepared for how incredible this would be."

She meant it. Today had seen the fruition of two dreams Jill had long fantasized about. First—most important—making love with the man she loved. And she did love Seth. Sure, they were young. She knew, however, this was not a crush, not infatuation or simple hormonal lust. Seth wasn't a guy she'd wanted to sleep with. He was a man she wanted to spend her whole life with.

He felt the same way. They'd often talked about what they'd do after graduation. Marriage, kids, a house in the country. Of course, those plans might have to be delayed because of her news. Seth would understand. He'd see the chance she was being offered and support her wholeheartedly.

His encouragement and old-fashioned dreams were two of the things she liked best about him. Plus his charm. His gorgeous, long-lashed green eyes. His thick, sandy brown hair, which lightened to burnished gold in the summertime. His killer sense of humor. And oh…that smile.

"Is there anything else I can do to make your twentieth birthday your best yet?" He tipped her chin up with his index finger and stared at her with the kind of emotion she'd never seen in any other man's eyes.

Yep. That was love. He adored her as she did him. The time had come to tell Seth about the letter she'd received today. "I heard something amazing."

"I don't think I've ever heard anything more amazing than the way you were crying out twenty minutes ago," he said with a wicked laugh. "Good thing this floor's deserted or we'd have had somebody breaking down the door for sure."

She playfully punched his arm. "I'm talking about something else. Do you remember the flyer on campus about a company looking for a fresh-faced college girl to be the spokesperson for a new line of skin care products?"

As he nodded, his smile faltered. Jill noticed, but pushed on. "I went to the interview a few weeks ago."

"I thought you weren't even considering it," he said. "I thought you said school was too important, and the company wanted someone who could take a few years off."

She bit her lip. "I changed my mind. I didn't say anything, because I thought nothing would come of it."

He pulled his arm out from under her and sat up in the bed. The late afternoon sunlight slanting in through the blinds on the window cast lines and shadows on his smooth chest and his handsome, youthful face. His smile remained conspicuously absent. "Tell me what happened."

Things weren't going the way she'd planned, but she couldn't back off. Sitting, she tugged the bedsheet up and tucked it under her arms. "I got a letter from them offering me the job. They want me to be the face of Mother Nature skin care products. I'll be their model and spokesperson for three years."

Seth didn't say a word. He just kept watching her.

"Seth, what's wrong? You know how much I've dreamed of this." True. Since she was a pretty little girl growing up in an Iowa town with four younger brothers, she'd been told she should try modeling. When she'd realized she would probably remain a five-ten, stick-thin blonde for life, she figured it was at least worth a shot. Though, at that point, she would have traded modeling dreams for a decent-size chest and some real hips.

"It's a new Seattle company nobody's heard of. But it's a start. I told you how much I used to dream of being a famous, world-traveling model, didn't I?"

"I thought you'd outgrow that dream," he said quietly, sounding deeply disturbed. He obviously saw her dismay. "Not that you couldn't do it. But you weren't out there trying to make it happen, trying to find an agent or anything. You're so gentle, not at all cutthroat. I figured it was a pipe dream."

She sighed. "Maybe deep down I thought it was, too. Which is why I was as surprised as anyone when the offer came. But you see, don't you, that I have to do this?"

Seth got out of the bed and reached for his jeans. He

looked vulnerable for a moment, not a boy, but not fully a man yet, his face showing his mixed feelings. And his hurt.

"Seth, what are you thinking?"

He snapped his jeans and reached for his shirt. "I'm thinking this isn't what we planned. You dropping out of college, being gone most of the time. What does that do for our wedding right after graduation? Our first baby as soon as I finish grad school?"

"It doesn't change anything," she insisted. "It only… pushes things back a little."

He donned his shirt, then looked for his shoes, which had gone flying in their frenzy to undress when she'd told him she wanted to make love. "A little? It could be years."

"Maybe a few. I can do this, then come back and finish school. Then we get married and start a family. Later."

He found one shoe, then knelt down and crawled under her cluttered desk. Digging through mountains of books, papers and what looked like a chemistry project but had once actually been a pizza box, he finally found the other. "Like how much later?"

"Five or six years," she admitted softly.

He sat up, gaping at her. "Five or six years till marriage? What does that mean for our first baby?"

Seth's love of kids and family, as exhibited by his delight in her siblings during their visit to Iowa last year, had been one of the things she loved most about him. Right now, though, she wished he'd think more like every other guy she knew here at Washington State…more interested in parties and homecoming than weddings and diapers. Still, something in his life made family deeply important to him. She'd always known it, so she couldn't hold it against him now. "Look, Seth. I'm only twenty. Is it so bad if I want to wait ten years to start having kids?"

He froze. "Ten years? That's forever—half our lifetime!"

Though she'd first been concerned, Jill found herself growing angry. "Get real, thirty is nothing for a woman to start a family." Even knowing she wasn't being entirely fair, she continued. "What's wrong with me taking a shot at doing something *I've* dreamed about, instead of just what *you* want?"

His look of dismay made her regret the words. They hung there between them, unable to be taken back. "I thought it was what we both wanted," he whispered. "I never thought you'd be the type to put dreams of being famous ahead of your dreams of family." Lowering his head, he tugged on his shoes.

"I'm sorry, I did *not* mean that. I do want everything we've talked about. But I want this, too. I want both."

He finally stood, meeting her gaze directly. "You can't have both, Jill. Not without one thing suffering. Believe me, I know what I'm talking about." He cleared his throat. "I won't take second place with the woman I thought loved me. And I don't ever want my children to come second to any job…mine or their mother's. Trust me on this. With a mother working as an international model, they *would* be made to feel second place." He looked away and she saw him gulp. "So I guess you need to decide what it is you want more. The job. Or me and the future we've been planning."

An ultimatum? He was giving her an ultimatum? She could hardly believe it. Seth, the nicest, most wonderful, romantic, thoughtful guy she'd ever known, had gone caveman. She blinked rapidly as tears rose in her eyes. "Don't do this. Please. Don't make me think you don't care about my dreams. If you ask this of me, then you obviously can't love me like I thought you did."

She saw a suspicious sheen of moisture in those green eyes of his. But he wouldn't relent. "If you leave, then you can't love me as much as I thought you did, either."

Feeling her future slipping through her fingers, no matter which way she chose, she finally turned to look at the wall. ''Well, I guess we were both mistaken, then.''

He waited, not yet grasping what she meant. She made it very clear, her own heart breaking with two words.

''Goodbye, Seth.''

CHAPTER ONE

October, 2004

STARING OUT the window of his office at Seattle Memorial Hospital, Seth Nannery couldn't decide which was worse: the media vans circling the parking lot below like sharks around a chum line, or the face of the woman who haunted his dreams smiling down at him from the billboard across the street.

"That face." He shook his head in disbelief, as he had the first time he'd seen his new office, for his new job, less than three weeks ago. Of all the sights to greet him every day at work, it had to be one that made his gut tighten and his heart ache.

Keeping his gaze from returning to the sign proved physically impossible. "Natural Girls give thanks to Mother Nature," he read for the thousandth time.

Natural girls. Natural beauties. Like this one, this incredible woman with the waist-length, pale blond hair, sea-blue eyes, peaches-and-cream complexion, and the tiniest, sexiest little beauty mark beside her lip.

The world knew her only as J.J., spokesperson for Mother Nature skin care products. The epitome of the Natural Girl.

Seth knew her as Jill Jamison, breaker of his heart. The epitome of the one that got away.

He hadn't seen Jill in eleven years…almost *exactly* eleven years. She'd be thirty-one next week. Seth had walked out of her dorm room on her twentieth birthday and hadn't seen her in person since. She'd gone off to start her big career. He'd gone home to Ohio for the holidays and transferred to a university there, not coming back to Seattle until last spring.

He had to give her credit…she'd really done it. Jill had followed her dream and launched herself a modeling career, setting a new standard for female attractiveness. She was the image of the woman whose natural beauty didn't need much adornment. Though stunning on the outside, Jill also preached through her company about the beauty that shone from within. To the world, J.J. represented the classic earth mother, a nurturer, a sweet, untouchable, wholesome goddess of nature.

"Untouchable?" he muttered, remembering their last meeting. In her bed. *Don't even go there, man.*

Seth yanked the blinds shut. He had no time to reflect on Jill and the way things had turned out. Not now in the middle of a crisis in his new job at the hospital. He'd never imagined when he'd decided to start a new life, in a new city, working toward what he'd always wanted, that things would be like this.

Two homes in the six months he'd been here. Worse, two *jobs* in the six months he'd been here.

Coming to Seattle from Ohio after his father died was supposed to be a positive move. It was the first step in achieving the goals he'd once thought were a given—goals that had eluded him. At thirty-one, an age when he'd once been sure he'd be coaching his son's Little League team and going to his daughter's dance recitals, he not only was childless, but had never been married. The successful career he'd always wanted had been a breeze. But he'd never nailed the family part.

That was supposed to be what this move was all about. He'd set his sights on Seattle, the city he'd fallen in love with when he'd come here to start college. Landing a job with a major vegetarian food company, he'd moved west and found a great apartment not far from prestigious Forrester Square.

Then he'd started pursuing his other dream. Seth wanted a family of his own. Not having been able to get it the way he'd always expected, through marriage and biological children, he'd decided to go after it the way he'd gone after whatever he wanted in life: with a plan, and sheer determination.

He didn't have to conceive a child to raise a son or daughter—though he knew he would, someday, when he found the right woman. But in the meantime, he could build his own family, work toward his own future. There were plenty of children out there who needed a good home, one he had the means and the desire to provide. So he'd contacted an adoption agency.

New city. New job. New home. New life. And someday soon, he hoped, a child. Everything had seemed perfect. And if, in the back of his mind, he'd wondered whether Jill was still here, if she was single, if she thought about him and if he might run into her, well, no one else had to know that.

Once he got here, he'd used every connection he had to learn what he could about her. Yes, she was still here. Yes, she was single. No, he hadn't yet run into her. No, he couldn't find anyone who actually knew where she lived.

Other than that stumbling block, things had been smooth sailing. Right up until the minute they started to fall apart.

Subterranean termites in his historic apartment building had meant a sudden move to a less desirable home.

Pork fat in his employer's veggie burgers had meant sudden unemployment.

Seth could sell snow to Alaskans, but the greatest spin doctor alive couldn't sell pork-tainted burgers to a vegetarian. Nor would he want to. Once an investigative news show had exposed the truth, the company had sunk like a stone, taking its unwitting employees down with it. The hospital job had been a godsend, considering that the stink of the porkie burger brouhaha followed anyone who'd ever worked for the company.

As if his world wasn't already screwy enough, he'd gotten a call from the adoption worker today. They were having doubts about his suitability as an adoptive parent. Seth's bachelor status was a strike against him; he'd always known that. Now his employment and residential instability added more concerns. "But this job is stable," he mumbled. "It has to be."

He'd been lucky to get this job, and would succeed. Seth had been brought in to eventually replace the retiring PR director at Seattle Memorial. *Eventually*—like after a few months' training. Sure, Seth had been in PR for nearly a decade. He knew the score, knew how to work the media and soothe the public. But he'd never been in a hospital environment, with its convoluted procedures, or the colossal egos of its physicians and administrators. It was as bad as Washington, D.C.

Thanks to his predecessor's desire to prove that sixty-one wasn't too old to try out his teenage grandson's motocross bike, however, Seth had been thrust headfirst into the lead position on his second day in the building.

Marty was still in traction.

Turning in his chair, he opened the blinds again to look out. Not at the face of Mother Nature, he told himself, but only at the media circus. "Isn't there any other story in the city of Seattle other than one poor baby who survived a car crash?"

Apparently not. The reporters weren't leaving until they got the answers everybody wanted: who was the baby who'd been brought to the emergency room after an accident on the Columbus Day weekend? Even more titillating—did Seattle Memorial have anything to do with the mix-up in the baby's identity? The answer to that was no, of course, but try to convince the media.

The case had it all. An orphaned child. A dead couple, who were conclusively proven not to be the parents. A hospital trying to stay out of the scandal, especially because these days the words *baby mix-up* and *hospital* in the same sentence were enough to ruin any major metropolitan facility.

And Seth at the center of it, trying to keep the hospital squeaky clean in the midst of his own personal upheaval.

"Marty, you sorry bastard, if you hadn't broken your legs, I'd be tempted to break them for you," he muttered.

"You're not supposed to say bad words. That's cursing."

Seth jerked around and saw the door to his office standing open. A kid stood there. A curly-haired, freckle-faced kid. A *familiar* curly-haired, freckle-faced kid. He lowered his face to hide a grin, then raised it to stare sternly at the boy. "Aren't you supposed to be somewhere else?"

Crossing his arms, he waited for the child's answer. How had Todd the Terrible escaped from Round the Clock, the in-hospital child care center, which was supposed to be as secure as Fort Knox?

"If you say bad words, your tongue will freeze up and fall off and you'll talk like this." The boy stuck his tongue out, clutched it between his thumb and index finger, and mumbled, "Thee? Efrybody'll know you're a curther."

Saying a silent prayer that the boy didn't know the old naughty-kid chestnut about his daddy working at the shipyard selling ashes, Seth rose from his seat. "You didn't answer my question, young man. Aren't you supposed to be someplace else?"

Todd shook his head with all the confidence of a four-year-old going on forty. "Uh-uh. I'm allowed to be here. I got a hall pass so I could come see you and teach you about cursing."

Seth tsked. "Too easy to disprove. There's no such thing as a hall pass at Round the Clock. Try another one, kid."

Inviting Todd to tell another fib probably went against every rule his poor parents and the harried child care staff had. Seth couldn't help it. Todd the Terrible cracked him up. He reminded Seth so much of himself as a boy, an outrageous smooth-talking little shyster, that he found him irresistible.

Yesterday, the day he'd made the acquaintance of the most infamous child at Round the Clock, Todd had been trying to sneak out of the four-year-olds' room. Seth had stopped in to talk to Shana Devlin, the child care worker, about the mystery baby currently in her care. He'd seen Todd shimmying on all fours, his little rear stuck up in the air, as he tried to crawl past the reception desk inside the center, where Shana had been fielding calls and ordering supplies. Picking him up by the back of the crisscrossed shoulder straps of his overalls, and holding the boy dangling eye to eye with him, Seth had asked him where he was going.

"To the Nintendo room," the boy had explained.

"Nintendo room's only for the big kids."

"I'm big. I'm seven. I just went to the bathroom and now I'm going back where I belong."

The kid, obviously no more than four or five, lied like a pro. Or a spin doctor. Seth had liked him on sight.

Funny that Todd had sought him out again today, especially after Seth had handed him over to Shana, foiling his great Nintendo plot. Maybe Todd had recognized a kindred spirit. "Okay, buddy, let's get you back where you belong. Shana's got to be upset." *She'll be more upset if the admin office finds out a little one got away from the center.* That's all the hospital needed. Another scandal involving a child.

"She don't know I'm here. I already got checked out by

one of my uncles. But he got busy so I came to say goodbye to you.''

With his office one floor up from the center, Seth wondered how Todd had tracked him down. ''How'd you get up here, anyway?''

''You told Shana your office is right upstairs. I'm big, I know my numbers. Even a baby knows one, two, three, four.'' The boy grinned. ''I like riding the elevator.''

A four-year-old alone in the hospital elevator. Seth prayed none of the reporters had been lurking around downstairs. ''So how'd you figure out which office was mine?''

Todd shrugged. ''You told Shana somebody put a duck on your door. I guess that's okay. But I don't think you look like a duck, even if you're sitting.''

Seth nearly groaned. As a joke, one of the staffers had put a picture of a duck between crosshairs on Seth's door. ''You're a smart one, aren't you?''

Todd nodded, the movement sending a thick shock of curly brown hair dangling into one eye. Unable to resist, Seth brushed it back. ''Now, what's this about your uncle?''

''I got *lots* of uncles. Lots and lots and lots. I can't keep 'em straight,'' the boy said with an exhausted-sounding sigh.

Seth rolled his eyes. ''Right. Do you have a mommy, too?''

''Yep. She's an angel in the sky.''

Suddenly worried the child's mother had passed away, which might explain his tendency for outrageous behavior, Seth gently took Todd's hand. ''Okay, let's get you back to your uncle.''

The boy tugged his hand free and ran over to the window. ''There's my mommy.'' He was pointing at Jill.

Seth began to laugh, unable to think of a more outrageous possibility. J.J., the Natural Girl, who reportedly lived out at the beach, jogged five miles a day, didn't own a car because it was bad for the environment, and had never had a serious relationship with a man, so far as any of his connections knew, was a mother? The thought amused him nearly as much as it hurt him.

He'd lost a lot through his own stupidity and immaturity.

"Hi, Mommy," Todd said with a wave at the billboard.

Man, the kid's good. He'd almost had Seth with the angel in the sky bit. "Rule number one little buddy—keep it plausible."

When Todd raised a questioning brow, Seth shrugged. "Never mind, Todd. Let's go."

THAT EVENING, while Seth carried a few bags of groceries up the stairs to his new—and not nearly as nice as the old one—apartment, a woman stepped out of the doorway of the unit directly below his. "Hi, Rhoda."

The gray-haired seventy-year-old, who'd been at his door with a bag of bagels and a package of mouse traps the day he'd moved in, gave him a grin. "Hiya, pal. How's the new job?"

"Stinks."

"How's the love life?"

"Worse."

"How's the mouse situation?"

Seth grinned. "Better. Thanks for the traps. Want a beer?"

Rhoda followed him upstairs. "I thought you'd never ask."

Ten minutes later, with cold bottles of beer in their hands, they sat in Seth's living room. Funny, the best friend he'd made in his new home town was old enough to be his grandmother. He didn't mind, though. Rhoda was a gem.

After he filled her in on the latest details in the mystery baby case, which was enthralling the city, Rhoda said, "Anything else interesting happen today?"

He thought about his run-in with Todd. When he'd walked the boy back down the hall to Round the Clock, he hadn't found a hysterical Shana. As the boy had claimed, Todd had already been checked out safe and sound. Shana had had no idea he hadn't left the building with his uncle, so at least the hospital bore no responsibility in this instance.

The uncle in question, a very young-looking guy with a long blond ponytail and a foreign accent, came frantically around the corner just as Seth and Shana decided to go looking for him. Todd had raced toward the man, who'd been dressed in nurse's scrubs, and thrown his arms around his neck.

Though happy Todd had been reunited with his uncle, Seth had been surprised by the sudden stab of longing he'd felt watching the scene. He still felt it now, hours later.

He wanted that for himself. He wanted a chatty little guy to tell outrageous stories, then give him a great big hug at the end of a long, tiring day. He wanted a giggling daughter who screamed for him to push her higher on the swings.

He wanted to be a dad, wanted to love his kids just as his father had loved him. Which was why the adoption was so important. His own father was proof a man didn't have to be a biological parent to be a great one. As an adopted kid himself, Seth had a special place in his heart for needy kids. Even if he married and had natural children, he'd always thought of doing for another child what his adoptive parents—who were, in truth, his biological aunt and uncle—had done for him.

He could be a great parent. He only needed the chance.

After another beer, he found himself pouring out the story to Rhoda. "So, as you can see, I think I'm in line for some good luck for a change. I definitely need some."

"No, what you need is a wife," the older woman said between sips of beer. "If you had a steady woman in your life, I bet the adoption agency wouldn't bat an eye before approving you.''

Seth snorted. A steady woman in his life? Oh, there'd been boatloads of unsteady ones over the years. Probably more than he'd care to admit. But none that had lasted more than a few months. Somehow, he'd never found Mrs. Right, though he was the first to admit he'd had a lot of fun going through a slew of Ms. Wrongs. What could he say? Seth *really* liked women.

Unfortunately, he hadn't met anyone who knocked his socks off since moving to Seattle. The last woman he'd dated—a reporter from a local TV station—had sent visions of *Fatal Attraction* running through his head after she'd become slightly whacked when he'd told her he didn't want to see her again. So he hadn't been looking real hard, either.

Besides, deep down, he knew he'd already found Mrs. Right. A long time ago. He'd just been stupid enough to let her go, unable to separate the long-buried insecurities left over from his childhood from his adult dreams.

He and Jill could have made it work. They could have had it all. After all, she was not like Seth's real mother, who'd valued her career more than her son. Jill would never have made the same choices Gina, his biological mother, had made.

Though he'd never completely understood those choices, he'd at least reached a point where he and Gina could be friends. Another piece of proof, as far as he was concerned, of the importance of family and his own suitability to be a parent. If he and his mother could have a fairly good, loving relationship after she'd pretty well dumped him as a kid, he felt damn sure he had a big enough heart to unreservedly love any child he was fortunate enough to welcome into his life. Biological or not.

''Most of the women I've gotten to know since coming to Seattle aren't mother material,'' he finally replied. He let her see his somewhat wolfish grin, and she responded by clinking her bottle against his. "Except you," Seth continued. "Interested?"

She winked. "Boyo, if I were even ten years younger, you'd have your hands full right now."

He chuckled. "Anyway, I don't think I can meet and marry the right kind of woman soon enough to help my case."

"Who says you need to marry one? You have to *seem* like you're involved with someone, maybe heading toward marriage."

"What good would that do?"

"Well, it'd show you're a stable, family kind of guy. That you have plans to put down roots here. But you don't have to get married. Get…involved. Or pretend to get involved." Rhoda popped the top off another beer and began to shuffle a deck of cards for their poker match. "Now, are we gonna order a pizza before we start dealing, or what?"

HE WAS STILL thinking about Rhoda's words hours later, after she'd fleeced him at poker. Okay—he'd *let* her fleece him. Jeez, the woman was a doll, with no close family, no real friends. She'd been the kindest person in his life since he came out here to Seattle. Losing to her at penny poker was easy enough payback.

Besides, Rhoda had dispensed worthwhile wisdom tonight. *Get involved.* Find a woman who'd lend stability and normalcy to his life. One image came to mind: Jill. She was the best-known "natural" woman in the country. A perfect maternal image.

Unfortunately, she probably still hated his guts.

That didn't mean he wasn't going to track her down to see her. He had to, because of the other lesson he'd learned from his father's death. Though you might have thought there would be time to right the wrongs, to make up for the crappy, stupid things you'd done, life was a fickle thing. It could be cut short anytime by a drunk driver or, in his father's case, a bad heart valve.

So, finding Jill was not merely about wanting to see her one more time. It was also about making amends for something stupid he'd done. Giving her an ultimatum on what he knew had to have been one of the happiest days of her life had been rotten of him. Now, eleven years later, it was easy to see, though it had taken him a few years to realize it. Mending his relationship with his own mother had helped put a lot of things into perspective for him in the past decade.

Just make things right. He'd find Jill, see her, apologize and wish her well. If she was happily engaged, or involved, he'd drink to her happiness and walk away. But if she wasn't...

He'd what? Try to win her back? Try to make her not hate him? Try to make her understand? Tell her he'd never loved another woman in his adult life because he was a one-woman guy and it was her or nobody?

"That's a pretty depressing thought," he told himself as he stripped for bed. But he sensed it might be true. Which made adopting a child, building a family in a nontraditional way, all the more important.

Rhoda's suggestion rang in his mind as he tried to get to sleep. Get involved with someone. Or pretend to get involved with someone. Someone like Jill.

Remembering her kindness, her gentle nature and her generosity, he suddenly realized there was one surefire way to get her back into his life. All he had to do was tap into the sweet part of her that couldn't resist someone in need. Telling her he missed her might get him nothing but a closed door. Telling her he *needed* her might give him a shot at winning her back. He just had to ask for her help and see what happened.

Years in the business had taught Seth one thing: anything was possible when you put the right spin on it.

CHAPTER TWO

SOME DAYS, it just didn't pay to get out of bed. Today was one of those days, Jill Jamison decided as she hung up the phone after speaking with her agent. Her appearance at a store opening at City Center was canceled, her schedule empty, and she was here in her big beautiful house on Lake Washington with a day of freedom. All alone.

"This stinks." She missed her baby. If she hadn't sent Todd off to the hospital child care center with Bjorn again this morning, they could have spent the day making Play-Doh French fries or Lego spaceships. Or else curled up in her bed, making up stories as they so loved to do.

Today was the third day this week she'd had to send Todd to Round the Clock, and she wasn't happy about it, not one bit.

"Rats," she muttered as she went to the bathroom and scrubbed her face clean. Changing out of her designer suit and into comfy old sweats, she padded into her room, picked up the phone and dialed a familiar number.

Chinese food. Mountains of it. Delivered ASAP. If she couldn't spend the day playing and goofing off with her son, a food orgy would have to do.

Throwing herself onto the bed, she flipped on the TV, not at all surprised to see a teaser for today's news, promising the latest details on the mystery baby case at Seattle Memorial.

"Piranhas," she muttered at the reporters. If they weren't there, staking out the hospital, ignoring the drizzling rain because they smelled something juicy, she could go down and pick up Todd. She had hats and wigs that had sufficed on earlier occasions. But she doubted a lame disguise would fool some bloodhound reporter looking to scoop the rest of his titillation-seeking brethren.

The media would be on her immediately, wondering why J.J., the nationally known Natural Girl, was walking out of the hospital with a chattering four-year-old. Especially a four-year-old like Todd. With her luck, he'd tickle her mercilessly until she let him go, then run and hide in a media van, or stick his face up in front of a camera asking if the people at home could see his loose tooth. Not that he actually *had* any loose teeth—though, if he kept up the incessant wiggling, he soon would.

Jill made a mental note to ask the dentist if it was dangerous for a four-year-old to work his teeth out prematurely. And another one to check the going rate for the Tooth Fairy.

She couldn't help grinning when she imagined what the reporters would make of her baby. He'd cavort, he'd scamper, he'd talk a mile a minute. He'd be…Todd.

Her son simply didn't know the meaning of the word *discreet.* Jill, possibly because she was so tired of being forced to be that way herself, didn't have the heart to make him learn it.

There were times—not very often, but occasionally—when she really resented J.J. What did that say about a person, that she resented a part of herself? She did, though, particularly when she realized how her public persona wouldn't allow Jill to acknowledge the truth about herself and her life. Or her son.

J.J. was supposed to be single. J.J. was supposed to be sweet and wholesome. J.J. was supposed to love to jog on the beach with her perfect, purebred whippet. Speaking of which… "Scoot!"

Ah, company. Her mixed-breed retriever-shepherd bounded

down the hall and leaped up on the bed, laying a bunch of slobbery, but enthusiastic, kisses on her face. She began to scratch his back. "You're not much of a purebred, are you? I guess we're both frauds."

Definite frauds. J.J. was also supposed to eat only the healthiest vegetarian foods, listen to lyrical music and never raise her voice.

It was a miracle she was allowed to go to the bathroom.

"And the sweet, unattainable stuff. Gag me," she muttered as she glanced at the clock, willing the delivery guy to hurry up. Though, if she were to be completely honest, since there was no one here to be shocked by her confession, the sweet, single, wholesome stuff was probably closer to the truth than anything else, at least lately. Her love life currently hung on the border between boring and nonexistent.

But the toughest part really didn't have so much to do with her persona, J.J., as it did with her role as a public figure. Whether she'd landed this job, or any other one that put her in the spotlight, she'd be faced with the same concerns about her son's physical well-being. There were too many whackos out there who got their kicks sending her creepy mail or showing up at her appearances, even frightening her once or twice. No way did she want them to know about Todd.

That, more than anything else, had gotten her thinking about what she might do next with her life. She couldn't stay J.J. forever. It had been a fun ride, had made her enough money to live comfortably for quite a while. But it might soon be time for the Natural Girl to move on and play up her role as happy, devoted mom.

Finally hearing a car pull up outside, she grabbed her wallet, pulled a wig on her head and shoved some big glasses on her face. It wouldn't pay for the regular delivery man to know when he brought out lo mein by the quart that he was contributing to the delinquency of a model.

He didn't ask why she was wearing dark sunglasses indoors on a rainy day, and she gave him a big tip. A mutually beneficial relationship.

After he'd gone, Jill spread her feast out on the expansive coffee table in her living room and raided the video cabinet. If Todd had been here, they'd be watching the superhero cartoon du jour. They owned every Disney movie available, but would the kid ever relent and watch something with princesses, enchanted castles or mermaids? Heavens, no. If it didn't involve flying heroes, karate moves, evil villains and bad Japanese animation, Todd wasn't interested.

That was one good thing. She got to choose today. And she chose *Sleeping Beauty*.

Opening her lo mein and sipping her diet soda, she fast forwarded through the previews.

"Prince Charming, you rock," she mumbled as she sampled a gooey noodle. She sat cross-legged on the floor in front of the coffee table. "This is how a prince should behave."

Battling witchy dragons, hacking through thorny bushes, loving a girl he thought was a simple commoner rather than a supermodel…er, princess… Yeah, he had it all. Good-looking without being perfect, great smile, a charmer—this prince was her ideal man. Well, all except for the being animated part. Anyway, he was much better than Cinderella's prince. Heck, all that guy did was pick up a smelly shoe.

All set to indulge in celluloid romance and fattening food, Jill flinched when she heard the doorbell ring.

Checking the table, she made sure the delivery man hadn't forgotten anything. "Lo mein, check. Egg rolls, check. Hot-and-sour soup, check. Fortune cookie…" No fortune cookie. He'd forgotten her fortune cookie?

Surprised the restaurant would send the guy back out to even their most regular customer just to deliver one lousy fortune cookie, Jill grabbed her wig and glasses. She yanked them on as she hurried to the door, so hungry she didn't really care that the wig was crooked and blond hair probably stuck out all over the place. At the door, she didn't even glance through the peephole. As she opened it, she said, "Wow, that's what I call service."

A man stood on the porch. He was facing away from her, glancing at the rocky shoreline at the bottom of the hill on which her house perched, watching the rain hit the water below.

When he turned around and she got a good look at him through her dark-tinted glasses, Jill sucked in a breath.

Then she slammed the door in his face.

"Seth Nannery," she whispered as she leaned against the closed front door, feeling her heart pounding out of control and her hands shaking wildly.

Seth was here. At her door. Looking as sexy, charming and appealing as ever, with his tousled, light brown hair, his rugged, handsome face and his endearing dimples.

"The rotten creep."

Of all the ways she'd envisioned seeing him again, it wasn't when she was barefoot, dressed in her nastiest old sweats, with a scraggly black wig hanging over her eyes and not one dot of makeup on her face.

She thought fast. Just how much time would it take to flush a carton of lo mein down the toilet, slather on a half pound of makeup, and pull on her sexiest, tightest cat-suit?

Well, okay, she didn't own a cat-suit. And tight probably wasn't a good idea, anyway, considering she was as skinny as a beanpole these days. She'd certainly never been curvaceous, but her recent stress level and manic schedule had caused her to drop a few much needed pounds. Unfortunately, they'd been her very few curvy pounds.

He rang again. "Jill, it's me, Seth. I know you're in there. I only want to talk to you."

Yanking the wig off her head, she stuffed it into a gigantic floor vase in the foyer. She sent a mental apology to the silk birds of paradise she shoved out of the way. Flicking a tiny piece of lo mein noodle off her sweatshirt, she took a deep breath and slowly opened the door again.

Calm. Cool. Collected. "Why, hello, Seth, this is such a surprise." *Can't you see my surprise? This tight smile on my face caused by my teeth being clenched together tightly enough to crack is most assuredly surprise. Not stress. Not embarrassment. And certainly not terror.*

"Hi, Jill."

Just that. Just *Hi, Jill.* As if those two words and his adorably sexy grin, complete with requisite dimples, were enough to make her welcome him with open arms? *Not likely, pal.*

"Are you lost? Seattle's an awfully long way from Ohio."

He shrugged. "I live here now."

His comment surprised her. She'd never expected Seth to return to Washington. Somehow she'd pictured him all cozy and paternal in a small Ohio town, where his wife was the head librarian-slash-perfect-homemaker, and his kids honor students at their private elementary school. "Since when?"

"Six months ago. Look, could I maybe come in?"

She thought about it. Let him in? Or shut the door again? Life was too complicated, she didn't need to add one more stressful thing to her world. And her convoluted feelings about Seth Nannery were definitely stress inducing.

The Jill whose heart he'd trampled on eleven years ago told her to shut the door and lock it.

The Jill whose heart was racing wildly out of control as she looked at the face of the man she'd so deeply loved told her to grab any time she could with him and deal with the stress and heartache later.

How twisted was that?

Finally sighing, she took a step back and opened the door wider. "Yes, of course."

She watched him enter her house, acknowledging the years that had passed by the changes in his face and in the way he carried himself.

Seth as a young guy had been really good-looking. Lean, lanky, with a ready laugh and a twinkle in his green eyes.

Seth as a grown man was totally drool-worthy. The lean boyishness had given way to one finely built six-foot-tall man. Remembering his passion for working out, she wasn't surprised at the thickness of his chest and arms, nicely outlined in a long-sleeved green jersey. His hips were still lean, his legs—well, she couldn't tell due to the loose khakis, but she imagined they were as toned and perfectly sinewed with muscle as the rest of his body.

His eyes still twinkled. His knowing grin was still enough to make her want to kiss him senseless. His thick, gold-tipped light brown hair still made her want to bury her fingers in it.

And she still wanted to punch him for what he'd done to her eleven years before.

"I'm sorry if I'm disturbing you," he said as she closed the front door and flicked the lock. "I should probably have called, but I couldn't get your number."

"How'd you get my address?" she asked suspiciously.

"I called in several favors, and someone from a PR firm here in town finally came through with it just this morning."

Must have been important to get him out here so quickly. That raised her curiosity and kicked her heart rate up a notch.

"Were you wearing a wig when you answered the door?"

She nodded, feeling heat rush to her cheeks. "I try to live incognito."

He glanced at the giant vase, with the crooked birds of paradise. The wig lay there between the silk plants like a hairy dead rat. Seth's eyes shone with amusement. "It didn't work really well. You might want to put your hair up in a towel or something next time."

"Thanks for the advice." She meant the exact opposite, of course. "Can I get you something to drink?" she asked, forcing herself to remain nonchalant as she led him into the living room. "Soda? A glass of wine?"

"Uh, it's only ten o'clock in the morning," Seth replied. He paused in the doorway, glancing at the banquet spread out on the table. "Breakfast?"

She nibbled the corner of her lip. "I had a craving."

"Never cured that junk food habit, did you?" he asked with a gentle laugh. "I never understood how you existed on pizza, Diet Coke and lettuce in college."

"Yeah, well, I never understood how you believed raw carrots qualified as a snack." She shuddered, remembering the times he'd drag her out to jog around campus, then insist on making her a nasty, healthy, green-and-grainy smoothy when they were done.

Funny, no one else in her life had ever cared enough to try to make her take better care of herself. She might have resented it, if he'd been obnoxious about it. But Seth never had been. He'd never pushed, just gently encouraged. Plus, he'd always given in to her whenever she wanted to blow off the jog for a movie, or the smoothy for a milkshake.

"You must eat healthy food occasionally," he said. "Your press says you're a vegetarian and only eat organically grown foods." He cast a pointed look at her Oriental breakfast.

"You should know more than anyone not to put too much faith in PR." She raised a brow. "Wasn't that your major?"

"Do you take care of yourself?" he asked softly.

His tone clearly revealed his concern, so she took no offense. "Yes, I do." The lie didn't even stick in her throat. "I don't usually do this. I had an appearance canceled and decided to stay home and be a slug since I had a free day for a change. I actually have a very active lifestyle." *Chasing after a four-year-old…*

He studied her intently, looking at her pulled-back hair, her clean-scrubbed face, her shapeless clothes. His brow tugged down in concern. "So you're really okay? You haven't been…sick or something?"

Sick. Yeah, sure, didn't everyone know twenty dollars worth of Chinese food was always the cure for the stomach flu? "I'm fine," she snapped.

She didn't need the concerned look on his face to tell her she looked like crap. Yes, she'd lost a few pounds. She was tired and it probably showed. Once in a while she even had dizzy spells and found it tough to keep up with Todd when he went running off down the beach for one of their daily walks.

The stress of the extra appearances to launch the new Mother Nature fragrance line, combined with the pressure of living a double life, all while trying to raise a four-year-old, had been brutal lately. When she remembered to eat, she ate lousy food. When she was able to sleep, she slept fitfully.

But, hey, even superfamous models should be allowed to look like crap every once in a while. It was her bad luck to have done it in front of the one guy she'd ever really loved.

"You don't seem fine. You seem tired and you're awfully thin. There are dark circles under your eyes."

"Well, you obviously cured that charm habit *you* had in the old days," she muttered as she walked to the coffee table. She closed the boxes of food, stuffing everything back into the brown paper sack in which they'd been delivered.

So much for her feast—she'd only eaten a few noodles, and never even nibbled on the crispy edge of an eggroll.

"Jill, I'm not trying to offend you."

"You're doing a bang-up job of it, anyway."

He sighed deeply. "Can we start over?"

Start over? What a lovely idea. Unfortunately, he was eleven years too late for that.

"Can we pretend I just arrived and I didn't make you feel like I don't think you look as beautiful as ever?"

He thought she looked beautiful? She mentally snorted. *Probably in the same way people think bizarre modern art is beautiful…interesting to look at, with clean lines and an unusual concept, but isn't the end result just one big mess?*

Rubbing a hand over her brow, Jill sat on the leather sofa and tucked her bare feet beneath her. "Why don't you tell me what you're doing here, Seth?"

He sat opposite her. "I moved to Seattle six months ago to try to get a fresh start after my dad died."

Remembering how close he'd been to his father, whom she'd met only once, Jill leaned forward and touched his hand. "I'm so sorry. I had no idea. He was awfully young, wasn't he?"

Seth nodded. "Early fifties. It was a shock. Really made me evaluate what I was doing with my life."

"Oh?"

He nodded. "Things haven't quite gone the way I thought they would."

She wondered what he meant, but didn't ask. It seemed too personal, too raw and intrusive, considering this was the first time they'd spoken in more than a decade.

"What about the rest of your family? Still in Ohio?"

"My sisters are both married, with kids. Mom decided to go to New York to stay with my…" He cleared his throat and glanced away. "I mean, she's staying with her sister for a while. I wanted to make a change, too."

"Moving from Ohio to here...quite a change," she murmured.

"Not really. I always loved Seattle. Besides, don't you follow the press? Seattle's the most livable city in the U.S. So, I applied for a job and moved out last spring."

How'd your wife feel about that? She thought the words. But wild horses couldn't have dragged them from her lips.

"I'm not married."

Oh, hell, she *had* said them!

Thinking quickly, she pasted a passive look on her face. "Really? I would have figured you'd be a family man by now. Two-point-five kids, the SUV, all that."

He shook his head. "No kids. No house. Just a new apartment, a new job and a whole lot of stress."

"I can understand stress," she admitted.

"How about you?" He cast a quick glance at her left hand, probably immediately noticing the absence of a ring. "Not married?"

She shook her head. "No, never."

"So the PR has that much right. You live here all alone?"

Before she could reply, Scoot bounded into the living room, jumping onto the couch to greet Seth with enthusiastically slobbery dog kisses. "Scoot, get down!"

"It's okay," he said with a laugh, scratching the big dog behind the ears. Scoot immediately flopped onto the couch, his big head on Seth's leg, as he reveled in the attention.

The traitor.

Jill sat quietly for a minute, watching those strong hands of his stroke the dog's thick black fur. Parts of her body perked right up, remembering his touch. She thought of the way he'd tangle his fingers in her hair to cup her head when they'd kiss. Then of the way he'd hold her hips when they embraced, his hand resting with light, easy possession on the curve of her rear, teasing her, arousing her with just a touch.

The way he'd reached a place deep inside her the one time they'd made love.

He'd made her feel adored. Like the world's most perfect woman, like a delicate piece of china he had to handle with the greatest care. No one had ever touched her the way he did. Before, or since.

As she focused on the slow, smooth strokes of Seth's hands down the dog's back, her heart skipped a beat or two and her breaths grew shallow. She closed her eyes briefly, unable to watch him.

His hands…Lord, those hands…they could be exquisitely tender, or strong and deliberate. He'd always seemed to know when she wanted sweet. Or when she'd wanted *hot*.

The first time he'd been incredibly patient, gentle and tender. That didn't mean it would have been that way all the time. Because in spite of the fact that they'd refrained from going all the way until her twentieth birthday, they'd done a lot of exploring in other ways before then. Her body reminded her of all that delightful exploration, going soft and liquid deep inside. Her mind betrayed her, filling with a collage of sultry images. Long, heated nights when they'd drive each other wild with intimate touches, caresses and kisses. Hot days when they'd go out to the mountains, spread a blanket and worship each other's bodies under the clear blue sky.

Sweet and tender the first time. But judging by the way they'd been so hungry for each other for so long, their next time would have been mind-blowing and erotic.

Unfortunately, there hadn't been a next time. Not for her and Seth. And she'd never completely stopped wondering about what might have been.

He met her eyes, catching her staring. Jill couldn't tear her gaze away, though she knew the high color in her cheeks and her quickened breathing probably betrayed her thoughts.

"Scoot, get down," she murmured, hearing the choppiness in her own voice. "You're not allowed to slobber on the guests."

"Better do what she says, dog. She can be dangerous." A grin brought a twinkle to those green eyes of his. "She might come after us with a spoonful of macaroni and cheese."

She couldn't prevent an answering smile, remembering the day she'd flung food at him for admitting he'd helped another girl in their English Lit class with a paper. "You deserved it."

"She only got a B. As I recall, you got an A minus," he replied in his own defense, making her laugh out loud.

Damn, she was sitting in her living room, laughing with Seth Nannery. Feeling all warm and gushy, when she should be stiff and cold. She should hate the guy, shouldn't she?

Somehow, though, over the years her emotions toward Seth had mellowed. They'd burrowed into one small corner of her heart where there was a bit of anger, a lot of regret, a tinge of sadness...and a miniscule piece of hope.

The anger hadn't been too difficult to dispel. Once she'd had Todd—once she'd realized how much she might have lost had she not chosen to go ahead and have a child in spite of her medical condition—she'd understood Seth's position more. Sure he'd been young to be so focused on children and family. But he'd been right about one thing...nothing in life was a sure bet. There was no way of knowing if you were going to get what you wanted way off in the future, so if something was really important to you, you'd darn well better grab for it while you could.

That's how he'd felt about kids. And he'd been correct—Jill knew that better than anyone. If she'd waited, if she hadn't regularly gone for medical checkups and really listened to her doctors, she might have missed out on motherhood. That would have been the greatest regret of her life.

So, no, she couldn't blame Seth for going after what he most wanted.

Besides, there had been two of them in her dorm room on her twentieth birthday. She could have talked, she could have explained, she could have tried to make him understand and negotiate. Instead, she'd kicked him out. She'd been every bit as quick to react, as slow to think things through.

But it was too late—*years* too late—to wonder how they both might have changed the outcome of that day. Besides, had the outcome been different, she might not have Todd now. And she wouldn't trade her son for anything in the world.

"So," she finally said, leaning back on the sofa and resting her elbow on her raised knee, "this really is quite a surprise. You haven't changed much."

"Neither have you. You're still so beautiful."

Self-conscious, she ran hand through her hair. "I'm a mess." *In more ways than one.*

"You have so much to be proud of. I see your face everywhere. You really made it. And I'm happy for you."

His genuine warmth surprised her. "Honestly?"

He nodded, his simple smile showing his sincerity. "Jill, I'm really glad things worked out for you. You should be proud. But I also came to tell you something else."

He hesitated, and she held her breath. "Yes?"

"It's been so many years, you've moved on, your life is great. Probably you don't even think about the old days."

Try all the time, sweetheart!

"I think about them," Seth said honestly. "Like everybody, I have regrets. The biggest one is the way I treated you our last day."

She thought about playing dumb, acting as though she could barely remember such ancient history. Somehow, though, she knew Seth wouldn't buy it. Nor did she feel like hiding the emotions causing her throat to tighten and her eyes to sting even now. "I can't lie and say I don't think about it. About the way things ended, and how they might have turned out."

He rubbed a weary hand over his brow. "Yeah, me, too. What can I say? I was young and stupid. I ruined what probably should have been the greatest day of your life because of my own selfishness and insecurity."

Her mouth fell open. Seth had always been an open, genuine kind of guy, who wasn't afraid to talk things out. Still, not everyone could admit such failings about themselves, even years after the fact.

"I think we both overreacted," she finally replied, long since able to recognize her own culpability in their breakup. "We should have done some thinking, then talked about it later. Instead, I pushed you out the door, then I got on a plane and left to go start filming commercials in New York."

"We were pretty young." He raised a wry brow. "And, as I recall, rather hormonal at the time."

She chuckled, knowing that much, at least, hadn't changed, if the last few minutes were any judge. Every female molecule in her body reacted to having Seth in the same room. "I'll say."

"So," Seth continued, "I want to apologize. My dad's death made me realize these kinds of things should be said while you have the chance. I'm asking you to forgive me."

Jill shook her head in disbelief. "That's why you're here? You tracked me down, sought me out and showed up at my door just to say you're sorry for something a lot of men wouldn't even remember all these years later?"

He glanced away. Obviously something else was on his mind. Her guard instantly shot up.

"That's not the only reason," he admitted.

Now we get to it.

"Seth, tell me what you're really doing here."

He patted the dog, then glanced at the TV, still silently running *Sleeping Beauty,* who was, at this moment, reaching out to prick her finger on the spindle. Then he met her eye. "I came to ask for your help, Jill."

Feeling as though she was reaching out to prick her own finger, but unable to help herself, Jill said, "Then ask. What is it you want me to do?"

A small smile crooked his beautiful, kissable lips as he rocked her world. "I came here because I need your help to have the child I've always wanted."

CHAPTER THREE

WELL, THAT WASN'T exactly tactful. Seth hadn't intended to just come right out and ask her like that. He'd planned to rationally discuss things, tell her what had happened with his life, his job, his apartment, then ease into his idea. But ever since he'd walked through the door and seen those incredibly expressive eyes of hers, he hadn't been able to keep a straight thought in his head. He was off balance. Confused. A little tongue-tied.

And now he was being stared at as if he had three heads, and not one brain between them.

She gave a dry chuckle. "Well, Seth, considering I spent a couple of years being pretty ticked off at you, I could probably hold the scalpel for the operation. But I don't think they've perfected those sex changes enough for men to be able to conceive babies."

He shook his head as a reluctant grin crossed his lips. "I didn't word that well."

Obviously, and thank goodness, Jill hadn't lost her smart mouth and quick wit. She had, however, changed in other ways. The years had transformed her from a pretty, whole-some-looking girl to a stunning full-grown woman.

Her hair was longer, still the same silky gold, but it now reached almost to her waist. He couldn't prevent a quick, heart-pounding longing to feel it wrapped around his naked chest.

He swallowed hard.

Jill still moved with the same innate grace she'd always

had. Though she remained slim, she definitely had a woman's curves, with gently flaring hips, an enticingly rounded backside, and endlessly long legs. Following her into her house, he'd nearly tripped over his own feet, just watching the sway of her body.

He'd lay money she wasn't wearing a bra. Remembering the sensitivity of her perfect, delicate breasts, he suspected the soft fabric of her shirt had rubbed her nipples into those heart-stopping points. He remembered how her dark nipples had tasted on his tongue, and wondered whether he could still make her come by sucking her there while cupping the sweet, tender hollow between her thighs.

Probably.

She was all soft and womanly, making him remember all sorts of things he had no business remembering. Like the way she'd moved in his arms. The way she'd arch her back and fist her fingers in the sheets when he kissed her belly. Lower. The way a delicate blush had pinkened her entire body the first time they'd…

Get a grip.

Seth forced his thoughts out of his pants, and hers. Clenching his jaw, he focused on the hollows in her cheeks, her sweetly curved lips. Anything except the erotic memories that had pounded him from the minute she'd opened the damn door.

"I'm sorry, I didn't mean—"

"If you're looking for a vacant uterus," she said, this time shifting her gaze and not meeting his eyes, "you can walk on out and look elsewhere. Mine's not available."

Stupid, Seth! He shouldn't have sprung it on her like that. It was no wonder she'd leaped to the wrong conclusion. In spite of her jabs, she was upset. Her hand shook as she lifted it to her brow to brush away a few errant wisps of hair.

He'd known something was wrong the minute he walked into the house. Yes, her heart-shaped face had gained maturity without losing its loveliness. But Jill also looked wan and washed out, as if life had been beating on her lately and she'd gotten tired of fighting back. Absent was the sparkle in her sea-blue eyes, and her saucy wit seemed a bit forced. His instant lust had simply blinded him for a few minutes.

"Jill, I went about this all wrong. It's not what you think. I'm sorry."

She still wouldn't meet his eye. "What I think is that it's time for you to go," she said, rising to her feet. "Thanks for the apology, and I hope you have a great life. But I'm just not in the mood for any practical jokes today."

"It wasn't a joke, Jill." Wondering how to backpedal his way out of the quagmire he'd created, Seth rose to his feet as Jill swayed on hers. She looked dizzy and blinked a few times as if light-headed.

"Hey, whoa there," he said, quickly reaching out to catch her around the waist and steady her. Beneath her clothes, her body was amazingly light. "Good God, babe, you weigh next to nothing. What have you done to yourself?"

She shook her head and raised her fingers to her brow. "I stood up too quickly," she insisted, not answering his real question.

"Sit down," he ordered, gently pushing her back to her seat on the couch. "When's the last time you ate a real meal?" He nodded toward the take-out bags. "And I don't mean *that*."

She shrugged. "I'm fine."

"Bullshit. In no way are you fine."

Back in college, Jill had been notoriously bad about taking care of herself. She'd been the first one to volunteer to help anybody else in need, whether that be a family member, friend or stranger. But when it came to doing something as simple as remembering to eat a decent meal once in a while, she'd been neglectful. Things obviously hadn't changed much.

"I just need a sip of something cold."

He glanced at her can of diet soda on the table. "Don't move," he ordered.

Not even asking her for directions to her kitchen, he bee-lined for the nearest archway and instinctively turned toward the correct room. Grabbing a bottle of orange juice from the fridge, he yanked open a few cabinets until he found her dishes. After pouring her a healthy glass of juice, he returned to the living room.

Jill sat on the couch, her legs crossed in front of her and an embarrassed expression on her face. She was holding her soda can to her temple, wiping away the condensed moisture with a napkin, as if trying to ease a headache or just perk herself up. "You don't have to take care of me."

"Well, you're obviously not doing it for yourself. What's with this dizzy spell stuff?"

She put the can and napkin back on the table, then reached for the glass of juice. "Thank you."

"Drink it all," he ordered.

While she did so, he noticed a bit of lo mein noodle sticking to a wisp of golden hair at her temple. It dangled like a tiny tentacle, obviously left behind by the napkin. Reaching over, he plucked it out, unable to prevent an amused grin from crossing his lips. If they could see her now... *Natural Girl J.J. unveils the latest all natural hair fashions. And they're edible, too!*

She groaned, obviously noticing his amusement. "Can today possibly get any worse?"

"I dunno, I'm kind of enjoying this," he said with a chuckle as she shook her head ferociously, probably worried about more noodles. Then he grew serious. "Except the dizzy spell part. Since when does Jill Jamison get light-headed? I've known you to face down a mugger and not flinch!"

Her eyes widened at the memory. "I'd forgotten all about

that guy. I hope he went to the shelter I suggested. I should have driven him to make sure."

Seth sighed. "You'd have gotten arrested for driving without a license, since he'd just stolen your wallet."

"He gave me back the wallet, remember?"

"Oh, yeah. Just not the money." Seth shook his head ruefully. "There's the Jill I remember. Always trying to save the world."

"While you always wanted to run it." Her pointed glance dared him to deny it.

He couldn't. She'd pretty much summed them both up. They'd made one awesome team once upon a time.

Seth sat next to her on the couch. Telling himself it was only to make sure she was okay, he figured he'd be right there for her to land on if she got dizzy again. Though, he honestly couldn't say how he'd react if she fell on top of him. Light-headed or not, he didn't know if he'd be able to prevent himself from kissing her, to see if she still tasted the same—like sweet peaches and summertime.

With, of course, the added flavors of spicy lo mein and tangy orange juice.

"Now, stop changing the subject. Have you had problems with dizziness before?" he asked as he stretched his arm out along the back of the couch.

"I stood up too quickly," she repeated with a frown. "I'm perfectly fine."

"Liar. You look awful."

"My, you still know how to charm a girl," she muttered.

He had no right to do it, but it still seemed completely natural for him to drop his arm over her shoulders and pull her close to him. "Just because I haven't seen you in a long time doesn't mean I don't know when you're BSing."

He figured the odds were pretty good that she'd toss his arm away, stand up again and order him out. He hoped she didn't. Because, while he definitely felt his heart trip a beat or two at the feel of her against him, he also believed, deep down, that she could use a friend right now. A shoulder to lean on. A body to relax against.

She seemed to agree. Curling into his side, she sighed deeply. Seth tried not to think about how perfectly she fit there, against him, and focused only on trying to find out what was wrong.

"I probably haven't been taking very good care of myself," she told him, sounding slightly disgruntled at having to admit it.

He stroked her shoulder lightly, offering support and encouragement. "Somehow, I'm not surprised. How'd you survive without me chasing after you, trying to shove food down your throat all these years?"

She chuckled, evidently hearing the note of teasing in his voice. "I'm still here, so I guess I managed. And can you believe I even eventually learned how to balance a checkbook?"

He gave an exaggerated gasp. "No! I'm completely shocked." Glancing around the expensively decorated room, he continued. "Then again, I guess you've had to learn how to handle money. It looks like you've had a lot of experience."

She nodded. "Yeah. Money is one thing I haven't had to give a second thought to. Three square meals a day? Well, that sometimes takes effort."

"You can't do that, Jill. What if I hadn't been here?"

She tilted her head back and stared into his eyes. "But you were."

The same sense of awe he'd always felt when Jill was in his arms made his blood pound in his veins. "God, it's good to see you," he muttered, unable to keep a husky note of physical awareness out of his voice.

After all, how could he not be aware of her when she put every one of his five senses on overload? How could he not be aware, when she was curled against him, her hair brushing his cheek, her hand on his leg? He felt her body move with every gently inhaled breath, and smelled the sweet vanilla-tinged fragrance of her soft skin.

"It's good to be seen," she replied softly.

Then, knowing it was crazy but unable to help himself, he lowered his mouth to hers. Whether he meant a kiss of friendship, of hello, or just a tribute to memory, he couldn't say. Nor did he care, once he tasted her lips. She sighed softly, deep in her throat, then lifted her hand to tangle her fingers in his hair, tugging him even closer, tighter against her.

Seth didn't think, didn't analyze, didn't plan. He only felt, sharing emotion as easily as they shared every breath.

She tasted the same. Sweet. Soft. Intoxicating. How had he survived for more than a decade without Jill's kiss?

Finally, their lips parted. She didn't lower her eyes, stammer or pull away. She merely smiled that gentle, confident smile of hers that told him she didn't regret a thing.

Neither did he. "I really didn't come here to kiss you. But, damn, I'm glad I did."

"Me, too."

They shared one long, understanding stare that both mourned and forgave the past. And perhaps—just a little—questioned the future.

Then she suddenly sat upright, as if remembering something. "Wait a second, let's get back to the reason you're here." She turned on the couch to face him, cocking her head to one side. "You're the one who has some explaining to do. So tell me, what is this whole thing about you having a baby?"

"Never mind…"

"Uh-uh," she said with a firm shake of her head. "I want to know what you were talking about, Seth. You can't mention something like that and not follow through."

"It's not what you think, I swear. I honestly didn't come here to ask you to play brood mare. I'm not looking for a surrogate mother."

She again shifted her eyes away, not meeting his stare. He saw her body grow tense, which surprised him. He'd meant to set her at ease.

"So what did you mean?" she mumbled. "Oh, God, please tell me you're not getting married and you came here to ask me to be godmother to your child or something. I'll simply have to shoot you if you do."

He chuckled softly, wondering if there was a tiny bit of jealousy beneath the humorous suggestion. "No, not engaged. Not involved at all."

"So how are you planning to have a baby? This isn't going to turn out to be some scientific experiment gone awry like that Arnold Schwarzenegger movie, is it?" She cast a suspicious glance at his stomach.

Seth let out a bark of laughter. "You still have such an active imagination.... Look, Jill, it's not such a big mystery. I'm trying to adopt."

"A puppy?" she asked doubtfully.

"No," he explained. "I'm trying to adopt a child."

She sat back in the couch, her mouth hanging open and her eyes wide. Finally she said, "You're serious. You're an unmarried bachelor, a man in the prime of his life, and you're trying to adopt? Ever heard of having a baby the good old-fashioned way—something I know darn well you're rather good at? What is wrong with this picture?"

Though her admission that he was good at the activity of conceiving babies sent a rush of heat through his body until it settled in his groin, he ignored it. Instead, he nodded, wondering if he could make her understand. Since Jill didn't know the full story of Seth's childhood—no one did, outside his immediate family members—he didn't know if he could make sense of it for her. "Look, I decided when my father died to work on having a child of my own. You know that's what I've always wanted—a family."

Her face tightened. *Wrong thing to say.* His desire for a family had been a big part of their breakup eleven years before.

"Yes, I remember," she admitted softly.

"I never told you, but the truth is, I was an adopted kid myself."

"Really? Why did you never tell me?" She sounded almost hurt, probably wondering why he wouldn't have revealed something so personal about himself when they'd shared so many other secrets, wishes and dreams.

He couldn't explain it. Even now he wasn't ready to tell the whole story. The unconventional way he'd been raised during his early years, before his aunt and uncle had taken him into their home and their hearts, was still almost too far-fetched to be believed. Gina, his biological mother, would have to be seen in the flesh to be appreciated.

Then again, Jill probably *had* seen her…maybe not in the flesh, but certainly in celluloid. Her hack-em-up screamer movies still ran with regularity during the Halloween TV season, particularly late at night on creature-feature type shows hosted by small-town vampiresses. And heaven knew her face filled the boob tube every day at one o'clock on one of the longest running soaps on TV.

But he really did not want to talk about his mother. "I don't know, I guess I just don't like to talk about it. But it's true. My aunt and uncle adopted me, becoming my legal parents, when I was eight."

"Wow."

He continued. "I've recently realized a lot of things. I'm thirty-one. I'm nowhere close to being married and having my own kids." *Maybe because I've never pictured having them with anyone but you.* "Life's too fragile. I can't just wait around forever. A person can love an adopted child as much as a biological one—my parents were proof positive of that.''

"Your sisters? Were they adopted, too?''

He shook his head. "No, but my parents never showed any difference in the way they treated the three of us. They loved us all equally.''

Entirely true. His parents had been wonderful to him as their nephew for the first eight years of his life. And after that, they'd adored him as their only boy. His bond had been especially tight with his father, who'd never made Seth feel he regretted not having his own biological son.

He wanted to do the same thing. Now more than ever. "So, this move to Seattle was about making all these things I've been wanting a reality. First, a baby through adoption. And later, more children.'' He grinned wolfishly. "The *regular* way.''

She took a deep breath, saying nothing. Seth watched her, glad to see the color returning to her cheeks, even though she wouldn't meet his eyes. She lifted a hand to her hair and swept her fingers through it in a familiar gesture he'd seen a hundred times.

Then she made a face. "Ugh.'' Tugging a few long strands of hair down over her forehead, she peered into it and frowned. "I have noodle gunk in my hair.''

He chuckled. "Why don't you go get cleaned up and I'll make you something to eat.'' He cast a pointed glance at the brown sack. "Something good to eat. Maybe involving a real vegetable or two?''

She smirked. "I'm not sure I'm familiar with the word…*vegetable,* did you say?''

"You're pathetic.''

"I know. And I'm also hungry,'' she admitted. "So, okay, I'll go wash up and change while you make me something disgusting and green to eat. Then we'll talk about this whole adoption thing some more. And you can tell me just what it is you want me to do.''

Pretend to be madly in love with me, act like we're going to get married so I can qualify to adopt.

''So you'll help?''

She shrugged. ''If I can.''

As simple as that. *If I can.* She'd help the guy who'd hurt her so badly eleven years before, simply because he'd asked her to.

Jill might be a superfamous model. She might live in a pricey house on the beach. She might stare down at the city of Seattle from dozens of billboards. But she hadn't changed. At heart, she was still the most giving person he'd ever met.

As she walked away, he thought about what he really wanted to ask of her. *What are the chances of not having to pretend the falling madly in love part?*

TEN MINUTES LATER, Seth stood in her kitchen, chopping vegetables he'd found in her refrigerator. Jill might say she didn't have time to eat right, but she had a well-stocked fridge. Lots of fresh fruits and vegetables competed with the junk food for shelf space. In the pantry was another odd assortment of nutritious grains and sugar-laden kid-type snacks. It was as if she lived a double life.

Figuring she could use the protein, he dug out the ingredients for an omelette and found her pots and pans.

The kitchen, as well as the entire house, was immaculately clean, which surprised him. Jill had never been what could be called a neat freak. No, *sloppy* would probably be more accurate. He'd never known a girl who could keep a two-foot-tall stack of notes under her desk, yet always be able to find the report or paper she needed.

''She must have a maid.''

Not only clean, her house was also beautiful. That had

made him hesitate when he'd arrived. It hadn't really hit
him how successful she was until he saw the evidence of it
with his own eyes. This part of the beach area was reserved
for the millionaires who looked down at the world from their
lofty, hillside perches.

It amazed him that she was still single. For the first time
in weeks, he began to feel a little more hopeful. Things had
to be looking up. Fate, karma—whatever it was called,
something had conspired to bring him back to Seattle, right
here to Jill's door, at the perfect time.

Because it was obvious to Seth after one hour in her company that she needed him as much as he needed her. Maybe
even more so.

While looking through her spice cabinet for the pepper,
Seth found a crumpled old cigarette pack with a few bent
smokes still inside. "Same old Jill," he muttered. She'd
never been a smoker, but when things got really bad—at
exam time, for instance—she'd sometimes sneak away for
a single cigarette.

"The Mother Nature fanatics would have heart attacks if
they could see this." Resisting the urge to toss the pack in
the garbage, he put it back where he'd found it, behind the
paprika jar.

As he finished the omelette and saw the whole wheat toast
pop up in the toaster, he heard a noise behind him. Expecting to see Jill walking into the room, he turned. "Just in
time."

Then he realized the noise he'd heard was the back door
opening. A man stepped in. A rugged, massively built *young*
man with close-cut blonde hair, a big smile, and a half-
dozen earrings in one ear. "Joost in time for vhat?"

Seth stared, noting the guy's gravelly thick accent. Swedish? Norwegian?

"You cooking something for Jill? Is she here?"

He nodded, still saying nothing, wondering who this guy

was. He hoped with every ounce of his strength that this wasn't what it looked like.

Could Jill have a live-in lover? A very *young* live-in lover? Hell, the guy looked like a teenager!

"Good," the blonde said, though it sounded more like "gutt." The man held out a hand. "I'm Sven. You are…?"

Common courtesy dictated he shake the man's hand, even when he'd have preferred to pretend he didn't exist. "Seth."

"So, Jill's home, ya? She no do the mall thing today?"

Deciphering, Seth shook his head. "She's home. Her appearance was canceled."

"Too bad," the other man muttered. "Woulda told the guys, and gone by the center before I come home if I knew, so we could have one of our rainy-day-off parties."

Come home. Yep. The guy lived here. *Please tell me she's baby-sitting you.*

He somehow doubted it.

Seth began to feel like the poor lousy sap who'd discovered the lightbulb a week after Edison, or the airplane a week after the Wright brothers put Kitty Hawk on the map. He was a day late and a dollar short. He'd lost her. Jill had moved on. Moved on with a young meathead from Sweden, but who was he to judge?

"She's upstairs getting cleaned up."

Sven nodded. "Okay, I gotta hit the sack. Long night. Goot to meet you," he said as he walked out of the kitchen.

Hit the sack? Jill's sack? *Jill's bed?*

He didn't realize he'd bent the fork he was holding completely in half until its tines pricked his palm.

Seth had no right to be jealous, no business being resentful. She'd moved on. Hell, he'd certainly moved on, had been involved with other women since college. She had every right to do the same thing. He had no claim on her whatsoever, in spite of the kiss they'd shared on the couch earlier—in the very home she shared with her lover.

Except for the little fact that she'd always owned a piece of his heart. Didn't that entitle him to something?

"No," he muttered. It just meant fate, karma or whatever had a really twisted sense of humor.

"No what?" Jill breezed back into the room, looking like a bright ray of sunshine on a cloudy Seattle morning.

She'd changed into a lemony yellow pantsuit. Freshly applied makeup hid the hollows in her cheeks and the dark circles beneath her eyes. Her hair was still damp where she'd had to wash out the noodles, but otherwise she looked like the billboard image, J.J., whose face was a national commodity. God, she was stunning.

Maybe she was getting ready for one of her rainy-day parties.

"Nothing," he muttered. "Great timing, your breakfast is ready. Have a seat."

She sat, casting a pointed look at the empty chair opposite her at the table. Seth remained standing. "I've taken up enough of your morning. I probably ought to get going. I have to get back to work."

"Where are you working, anyway?" she asked as she took a bite of mushroom.

"Seattle Memorial."

She started to cough, as if the food had gone down the wrong way. Seth grabbed a glass from the counter, filled it with water and shoved it into her hand. She gulped it, then looked at him with watery eyes. "Thanks."

"No problem. Are you okay?"

She nodded. "Fine. You said you work at the hospital?"

"Yeah. I'm their new public relations director." He figured Jill knew about the mystery baby case—didn't everyone in Seattle? Thankfully, though, she didn't bring it up. "Like I said, I should really go. I've only been on the job a few weeks and can't afford to be out of the office right now."

She tilted her head, looking confused. "Seth, what's wrong? I thought we were going to talk about this whole adoption business."

He was enough of a typical jealous guy to be tempted to walk out and tell her to have a nice life with Sven the burly boy toy. But he couldn't. He had absolutely no right to pass judgment on Jill. She was her own woman.

As it turned out, it was just as well he hadn't made his request earlier. Because he somehow doubted the adoption agency would look with favor on a potential mother who lived with her hulking foreign lover, who appeared to be a good decade younger than she.

Enough!

"Yeah, that…"

She put her fork down. "What is it? Do you need a reference or something? Somebody from here in town who's known you a long time?"

Silently blessing her for coming up with a logical explanation for his idiocy, he nodded. "Right. Yes. Exactly. I need a local reference."

She shrugged. "Good grief, is that all? Of course I'll give you a reference." Rising, she walked over to the counter and opened a small plastic case stuffed with envelopes. She dug around for a second, then held up a small white business card. "Here's my number, e-mail and address. Have them reach me any way they need to and I'll vouch for you." She gave him a wistful smile. "I remember how great you were with my brothers. No matter what else happened between us, and the way I might feel about how things ended, I have no doubt you'll be a wonderful dad. I know you always dreamed of being one."

Thinking of how close he'd come to sharing parenthood with Jill, he gave her a tight, sad smile. "Bye, Jill. I'm glad I got to see you again."

"Me, too. Hey, now that you're here permanently,

maybe…'' She glanced around, as if suddenly uncomfortable with what she'd been about to say. Then she rushed on. ''Maybe we could see each other more often? I have someone I'd like you to meet. Someone very special to me. A young man…''

God, just kick me and get it over with!

''I don't think so.'' He couldn't picture sitting with Jill and her baby boyfriend, pretending he didn't want to shove the guy's pearly-white teeth down his throat or ask him if he knew his *A-B-C*s.

Her eyes widened in shock. Damn, he hadn't meant to hurt her. But pride wouldn't quite let him admit why he thought it best for them to remain apart. ''I know you're really busy. I am, too. I see the kind of life you're living, and I—I really hope it makes you happy.''

Her shoulders stiffened and emotion snapped in her expressive eyes. ''Yes, actually, I am very happy. Incredibly happy, thanks so much for your concern. I have everything I ever wanted in my life.''

Yeah. A big house, a great career and a young stud. He stood up and headed for the front door. ''Great,'' he muttered, needing to get out of here now before he did something really stupid. Like grab her and kiss the hell out of her, just to show her what she was missing. To remind her of the way that side of their relationship had always been. Hot. Intense. Intoxicating.

''Life's perfect,'' she insisted, following him. When they reached the foyer, she grabbed his arm. ''I don't need another thing.'' She squared her shoulders and stepped closer, until they stood toe to toe. ''Or another person. I am completely fulfilled, Seth Nannery.''

''Fulfilled?'' he snapped, unable to hold back his emotion as he swept an angry, derisive stare over her too thin, tired-looking form. ''Keep telling yourself that and maybe you'll start believing it.''

He reached for the doorknob—but didn't quite make it.

Seth's conscious mind gave control of his body to a more basic, primal part of himself. Without being fully aware he was going to do it, he turned away from the door. Grabbing her shoulders, he hauled her close, catching her surprised mouth in a demanding, hungry kiss.

This was nothing like the sweet embrace they'd shared earlier. This was driven by anger, by buried emotion, by eleven years' worth of suppressed passion and the sparks they'd struck off each other from the moment they'd met.

She gasped once, and he seized the opportunity to lick at her lips, silently ordering her to part them. When she did, their tongues met in a hungry dance of heat and need. Possession and pure, unfettered desire.

When she tilted her head, grasped his hair and tugged him close, he knew she wanted this as much as he did. Their bodies melded against one another, touching from neck to knee. As she ground against him, deliberately seductive, Seth knew she felt his instinctive, carnal reaction. And wanted the same thing he did. This. Them. Now. Here. Hot. Hard. Immediate.

Finally the slamming of a car door brought him to his senses. He pulled away after making one final, quick imprint on his brain of the way she felt in his arms.

She backed up until she leaned against the wall, gasping, panting, raising her shaky hand to her lips.

"That's what a grown man kisses like," he snapped as he reached for the doorknob and twisted it. "Remember that the next time you try to convince someone you're completely *fulfilled.*"

She remained silent, wide-eyed, still breathing deeply, looking aroused and alive, passionate and full of need.

One step toward her and he'd be gone. They'd be on the floor, on the couch, up against the wall. Whatever. Not caring that her boyfriend was home, one floor above them.

He angrily swept his shaking hand through his hair. "I've got to get the hell out of here."

But before he could walk out, he heard a tiny sniff.

"Seth?"

Her sad whisper tore at his heart. The confusion in her beautiful eyes grabbed at his soul. Unable to leave with her so hurt, so dejected—no matter how angry he'd been—he sighed deeply, calling himself ten kinds of ass. "I'm sorry, Jill."

"You've said that a lot today." Her voice, shaky and soft, ripped at him, making him feel like a louse and a fool.

He met her eyes, urging her to believe him. "I meant it. I'm really sorry."

They exchanged one heavy, emotionally charged look. He knew she saw his genuine remorse…and that had to be enough. "I have to go. Promise me one thing, okay?"

She just stared.

"Please take better care of yourself. Eat right, slow down a little." *Cut back on the rainy-day parties with Sven and the guys from the center.*

"And I hope you keep finding your life…fulfilling."

The word stuck in his mouth, tasted bitter on his tongue. But he had no right to question her choices, no business wondering why she'd changed, why she'd changed from the warm, genuine person he'd once known into someone who could be happy living in a fast-paced world with a young stud on her arm.

No right. No time. No chance.

"Goodbye, Jill."

Without another word, Seth exited the house, hearing the front door click closed behind him. He didn't look back. Looking back, as he'd just discovered, could be a really bad thing to do.

Still, he didn't regret coming. At least he'd made his peace with her. He'd apologized, he'd wished her well. He'd made a serious error by kissing her—twice—but at least he now knew for sure that she'd moved on. Any dreams he might have entertained about the two of them were finished, no matter how hot they could still make each other.

It was time for him to move on, too. Starting today, he was going to look only forward.

CHAPTER FOUR

JILL STOOD inside the doorway for a solid minute after Seth walked out. She replayed every moment of their conversation, remembering his smile and good humor when he'd arrived, then his frenzied, almost angry passion before he'd left. "What changed in the fifteen minutes I was upstairs?" Still shaking, still hungering for more of his mouth, his hands, his body, she closed her eyes and leaned her head against the wall. "What happened?" Before she could think of an answer, the door opened. "Tony?"

"Hey, *cara*." Tony kissed her cheek in his usual, effusively affectionate European way.

Tony was the newest tenant in what she liked to call her house of boys. Whoo-hoo, wouldn't that give the public quite an image of J.J. the Natural Girl? She lived in a beach house with four gorgeous, single young men. Well, one of them was Todd, who was only four, but he was still gorgeous and single.

The rest were studly nineteen and twenty-year-olds. All three, Sven, Bjorn and Tony, were participants in the foreign exchange nursing program at Seattle Memorial. Here to study, take classes, and pull shifts at the hospital for a year, they had proven to be terrific tenants. Respectful, neat and hardworking, they were also loving and protective of her and Todd.

Todd even called all three of them Uncle. She allowed it, partly because he so missed his real uncles—Jill's younger brothers, back in Iowa—and partly because Sven and Bjorn had nearly unpronounceable last names.

Having the guys in the house was like having her own big family around again. Besides, the hospital staff had been so wonderful to her during her very hush-hush medical problems, as well as her pregnancy and Todd's birth a few years ago. She'd welcomed the chance to pay them back by providing low-rent rooms to some of the students. That all three of her current tenants were gorgeous young men was amusing, but not significant. Next year, she might end up with three female French bombshells.

Of course, not everyone might see it that way. Which was why she didn't go around telling anyone about her house-mates. George Wanamaker, the owner of Mother Nature skin care, might not be so understanding. He hadn't put up too much of a fuss over her decision to have a baby alone, because he knew her health had forced her to make the choice. But he probably wouldn't be thrilled if word got out that his wholesome princess rented out rooms to three young hunks. The tabloids, who already liked to take bites out of her in print whenever they could, would just love that one.

Tony shrugged out of his overcoat and shook off his hair, damp from the typical fall drizzle. In precise but heavily accented English, he said, "What happened to your appearance?"

"Canceled," she explained, glad to note her heartbeat was finally slowing and she could almost breathe normally again. "I wish I'd known you were coming home between classes. I would have had you pick up Todd at the center."

Tony frowned. "Sorry, I should have called. When I go back I'll tell Bjorn to bring him home, yes? His shift ends soon."

She nodded, acknowledging another benefit of her boarder situation. Her three tenants had easy access to the new Round the Clock child care center at the hospital and had no problem taking Todd to and from there whenever she had to work. Their assistance saved Jill from having to go to elaborate lengths to hide her identity when seen with her own child.

"Why didn't Sven bring him home?"

She raised a questioning brow.

"He's not back yet?"

"No, I'm alone," she explained.

Tony wagged his eyebrows suggestively. "Ah, not so alone, though. The man I saw leaving? He was an old friend coming to visit you on your unexpected morning off, no?" Tony was always looking for signs that Jill had a love life. Which she didn't.

Then she realized what Tony had said. "You ran into him?"

Tony nodded. "We met."

Nibbling her lip, Jill said, "I, uh, don't suppose you told him you rent a room here, did you?"

Tony appeared completely unconcerned. "No."

She wondered what Seth had made of Tony. Then she shrugged. No way could anyone mistake Tony for anything but the near adolescent he was. Jill might be a single, lonely woman, but she wasn't the type to get involved with a kid one year past being a teenager! "Doesn't matter."

Before she could ask Tony about Seth, she heard someone coming downstairs. "Ah, Tony, you didn't bring Todd home, eh?"

Jill's eyes widened. "Sven? How long have you been here?"

The Nordic youth smiled. "Hello, Jill. I have been here a while. Did you have a nice breakfast with your man friend?"

Uh-oh. Seth had met Sven. And he hadn't said a word. He'd merely retreated behind a cool mask, losing the warm sparkle in his eyes. He'd lost the devastating smile that could grab her heart and wring every bit of emotion she had from it. Then, when she told him how *fulfilled* she was, he'd gone completely caveman and kissed her like she hadn't been kissed in a decade.

To remind her of how a grown man kissed.

No, he wouldn't think… Yeah. He had. She froze, wondering how she felt about that. Was she a tiny bit satisfied that the guy who'd broken her heart in college now thought she was hot enough to interest a young hunk?

No. Not satisfaction. A slow boil of anger rolled through her. Just what did Seth think of her? Had he seen Sven and instantly assumed she was a cradle-robbing, gigolo lover? Then, when he met Tony outside, had he assumed she was some trashy supermodel living a wild, raucous life with her two studs?

What a jerk. He'd assumed the worst, not trusting the person he knew her to be.

"Boys, I've got to go." She grabbed her wig, tugging it out of the vase and plucking off some vines that were tangled in it.

"You're going out?" Tony asked.

"Yeah." One way or another, even if she had to wear a disguise, she'd pick up Todd at Seattle Memorial. But first she was going to make a stop in the hospital's public relations office.

SETH GAVE HIMSELF the twenty minutes during the drive from Jill's pricey lakefront neighborhood back to the hospital to consider the latest turn in the rocky road of his life. He'd been telling himself for months that he had it all together, had a plan, had the future all laid out. Those plans hadn't consciously included Jill…not for a long, long time.

So why the hell was he feeling as if he'd just lost out on the most important thing he'd ever had? *Again?*

"She's not the most important thing," he muttered.

She might have been once. But that train had left the station years ago. They'd both moved on to new lives. It wasn't his place to judge the direction hers had taken, even if it included a couple of hot young guys, a ritzy estate, and a fast-paced lifestyle that left her thin and exhausted looking.

He shook his head and forced himself to take a deep breath. No way did he really believe Jill was romantically involved with *both* the young men he'd met at her house. Rich superstar model or not, the woman had integrity and honor. She was too decent to have become so jaded. No one could have changed *that* much.

But judging by the second guy's comments—the one he'd met while getting into his car—she did openly live in a house with two young men. Meaning one was probably her boyfriend and the other…a roommate? A fellow model? Whatever. It didn't matter. A woman living with a lover and another partying guy wouldn't exactly impress the adoption caseworker during a home visit. Nor would she likely be interested in rekindling a romance that had died a painful death a decade before.

It was time for him to focus on his own journey toward fatherhood. He'd taken enough detours in the road. If he really wanted to be putting lights on a Christmas tree in front of a gleefully clapping toddler a little over a year from now, he needed to get his act together.

Step one, forget about Jill. Here and now. Not easy, given her face looking down at him from every frigging billboard in the state, but he could do it.

Rhoda's idea to get a mother figure in his life had been a pipe dream at best. Deep down he could admit, if only to himself, it had been more of an attempt to work his way back into Jill's life. But it was too late. She no longer had any room for him in her life, even if she'd had the desire.

Judging by the kiss, there was definitely still desire. But

hot, hungry sex up against a wall wasn't what he wanted from Jill. Well, okay, yeah, he *wanted* it…damn, he was still shaking from wanting it so bad. He also, however, wanted more in his life. A partner. A family.

She said she wanted to get together again.

"No." He tightened his fingers around the steering wheel. They couldn't be "friends," as she'd been suggesting when she told him she wanted him to meet her "young man." Especially not with the amazing chemistry they still shared.

Why on earth women thought their exes should be happy with *friendship* was something he'd never understand. A man couldn't be *friends* with someone who'd once owned a little—or, in his case, very large—piece of his heart. Especially not one who made him so hot and hungry he didn't know if he could hold on to his control with both fists and an anchor.

Women liked to keep things tidy and friendly, to bandage a wounded relationship until a new one formed in its place.

Men just wanted to burn out the pain, cauterize the wound into nonexistence and move the hell on.

She hadn't liked his response to her invitation to meet her boy toy. "I'm sorry, babe," he whispered, thrusting the image of her expression out of his mind. He hadn't meant to hurt her, but developing a friendship with Jill and her lover would cause him nothing but heartache. Bad enough to picture her sitting across from Sven the baby stud at the kitchen table. If he someday actually had to watch them together, to see them embrace or kiss, he might be tempted to break his own fingers by throwing a punch at the burly guy.

Besides, even if he could refrain from brawling over her, he would never be able to stay focused on his goals. She'd be constantly on his mind, in his thoughts. He couldn't afford that, especially not now, with so much at stake for his future.

Which reminded him of step two. He had to make sure the agency considered him suitable for fatherhood. That meant making a stable, reliable home for himself here in Seattle. It also meant no more casual dating for a while. Considering he had pretty much had Jill, and only Jill, on his mind for the past few months, that shouldn't be a problem.

Finally, it meant he had to not only keep his job, but wow the administrators so much they would never consider letting him go. That was step three: protecting the hospital. Keeping Seattle Memorial out of the line of fire in the missing baby case would probably ensure him employment for life.

Knowing the best way to keep the hospital squeaky clean was to keep pressure on the police to solve the mystery, Seth reached for his wallet. He retrieved a small business card, avoiding looking at the one Jill had given him. Grabbing his cell phone, he dialed the detective in charge of the case, with whom he'd become friendly over the past couple of weeks.

"Dorsey," the other man answered.

"Hey, Jaron, this is Seth Nannery. Any chance you can give me an update on the investigation?"

"I do have some new information," the other man conceded.

"Can you discuss it?"

The other man hedged. "It's not concrete...."

"Off the record?" Seth prompted.

"Is anything off the record with you PR media types?" Jaron said with a laugh.

Seth took no offense. He and Detective Dorsey had shared a beer or two and discussed how their jobs tended to cause some natural friction. But Jaron no longer saw Seth as the hospital mouthpiece, who hadn't much cared about the human aspect of the story. Once he'd gotten to know

Seth, he'd realized that the prospective father in Seth very much cared about the human aspect of the story.

"Yeah," Seth finally said. Then he sighed heavily. "Look, it's no secret I want the hospital to come out of this looking as innocent as possible, and I could use your help. But I'd also like to know what's going on, and to help *you,* if I can."

Dorsey was quiet for a moment, thinking it over. "All right," he finally said. "I'm at the hospital right now. Maybe I could stop by your office and fill you in."

Seth grinned in spite of his bad mood. Jaron Dorsey was at the hospital—but he'd lay money he wasn't talking to the staff or working the case. No, it was nearly lunchtime. Dorsey was probably somewhere in the vicinity of the E.R., spending time with Dr. Annabelle Peters.

It wouldn't have taken a genius to notice the sparks those two shot off each other from the time they met, a couple of weeks back. Even when Jaron had been hinting that Annabelle might know more than she was letting on about the orphaned baby, and could be hindering the case by keeping quiet, Seth had suspected the cop was interested in the lovely E.R. doctor.

Thankfully, Jaron had lately been telling the press that the hospital was cooperating fully. Though Seth figured the cop was, in part, trying to make amends for doubting his now fiancée, he still appreciated getting the reporters off his own back. They'd been relentless after the rumor had surfaced.

"That'd be great," Seth replied. "I'm returning to the hospital right now. I'll see you in a little while."

JILL DIDN'T imagine her wig, raincoat and big glasses would fool anyone on close inspection. But the crowd of reporters setting up their shots outside Seattle Memorial for the noon news weren't paying much attention. Inside, she followed the signs to the public relations office and found herself standing outside Seth's door an hour after he'd left her house.

She suddenly stopped to wonder what the heck she was doing. This was just stupid. She'd been crazy to come here, and would have to be insane to confront him again.

Let it go. Who on earth cared what Seth Nannery thought of her? They were long past the point of having any right to interfere in each other's lives. Confronting him, telling him off for assuming the worst about her would do nothing positive. It would put her in a room with him again, let her breathe the same air he was breathing, give her a chance to marvel over that deadly smile of his and lose herself in his heavily lashed green eyes. Remember that kiss…

Only a masochist would seek out someone who could still physically affect her so much she nearly shook when she looked at him. Hadn't he done enough damage years ago by insisting she choose between the two things she'd most wanted in her life, a modeling career and him?

Leave. You're a fool if you do this. Jill wasn't a complete fool. But she opened the door anyway.

Seth sat at a massive, paper-cluttered desk, busily typing on a computer keyboard. He didn't even glance her way. "Gimme one more second, okay, Detective?"

She cleared her throat.

He immediately looked up and saw her there. "Can I…Jill?" Immediately rising to his feet, he walked around the desk toward her. "Is that you?"

She forced a tight smile. "In the flesh."

"What on earth are you doing here?"

Knowing he'd never buy it, she pulled a small black comb from the pocket of her trench coat. "I found this and thought maybe you lost it this morning."

He raised a doubtful brow. "You drove all the way down here to see if I'd lost a fifty-cent comb at your house?"

She shrugged. "I had errands to do downtown. So, is it yours?"

Seth shook his head, still looking completely befuddled by her appearance in his office. Then he frowned. "Maybe it belongs to one of your…friends?"

Perfect. The opening she'd been looking for. "Friends? Oh, Sven or Tony? No, I don't think so. I'm sure they would have said something before I left home."

She watched Seth swallow as he crossed his arms and leaned against his desk, sitting on the edge of it. "Home. So, it is their home, too?"

"Uh-huh." Breezily pushing his office door shut behind her, she sat in a vacant chair. "Awfully misty out there today," she said, not answering his probing question. *Let him stew for a little while.* "This silly wig got wet and started sliding over my eye when I left the parking garage."

He watched with a slight smile on his face as she tried to tug the long black wig back into place. Finally he said, "You can take it off in here, if you want."

"Sure, just in time for the next reporter to zoom in wanting a quote about this crazy orphaned baby story." She saw him frown. "I assume, because of your job, you're right in the thick of that whole mess?"

He nodded. "Yeah. It's been a nightmare."

"How's the baby? Everyone's talking so much about *who* she is, I don't see much anymore about *how* she is, or even where she is."

"She's fine." A slight smile crossed his face, giving her a flash of those dimples she'd found so irresistible as a teenager.

They were still pretty darned irresistible.

"Physically, she's in great shape," he continued.

"She's really captured the hearts of everyone at the in-house child care center. Shana Devlin, the woman who helps run the center, is looking after her."

Jill hadn't heard that part. Obviously something the hospital wasn't leaking out to the press. "I'm surprised Social Services didn't take over."

"The Social Services director for the hospital, Keith Hewitt, is overseeing the case." His grin broadened. "He and Shana have apparently…*bonded* while taking care of the baby."

Jill got the impression Seth was hinting at more than bonding between Shana and her friend. Having met Shana a few times, she'd formed a lot of respect for the young woman. She did a wonderful job with the children at Round the Clock. Todd adored her. And after meeting with her privately when she'd first enrolled her son at the center, Jill had felt very confident that Shana would honor her word to keep Todd's parentage confidential.

"That's great. Poor little thing deserves some TLC, having survived that crash. Have they come any closer to figuring out just who she is, and why she was with the couple who died?"

Seth wearily ran a hand through his hair. "No. And the police haven't even been able to find out who the adults in the car were. No ID. No relatives reporting them missing. It's very mysterious."

She glanced out the window at the media vans. "Mysterious enough to feed the frenzied reporters."

He gave her a knowing look. "You're used to dodging reporters, I take it?"

"In my line of work, I have to be."

"Unless it suits you to get some press."

She chuckled, not offended. Seth knew the business. He was *in* the business. "Right. But it's a tightrope. The problem is getting the publicity you want, without sacrificing your personal life every time you walk out the front door." She rolled her eyes. "Or having something completely innocent misconstrued, blown out of proportion and reported as newsworthy.''

A wry grin crossed his lips. ''Does that mean you didn't throw a drink into Matt Damon's face when you got into a lover's spat at Spago?''

She grimaced. ''I'd never even met the guy. He was there, I was there. Someone introduced us, then he got bumped from behind and spilled his drink…on himself!''

He nodded. ''The bodyguard story?''

Jill sighed heavily. ''I don't have bodyguards. So I didn't get three of them to carry the bed out of a Chicago hotel room so I could replace it with Japanese screens and furniture.'' She shot him a glare. ''You saw my house. Was there a futon in sight?''

''I didn't see your bed,'' he replied evenly.

She swallowed hard, noting the way his voice lingered on the word *bed*. There was nothing sexual about the comment, nothing at all. But she still shifted in her seat as her mind filled with the image of the last time she and Seth had shared a bed. Eleven years ago next week. On her birthday.

Of course, they'd come close to not needing a bed today. Her tile floor would have done just fine.

''I don't have a futon,'' she finally said, hearing the weak, breathy tone of her voice.

Definitely time to change the subject. Mental note—no more bed talk with Seth Nannery. Not if she wanted to hang on to her sanity and refrain from throwing herself at him, inviting him to see where she slept for himself.

''And you didn't get arrested during an antifur rally?''

''Oh, that was true,'' she admitted sourly. ''But they rounded up practically everybody.''

He walked around and took his seat behind his desk. Picking up a pen, he began to spin it between his fingers as if striving for nonchalance. ''Well, in spite of some of the more outlandish stories, Jill, I'd say you've managed to keep *some* details of your private life pretty private.''

For a brief moment, she thought he was referring to Todd. Because yes, she had done a darn good job of keeping her son safely out of the spotlight.

Then she saw the tightness in his clenched jaw and knew he referred to her living arrangements. The anger that had driven her down here to the hospital to confront him built inside her again. Talking about the orphaned baby and the media had almost made her forget this infuriating man believed she was shacking up with a couple of young gigolos.

''Yeah,'' she said, intentionally goading him. ''It wouldn't be good for the world to know J.J., the wholesome Natural Girl, lives in a beautiful, beachfront house with her boy toys.''

Let him choke on that!

He didn't really choke, but he did snap…the pen. As she watched, he fisted his fingers, breaking the plastic pen and instantly getting black ink on his hands. ''Oh, hell,'' he muttered, reaching into his drawer for a bunch of napkins.

''Better watch your shirt, that'll stain,'' she warned, feeling slightly remorseful for having goaded him.

The napkins blotted up the ink, but his skin remained black where the ink had touched it. Seth sighed heavily and shook his head. ''Today isn't my day. Look, I should go wash up in the bathroom. Thanks for the…comb.''

He stood, as if expecting her to leave, but Jill wasn't going anywhere. Not until she'd had her say, nailing him for his stupid, sexist assumptions. ''I'll wait,'' she said with a sweet smile. ''I wanted to chat a little more, anyway.''

His expression said he'd rather chat with a matchmaking old grandmother or a loquacious geometry buff. But he finally nodded. ''Okay, I'll be right back.''

SETH TOOK several minutes to wash his hands in the men's room down the hall. He supposed it was too much to hope that Jill would get tired of waiting in his office and be gone by the time he got back.

Damn, it had hurt to sit there, looking at her across the desk. She was so beautiful, even in the ridiculous wig. There'd been genuine amusement in her smile once or twice, reminding him of how happy she'd been as a teenage girl. He suddenly remembered the way she used to sing a silly song from an old musical, calling herself a cockeyed optimist whenever someone commented about her constant good humor.

And her smile hadn't broken once when she'd talked about her *boy toys*. He grimaced, then bent over the sink to splash some water in her face.

"She's okay, moron," he told himself in the mirror, watching drops of water cling to his lashes and lips. He dried off with a paper towel and took a few deep breaths. "She's a grown woman and she's happy doing exactly what she wants to do."

In spite of her poor appetite and thinness, Jill seemed content with her life. Well, with her love life, at least. No matter that she'd kissed the lips off him an hour ago. She seemed perfectly *fulfilled* with things, just the way they were.

He splashed more water on his face, which he'd only just finished drying.

"Get a grip, Nannery," he told himself.

The fact that she didn't even consider he might be the tiniest bit bothered by her situation convinced him, more than anything else, that Jill had long since stopped thinking of him in any romantic way, in spite of their kisses today. She wouldn't be so completely blasé if she knew she was ripping his heart out all over again with every carelessly uttered comment. Because, while she'd always been something of a smart aleck, Jill had never had a mean bone in her body. Which meant she honestly believed they'd come so far from the old days that he would be totally unaffected by knowing she was living with a lover and another man.

"Not even close, babe," he muttered. He was very affected. He needed to concentrate on not letting her figure that out. And if she did bring it up, he'd have to explain away his hot, demanding kiss as a final farewell, a last hurrah.

A stupid bloody mistake.

As he finally left the bathroom, knowing he'd have to face her again sooner or later, he willed himself to play it cool. He had blown it, long ago. He had absolutely no right to question the choices Jill had made in her life since the day he'd forced her to choose between him and her future.

Maybe if he reminded himself of that often enough, he'd be able to keep it together the next time she mentioned her boy toys. If not, he might have to just throw himself out the closest window.

Before he reached his office, he glimpsed a flash of red out the corner of one eye. Pausing to glance down a corridor that veered off the main hallway leading to his office, he saw an empty cart, like one used to deliver flowers to patients. It was moving. Slowly. All by itself.

Curious now, Seth walked down the hallway, having a sneaking suspicion about what…or who…the flash of red had been. His suspicion was confirmed when he saw two small hands reach out from the concealed bottom shelf of the cart and start pushing the thing down the hall.

"Todd," he said as he hunkered down next to the cart and saw the curly-haired boy crouched on the bottom shelf. He wore a bright red sweatshirt with Spider-Man webbing across his shoulders. Seth had obviously caught a glimpse of the sleeve.

A curly head popped out. Todd gave him a toothy grin,

then raised his finger to his lips. "Shh. I'm playin' hide-and-seek."

"With who? Shana?"

He shook his head. "Nope. I got checked out early. So I'm playing with my uncle."

Seth breathed another silent relief that, once again, it hadn't been Round the Clock Todd had escaped from, but his own rather neglectful uncle. That made twice this week. "Uh, Todd, does your uncle *know* you're playing hide-and-seek?"

The boy scrunched up his brow. "Sure he knows. He's looking for me right now. I heard him calling out, 'Todd, Todd, vhare are yu?' when I got on the elevator."

Seth glanced away, hiding a grin as Todd mimicked a thick accent. "Did he also yell, Olly olly oxen free?"

Todd shook his head and raised a curious brow. "What's ol—ox—what's that?"

Had hide-and-seek changed that much since he was a kid? "Never mind, Todd. I have a feeling if your uncle was saying anything else, it was probably something along the lines of, 'Show yourself right now, young man.'"

The boy giggled. "That doesn't sound like Uncle Born. It sounds like Mommy."

Uncle Born? Not pausing to dwell over the strangeness of the name, Seth glanced at his watch and at the elevator. The noon news would be well underway. With his luck, he wouldn't lay odds on whether or not he could get away with bringing Todd back down to Shana to wait until the uncle could be found. It might be too late. The reporters might have already heard Todd's uncle yelling for the lost child.

He was not about to walk down there and say he'd found the boy roaming…or rolling…around upstairs. Alone. The media wouldn't pause long enough to understand the hospital was not at fault. They'd just report it, let the innuendo and rumors continue, then *maybe* issue a retraction weeks from now when nobody cared anymore.

"Come on, let's go to my office. We'll call Shana and have her find your uncle and send him up, okay?"

"If she tells him I'm up here, that's cheating."

Seth stared hard at the kid. "If she doesn't tell him where you are, you're gonna get in trouble. Because he does not know you're playing hide-and-seek." He frowned forbiddingly, going for the same tone his own father had used on him when he'd been telling whoppers as a kid. "Does he, Todd?"

Todd scowled, but did slide out of the cart onto the linoleum-tiled floor of the hall. "Well, he oughta," the boy mumbled, not giving up. "It's my favorite game."

He slipped his hand into Seth's and trudged along next to him down the corridor. As if sensing Seth was disappointed in him, Todd continued, "He's bored all the time and he likes to play games with me."

He was almost afraid to ask. "Bored all the time?"

Todd grinned and nodded enthusiastically. "Oh, yes, he's very bored. All my uncles are. That's 'cause they're called bordeds. Or something like that."

Before Seth could decipher the boy's comments, they reached his office. He was pushing the door open before he remembered Jill was inside. "There's a lady here, so can you be a good boy while we wait quietly for your uncle?"

Todd wasn't listening. He was staring into the office at the woman standing before the large glass window. She was silhouetted in the tiny bit of sunlight peeking through the heavy, gray afternoon clouds. Jill's perfect profile made Seth's heart skip a beat.

His skipping heart nearly fell out of his chest, however, at what Todd did next. The boy launched himself into Jill's arms, screeching, "Mommy!"

As the world started to spin off-kilter, Seth could only watch in amazement. Because Jill was hugging the boy right back.

CHAPTER FIVE

JILL WAS too thrilled to have her little boy in her arms to wonder why he wasn't safely down in the care of the hospital child care center. But after a big huge bear hug and some sticky, wet kisses that melted her heart, she finally paused to think about their audience.

Glancing across the room at Seth, she realized she had some explaining to do. He looked as if he'd seen aliens land and begin marching through the city, led by Elvis on roller skates. His eyes, as wide as saucers, shifted back and forth, staring at Todd, then at Jill, then back at Todd. His mouth opened, though he didn't speak.

Seth Nannery, who'd once sworn he'd be the slickest spin doctor ever, had been struck speechless. She almost giggled, but sensed he wouldn't appreciate it.

"I guess you two know each other?" she asked, glancing back and forth between Seth and her son.

"Sure. He's the duck man," Todd replied with a nonchalant shrug. "That's not as good as Spider-Man. Or Batman. Or the Incredible Hulk. But I guess I like ducks better than spiders or bats or hulks…whatever they are…so it's okay."

Duck man? She was afraid to ask. Todd had the most vivid imagination she'd ever encountered in another human being. No telling what stories he'd weave if she encouraged him. And she'd long since given up trying to get him to explain his convoluted reasoning or slow down on the mile-a-minute chatter.

"Jill," Seth began, still looking completely bemused. "He's…Todd the…I mean, Todd is really your *son?*"

She nodded. "Yep. Found him in the cabbage patch four years ago."

"Four and a half," Todd replied, looking offended. "And, Mommy, forget that cabbage patch stuff. There's lots of kids at Round the Clock, and we all know babies come outta their moms' guts."

Jill rolled her eyes.

"Your *son,*" Seth said, still shaking his head in shock. "He's really yours. He pointed to your picture the other day on that billboard and said he was, but I figured he was just—"

"Making it up?"

Seth nodded.

"He usually is. Mr. Imaginative, that's my boy."

Todd squared his shoulders with pride. "Mommy says I'll be writing books when I'm five."

Jill stared at her son. Hard. "Five? Don't you think we ought to master the alphabet first?"

"Okay, well, sometime," Todd replied.

Seth continued to look at Todd, studying him, as if almost unable to believe he was real. Jill, as proud as any mother, wondered what he was thinking. Did he view her son as the perfect little angel…okay, *devilish* angel…she saw when she looked into those innocent, laughing brown eyes?

"Wow," Seth finally said. "You're a mom. That's wonderful, Jill."

Wonderful. He sounded like he meant it, and she supposed, if any man would, it was Seth. After all, hadn't he confided in her just this morning how much he, too, longed to have a child? If he was serious enough to adopt a baby without having a wife to help share the responsibility of parenting, he obviously wanted it pretty badly. Since she'd made the same choice for herself, she respected his decision.

Having raised Todd alone since birth, Jill could have told him what he was in for. Weeks and weeks without a single uninterrupted night's sleep because of the late-night feedings. Tummy rubbings for colicky days. Letting her finger be used as a chew toy when Todd was teething. The trip to the E.R. for the never-to-be-spoken-of-again raisin-up-the-nose incident.

Of course, the tough times weren't the only occasions when she'd regretted not having a significant other to share the experience. There had been so much joy, so many happy moments, she often wished she'd had someone there with her, holding her hand, to also enjoy the wonderful ride called parenthood. Todd's first smile, the first time he'd rolled over in his crib. The first solid food, the first steps, the first word. The perfect little crayon art decorating the walls of his room. And oh, those gooshy wet kisses and good-night cuddles.

Todd made everything worthwhile. Everything she'd gone through—a cancer scare, the decision to have a child while she still could, Todd's birth and the surgery that had ensured he would be an only child—had been worth it. Since she hadn't had any choice about her body's decision to throw the *C*-word her way at the ripe old age of twenty-five, she knew she'd done the absolute best she could. And she wouldn't change one decision she'd made.

It hadn't been easy. Her family had been incredibly supportive, but there was only so much they could do from far away. Jill and Todd had been experiencing all the highs and all the lows by themselves.

Still, she couldn't imagine what her world would be like if Todd weren't in it.

She could have told Seth a lot about the step he was preparing to take. But she sensed Seth was no more ready for that conversation than she. She didn't know if she'd *ever* be ready to have that conversation with Seth. Telling him the story about how she'd become a single parent, and why she'd made the decision to have a baby in the first place, would be a major invitation for him to intrude in her personal life. And her past. Jill wasn't used to trusting many people with either of those things.

Besides, Seth hadn't lost his old habit of worrying too much about her. The way he'd been so concerned back at the house had told her that. Let him know she'd once had real health issues, and he might start treating her like a porcelain doll. The very last thing she wanted from a man who had totally rocked her world in bed once upon a time was to be handled by him with kid gloves.

Not, of course, that Seth was going to be *handling* her at any time in the near future. Definitely not! But that didn't stop her treacherous mind from remembering just how physical and passionate their relationship had been.

"Thank you," she finally replied, hearing a breathy sound in her own voice. She cleared her throat. "Now, where did you find him? He's supposed to be down at Round the Clock."

Seth exchanged a look with Todd, and Jill could almost see her son silently pleading with Seth not to bust him to his mom.

Finally, Seth crossed his arms and said, "Are you going to tell your mommy where you were?"

Todd nibbled his lip. "Maybe you better," he whispered. "Just watch out for the laser."

Jill sighed deeply, knowing her son had been up to no good. If he started worrying about the laser—a maneuver she'd made up to convince him she could "see" lies, to get him to stop telling stories—he had to have been doing something naughty.

"He was down the hall, hiding under a push cart," Seth explained. "He said he was playing hide-and-seek."

Todd piped in. "With Uncle Born. He was gonna take

me home early. I didn't run away from Shana. I got all checked out.''

"Bjorn," Jill explained, seeing the confusion on Seth's face. "He lives with us.''

Seth's jaw dropped. "Another one?''

Jill's entire body began to tense as she remembered why she'd come to Seth's office in the first place. To tell him off. But she was not about to have this argument in front of her son. As much as she longed to tell Seth Nannery where he could shove his nasty imagination, she instead snapped her mouth closed and took Todd's hand, fully prepared to walk out the door.

Then she saw a reluctant, amused smile break out on Seth's face. "Okay, Jill, one boyfriend I could believe. A boyfriend and another roommate, maybe. But you actually have *three* guys living in your house? Something doesn't add up.'' He glanced at Todd. "Right now, I'm doubting you're involved with even one of them—not with your four-year-old son under your roof. It's absolutely impossible— you'd be much too good a mother for that.''

She paused, the tension easing out from her stiff shoulders at the note of unequivocal certainty in Seth's voice.

"So, can you please tell me what the heck is going on in the house of boys you're living in?''

"That's what Mommy calls it,'' Todd interjected. "Her house of boys. I told you about them. They're my bored uncles.''

"Boarders,'' Jill corrected. "And not really uncles. Todd can't pronounce their last names. Todd likes thinking of them as his uncles, since my brother lives so far away.'' She shot Seth a serious look, daring him to disbelieve her. "They're all foreign exchange students enrolled in the nursing program here at Seattle Memorial. Todd and I are a host family, and Tony, Sven and Bjorn are our current students.''

Seth's green eyes sparkled as he grinned. He was either

amused...or happy he'd made an incorrect assumption about her. She somehow suspected it was the latter, and couldn't quite say how the realization made her feel. Considering the way her heart was racing, it probably wasn't a good thing. She was already way too vulnerable to Seth—hadn't she proved that back at the house when she'd been so easily hurt that he hadn't wanted to get together again? And God, even after he'd hurt her, she'd still fallen into his arms, been ready to say yes to anything he asked, just as long as he kept kissing her. And kissing her.

No, being warmed by anything about Seth Nannery was probably not very wise. Particularly not his smile. Not those dimples. Not those eyes the color of fresh spring leaves. Not those big, warm hands that had once touched her with both exquisite gentleness and erotic heat.

She gulped. Not Seth Nannery. Period.

"I thought..."

"Yeah, I know what you thought," she snapped, trying to hold on to her anger.

He didn't try to talk his way around it, justify his feelings, make excuses about how it was a logical mistake. He simply said, "I'm sorry, Jill. Truly sorry. I should have known better." He shook his head, sighing. "Actually, I *did* know better. I reacted from the gut instead of from the brain." His voice lowered as he stared into her eyes. "Or from the heart."

She stood frozen as she heard a note of something intimate and very tender in Seth's voice, then nodded. Once again Seth had surprised her. He'd also gone up a step in her estimation.

The man had changed, in a lot of ways. Seth had always been a talker, always managed to get himself out of scrapes with his charm, winning smile and sense of humor. But not this time. His honesty and genuine remorse reached her the way a quick grin and flirtatious explanation wouldn't have.

Once again, she was reminded of her son. Todd had moments just like these…quick smile, easy wit, and a never-ending supply of explanations. But once in a while, he'd startle her with some pretty deep understanding for a four-year-old.

How funny that she should have a child so much like the only guy Jill had ever loved…and yet they were in no way related.

She turned away, busying herself fastening her coat. "Apology accepted."

"Wow, two in one day," he murmured.

She shot him a look out of the corner of her eye. "And that's my quota. So watch your step, buddy."

"What's a quota?" Todd asked, looking back and forth between the two adults in the room with avid curiosity.

"It means the limit…the *most* you can do something and get away with it. As in you, young man, have reached your quota of running away from the guys, and it's time we talk about some consequences."

Todd dropped his head and gave an exaggerated sigh. "Consequences. I sure know what those mean."

Seth chuckled. "I bet you do."

"No TV and no computer games," Todd grumbled. "And no gummy fish in the bathtub."

Jill crouched in front of her son. "Todd, you're never allowed to eat gummy fish in the bathtub!"

"I don't eat 'em," he replied, looking offended. "They're just bait—they catch the monsters under the bubbles." He cast a wide-eyed look of fear at Seth.

Jill groaned. "Whether you eat them or not, you're not allowed to bathe with food. Remember the time you let some of your *bait* go swimming away? When you didn't take them out, they gummed up the drain so that man had to come out and tear out the pipes in our bathroom."

Todd wrinkled his nose in distaste. "That man's pants didn't go up high enough in the back."

Seth's shoulders shook with laughter.

"I should probably find Bjorn," Jill finally said, unable to prevent a laugh of her own at her outlandish little boy. "But the reporters…"

Seth glanced at the wig and obviously saw her concerned expression. "Let me call down to Round the Clock and ask Shana to direct him up here, okay?" He didn't wait for her reply, but went to the phone and dialed a few numbers.

While he talked to the child care worker, Jill sat down and pulled Todd onto her lap, holding him still as he tried to wriggle away to avoid the scolding he knew he was going to get.

"How many times have we talked about not running off? Uncle Bjorn is probably very worried about you." She gulped. Now that she thought about her son wandering around this huge building all alone—where he could be exposed to any number of ill patients or just plain weirdos— she cringed. Holding him tighter, she continued. "You promised, Todd."

He nibbled his bottom lip. "I'm sorry, Mommy. I forgot."

"Don't forget again, okay?"

He nodded. "Okay."

But she knew he would.

"Now, about those consequences…"

SHANA DEVLIN CAST a worried glance out the window at the reporters giving viewers their noon updates outside the hospital. The drizzly weather didn't seem to bother them. *Not rain, nor sleet, nor hail…will keep a scandal-seeking reporter off the beat.*

She tsked and turned away from the window. Thank heavens she'd found Todd Jamison's uncle right outside the center door not thirty seconds after getting a call from the new PR guy, Seth Nannery. She definitely wouldn't have wanted any rumor of a missing child circulating through the media pool. She'd sent the frazzled-looking uncle upstairs and gone back to peering out at the reporters.

At least they'd all gotten the message loud and clear that there were innocent children here who needed a routine. It was tough enough for some of these little ones with parents who worked crazy hours and long shifts. Round the Clock took care of children 24/7, and was therefore off-limits to the media.

The front steps of the hospital, however, were still fair game. "Don't those people have anything better to do?"

She had been speaking to herself, since she was alone in the reception area of the center, but a man's voice answered anyway. "Nope. Want to really give them something shocking to talk about?"

The shiver of anticipation running down her spine and the familiar warmth oozing through her veins told her who'd just entered through the glass doors. Keith Hewitt's arms were around her waist and he'd pressed a quick but hot kiss onto her lips before she could glance around to make sure no spying eyes were in the vicinity. "Well, hello to you, too," she said when they stepped apart. "Missed me that much?"

He nodded. "It's been a long morning. How about you? Everything okay here? How's Chris?"

Shana glanced toward the newborn room. "Fine." She couldn't prevent a tiny, heartfelt sigh when thinking about the precious angel who'd captured her heart. "Perfect."

The last time she'd checked, about three minutes ago, Chris, the foster baby she and Keith were caring for, was sleeping as peacefully as…a baby. A sweet-natured, adorable baby. Fortunately, she was completely unaffected by the frenzied whirlwind of interest surrounding her little life. And that's exactly the way Shana intended to keep it.

"I see they're still hard at work," Keith said, nodding toward the window. A frown tugged at his brow, and his beautiful, amber-gold eyes darkened. "Wouldn't it be nice if they put as much effort into helping find out who Chris is as they do into screaming about hospital cover-ups and stolen babies?"

She nodded in agreement, then purposely changed the subject. "So, have you come for lunch? I think we have dinosaur-shaped chicken nuggets on the menu today."

He grinned. "Got any of that cool purple or green ketchup to dip them into?"

"I think we could scare some up."

"I'm in."

She slid her arm around his waist to lead him into the small cafeteria, still finding it a little hard to believe that he was here. That he was *hers*. And that she could be so incredibly happy.

Before they could join the preschool-age children, already eating their noon meal under the supervision of staff members, the phone rang. "Can you give me a minute?"

As Keith nodded, they both heard a beeping sound. He sighed and reached for his beeper. As she answered her call, he glanced at his message, then mouthed, "I'm sorry, I've got to go!"

Hearing her stepsister on the phone, Shana nodded and blew Keith a kiss. He caught it in his hand and winked as he left.

Shana was still smiling as she greeted Alexandra. "Hey there, I was hoping I'd hear from you today. You home?"

"I'm home."

"How'd it go?"

Alexandra's silence said more than any words might have.

"That bad, huh?" Shana prodded.

"It wasn't great."

Not great. There was a big surprise.

Alexandra had gone to Nebraska to meet Shana's brother, Brett. Shana nibbled her lip, waiting to hear what had happened. She loved her brother, she truly did. But a more stubborn, hardheaded, self-protective man didn't exist anywhere on earth.

For Shana, discovering that she had another family connection—even if a tenuous one via marriage—had been like receiving a long-awaited gift. Since their mother's death, it had been just she and Brett. Their former stepfather had disappeared from their lives after he and her mother had divorced. No other family members lived close by. So finding out she had a stepsister living in Seattle—a stepsister who wanted to meet them and to welcome them into her life—had been, in Shana's opinion, a blessing.

Brett hadn't felt so blessed.

He hadn't been at odds with Gary Devlin, their stepfather. But after the divorce, Brett hadn't exactly been heartbroken. He'd hardly batted an eye at hearing from Alexandra that Gary's real name was Jonathan Webber, and that he'd been found living in Seattle and suffering from Alzheimer's.

Shana, of course, had been on the first plane west.

Thinking about the last few weeks of her whirlwind romance with Keith Hewitt, the hospital's social services director, Shana knew she'd never regret making the decision to move out here. She couldn't begin to imagine life without him.

"So," she asked, "Brett really wasn't interested in hearing all about how your dad became Gary Devlin through the witness protection program?"

Alexandra sighed. "Not particularly. I was at his place for less than half an hour. That brother of yours gives new meaning to the word *loner*."

Yes, indeed, Brett did. Shana sometimes wondered if he paid someone to remind him to call her every few weeks to make sure she was still alive.

"He said he was glad my father was doing better and he hoped he'd be okay."

Shana felt a tinge of hope at this hint of emotion in her rugged sibling.

"Then he asked why this should be of any concern to him and especially why I'd felt the need to fly all the way to Nebraska to tell him about it."

Shana's hope faded. "I'm sorry."

"Me, too," Alexandra replied, sounding genuinely regretful. "I mean, I do see his point. We're not blood relatives or anything. I just thought…"

Shana made a sound of agreement, knowing exactly what Alexandra had thought. The two of them, she and Alexandra, were a lot alike in spite of being raised in different worlds. They each wanted family, wanted connection. They loved that they'd found each other and developed a relationship that could someday be as close as true sisters.

Brett did not. And he probably never would.

"So, I don't imagine he'll be accepting your wedding invitation," Shana finally said.

Alexandra gave an unladylike snort. "He didn't want to hear anything about it. I ended up leaving the info on his kitchen table as I left. I told him I'd send him an official invite when they're ready, but I'm sure he won't come."

"I'm sorry. Really sorry." Glancing at the door as it opened, Shana saw Keith walking back in. He smiled broadly and rubbed his stomach, reminding her of their date for dinosaur nuggets. She laughed softly. "But then again, you never know, Alexandra. Sometimes things can happen that we never expect. Occasionally our lives turn in a completely different direction and we find we like the new road we're traveling on."

Keith leaned his hip against the counter, lounging in complete nonchalance, not at all looking like a man who knew he was traffic-stoppingly handsome.

And all hers.

"Who knows?" Shana spoke to herself as much as to her stepsister, still amazed at the change in her own life. "Maybe something unexpected will happen to Brett, too. I think his life could use a change in direction. I just wonder if he'll be able to handle it when he hits that great big detour."

Saying goodbye, she hung up the phone. She took Keith's hand to lead him into the lion's den known as the three-to-four-year-olds' lunchroom. A mere month ago she could never have even fathomed sharing a meal with the man. Much less her life.

So yeah, she knew better than anyone that sometimes life could take an unexpected turn.

She just hoped it would for her brother. Soon.

AFTER FINISHING his conversation with Shana, Seth stood at his desk, watching Jill and her son.

Jill and her *son.*

He didn't know why the news came as such a shock to him. Jill had been wonderfully nurturing with her own younger brothers. Still, throughout the years, he'd thought of her doing many things, all over the world, but never having a child. Never caring about another man enough to conceive a baby with him. Never blooming beautifully during pregnancy, giving birth, nursing an infant. Without him.

Judging by the way she was speaking softly to Todd, tenderly but firmly scolding him, Jill was a very good mother. That didn't surprise him, though anyone who knew Seth's background—the truth of his own mother and early years—would probably question why not. But he didn't judge other people by his own situation. Celebrity mothers balanced work and motherhood every day. Just because his *own* biological mother had been incapable of doing so didn't mean Jill couldn't.

As Todd giggled and wrapped his arms around Jill's neck for a bear hug, Seth's heart tightened a little in his chest.

God, they were beautiful. Both of them.

He was happy for her. So why did it hurt so damn much to think about it? Funny, it wasn't the conception of a baby that bothered him the most. Okay, so it wasn't pleasant to think of Jill being sexually involved with someone else. The very thought made him swallow hard and grit his back teeth.

Still, he reminded himself, they'd been apart for years. It was only natural they'd become involved with other people eventually. Heaven knew *he* hadn't been a saint, and he wasn't enough of a chauvinist to think she should have been.

No, what really hurt was her being a parent with someone else. Because that was the role he'd once envisioned her playing in his life. Though he'd lost her years ago, he'd never been able to picture anyone else by his side, a partner in raising his children.

Which was probably why he was thirty-one years old, unmarried, childless and looking to adopt. Alone.

She hadn't been alone, at least not the entire time, but he had the impression she was now. Still, some other man had been there to get the news of a positive pregnancy test. Another man's hands had been on her stomach, feeling the baby move while she was pregnant.

Had he been in the delivery room, urging her on during Todd's birth? And what about when she was ready to leave—had he wheeled her through the hospital, looking down into the face of their sleeping child, carefully cradled in his baby seat? Then, had he helped her into her car for their first ride home as a family?

Possibly. That's definitely where Seth would have been for every step of the way.

Two questions remained. Where was the other man? And how the hell could he have been foolish enough to let her...*them*...go?

She looked up and caught him staring. Jill flashed him a bright smile, taking his breath away, making him remember the way he'd always felt when she'd smiled at him like that.

Like he could do anything. Be anything. As long as she was right there beside him, smiling her beautiful smile.

CHAPTER SIX

DETECTIVE JARON DORSEY didn't feel entirely compelled to keep Seattle Memorial Hospital updated on the investigation concerning baby Chris—who she was, where she came from and where her people were. But he'd actually grown to like Seth Nannery, the PR director of the hospital. And he didn't mind throwing him a little help if he could.

"Talk about trial by fire," he muttered as he got off the elevator. Nannery seemed like a decent guy, and he'd sure been initiated into his job by a massive, uncontrollable firestorm. For those reasons—and because Annabelle believed the hospital was completely blameless and didn't deserve the raking over the coals it was getting in the media—he decided to fill their spin doctor in.

Unfortunately, as he walked down the hall, he was spotted by one of the most intrusive reporters on the Seattle beat. Perky and ruthless, Savannah McCain loved dirt and dug for it as deeply as her freedom of the press credentials would allow.

"Detective Dorsey, can you give us any more information on the case?" The reporter, a too loud, too smiley brunette, was wearing a choking tier of pearls above her silk blouse.

"No, I can't." *I won't.* He walked past her.

She and the cameraman, who struggled with his gear as he tried to keep up, followed. "Please, Detective…tell us the latest. I've heard the investigation is beginning to focus outside of the city. I'd think you would be with your team, away from Seattle Memorial. So why are you here?"

He shook his head in disgust, wondering who had passed that information on to the press. It was true. They'd tracked down leads that the couple killed in the crash over the Columbus Day weekend had stolen the car they were driving from a tiny town up north by the Canadian border. And yeah, because the investigation seemed to have stalled in the past couple of days, someone from Jaron's team would be going up there tomorrow to dig a little deeper.

Finding the owners of the car had given them no new leads, and the case was getting pretty damn cold, pretty damn quick. The leaky-as-an-old-faucet Seattle PD wasn't helping it get solved any faster. At the rate they were going, the baby would be walking and talking before they found out her real name.

"So, is it true, Detective? Are you leaving Seattle to follow up on a new lead? Does it have something to do with the car being driven by the couple killed in the accident?"

He clamped down on his back teeth to hold in a curse at how much the woman knew. "No comment."

"But, Detective Dorsey, don't you think it would be helpful in finding the baby's family if you keep the press informed? Someone out there might be able to answer your questions. We want to do our part to help by getting the details to the public."

She sounded so reasonable, so concerned. But the look in her eyes was pure, glittering avarice. She craved a story the way a junk food junkie craved potato chips.

Before he could answer, he heard a chattering voice and glanced up. Three people were leaving the hospital Public Relations office—a tall, hulking young man in nurse's scrubs, a curly-haired little boy and a woman with long, nearly jet-black hair. The three were laughing and talking, but when the woman looked up and saw Jaron there, talking with the reporter and the cameraman, her face went pale.

She whispered something to the young man, then rushed back into Nannery's office.

Interesting. The woman didn't want to bump into the reporter, and Jaron had a pretty good idea why not.

When the big blond guy and the boy went strolling past in the hospital corridor, Jaron recognized the kid and knew his instincts were right on. It was Todd Jamison, one of the children from Round the Clock and a good friend of his own four-year-old daughter, Tina.

"Hi, Tina's dad!" Todd said with a big, toothy grin.

"Hey there, little buddy. Are you going home for the day?"

Todd nodded.

"Well, Tina's going to be sorry to hear that."

"I said goodbye already. Me and Uncle Born are hitting the road. Mommy was going to come…"

"We have to leave, Todd," the young blond man said in a thick accent as he started to lead the boy away. "I think these people are busy. Let's go now."

Todd waved and walked away, hand in hand with his uncle. Jaron watched them go. He knew Jill Jamison, Todd's mom, from their days at Forrester Square Day Care and now Round the Clock. Jill resorted to wigs and other disguises to keep Todd's existence a secret from a prying public, and the staff and parents in the know did everything they could to help her.

In spite of his more devilish qualities, Todd was one adorable kid. Keeping Savannah McCain away from the PR office and Todd's mom would be Jaron's good deed for the day.

"All right, Miss McCain," he murmured. "Let's go downstairs to the cafeteria, so I can grab a cup of tar masquerading as coffee. And I'll give you a detail or two you can feed to your viewers on the five-o'clock news."

AFTER JILL, Todd and the bored Uncle Bjorn had left his office, Seth stood at the window, staring through the blinds at the billboard across the street.

"The Natural Girl is a natural-born mother," he whispered. He found himself looking for signs of that in her massive photo, but saw nothing different. She was still the stunningly beautiful face of Mother Nature skin care. He wondered how she'd kept the world from finding out she was a mother for real.

Jill hadn't suggested they see each other again. Considering the assumptions he'd made about her, he couldn't say he blamed her. That didn't mean he wouldn't stop hoping she'd change her mind. Nor did he plan to just let her walk back out of his life completely.

Earlier she'd hinted she wouldn't mind a friendship. And while he'd thought trying to be friends with her would be too damaging emotionally, he now knew anything was better than nothing. Besides which, Jill looked as if she could use a friend. So, in a day or two, when they'd both calmed down from the ups and downs of their first meeting in eleven years, he'd call her and ask her to meet him for coffee.

"That'll work. Slow and steady, easy friendship."

Definitely no drama. No whirlwind. No passion. No frenzied attraction like they'd experienced from their very first date in freshman year of college. God, they'd been so incredibly hot for each other, it was amazing they'd both stayed virgins until Jill's twentieth birthday.

"Enough." He mentally swore for letting his mind go there.

This time, they'd work on being friends. Period. They were both adults, both in control of their physical desires, unlike when they were teenagers. They could have an adult relationship that didn't involve putting their hands on each other's bodies, even if that's exactly where Seth's hands itched to be, especially after what had happened at her house this morning.

"No," he snarled at himself. It'd be platonic. Period.

He'd almost convinced himself that was possible when Jill came bursting back into his office and threw herself into his arms. "Kiss me," she ordered as she wrapped her arms around his neck and tugged his face down to hers. "Kiss me quick, Seth!"

All his ideas about no passion, and no whirlwind, flew right out the window as he followed the most delightful order he'd ever received. "Yes, ma'am."

He met her lips with his, falling right back into the world where only he and Jill existed. She tasted sweet and minty, her lips so incredibly soft. As her arms tightened around his neck, Seth gentled the kiss, silently urging her to calm down, to relax, to enjoy the moment as one to be savored and appreciated.

They'd done the hot and hungry back at her house. Now it was time for languorous and erotic.

She seemed to get the message. Her body softened against his, he could practically feel the tension ease out of her as she melted into him, from chest to knee. Heat, insistent and unrelenting, swept through his body at the feel of her. He forced himself to focus on their kiss, just the sensation of shared breaths and the moist meeting of lips.

He'd forgotten how good this was. Slow, deep kissing. Earlier today he'd been too angry to enjoy having her back in his arms. And somehow over the years, he'd remembered the sex, that one afternoon in her dorm room. As well as all the heated encounters before it. But he'd almost let the achingly sweet intimacy of Jill's warm kisses fade away from his memory.

Her lips parted and he slid his tongue between them to gently tangle with hers. She moaned softly, tilting her head for a better fit, and returned every lazy, seductive stroke.

Somehow, not even aware he was doing it, he backed up to his desk, leaned on the edge of it and pulled her between his legs. She writhed against him, obviously feeling the re-action of his body, which was impossible to disguise.

Jill whimpered against his lips, pushing harder. He almost pulled her onto his lap, which was where she seemed to want to be. She lifted one leg and crossed it over his, bringing their lower bodies into achingly intimate contact.

Their kiss went on and on. They tasted and sipped… exploring, remembering, joining. Seth felt pretty sure he could do this, and nothing else, for the rest of his life and still die a happy man.

When she moved her hands to tangle in his hair, then stroke his shoulders, Seth groaned. He wanted to turn them around, to put her on the desk and step between her thighs.

"Oh, Seth," she murmured, not pulling her lips from his. "It's been so long since you've touched me."

A lifetime.

He moved his hands higher, hearing by her sighs and whimpers as they began to kiss again just how much she wanted to be touched. *Needed* to be touched.

Her silky yellow blouse proved no barrier to his hands, and he easily slid beneath it to caress the smooth skin of her waist. She mumbled something that sounded like a plea as his fingertips traced a delicate trail up the tiny protruding bones of her beautiful back.

"Way too long," he mumbled in agreement when he touched her higher and realized she wore nothing beneath the blouse.

She pressed against him, turning slightly, silently telling him she wanted more. Wanted his hands on her. Wanted whatever he had to give her.

He knew he should stop, knew someone could walk in at any moment, but he couldn't resist, couldn't prevent stealing one more moment, one more relived memory of Jill in his arms. Her body beneath his hands. Her mouth on his. Her sighs in his ears.

Her top would come off so easily, slide right off her shoulders with a few unfastened buttons. He could close his eyes and see the fabric dropping away, see himself reaching for her, tasting her collarbone with his lips. Testing the weight of her perfectly shaped breasts in his hands. And on his tongue.

No.

They were in a public office, in a public building, standing right in front of a broad window through which reporters and spectators could be ogling them from below right this very minute.

As much as it pained him, he had to back off, to get some physical distance between them before he started unbuttoning and unzipping.

With one last taste of her mouth, he ended the kiss and forced his hands to give up the sensual pleasure of her skin. Pulling away, he stared at her lovely, flushed face. Her long lashes brushed her cheeks, her eyes remaining closed. Her lips were reddened, moist, and her breath came in short little gasps.

She was glorious.

He swallowed, hard, holding on to control with everything he had. "Jill?"

"Mmm?"

He smiled lazily, liking the look of pure feminine satisfaction on her face…knowing he'd put it there. Still holding her around the waist, he supported her slight weight as she kept her leg curved around his. Their bodies were close, heat snapping between them. Although his mind was ordering him to pull away, the signal hadn't crossed all the wires down to his lower half and he remained hard and hungry for her.

He ignored the need, focusing on their situation. "You want to tell me what that was all about?"

Her eyes opened. "What?"

"That. *This*. Uh, care to explain what just happened here?"

She gave him a saucy grin. "I think it was called a kiss." She leaned closer, nibbling on the corner of his lip. "Don't tell me you've forgotten—in the past hour—what one is?"

He shook his head and swallowed hard. "Yeah, I definitely know it was a kiss. But that doesn't answer the question. Why did we kiss?"

Her throaty sigh of pleasure gave him the obvious answer. *Because it feels so damn good.*

"I always loved kissing you, Seth."

He appreciated her honesty and returned it. "I always loved kissing you, too, babe. But this…well, you definitely caught me by surprise." He ran a shaky hand through his hair, waiting for the slowing of his still-racing heart. "You left here three minutes ago heading home with your son," he finally continued. "And now you're back in my office, practically on top of me, on my desk. You kissed me like you want to get naked and horizontal right here and now."

Jill laughed, poking her index finger on his shoulder and pushing him back until he had to put his hands on the desk to support himself. "Looks like you're the one who nearly ended up horizontal."

He pulled her down to him until she sprawled across his chest. "Now we both are."

Unable to resist, he pressed another quick, seductive kiss on her laughing lips. This time, she was the one who drew away, sliding off him to stand beside the desk. "Oh, you tempt me to forget what a jerk you were to me, Seth Nannery. Besides, didn't you turn me into a quivering mess an hour ago at my house? You deserved some payback."

He straightened and hopped off the desk, standing next to her. "Was this payback?"

She shook her head, reaching out to cup his cheek. "No, I promise, it wasn't."

When she looked at him like that, hungry and aroused, as if ready to fall back into his arms and start all over again, he swore he could feel the earth moving beneath his feet. He couldn't help whispering, "Jill, you tempt me to forget the door's not locked and the blinds are open."

Her mournful little sigh told him she felt the same way.

Crossing his arms in front of his chest, he shot her a look demanding answers. "So quit distracting me. What is going on?"

She glanced out the window, busied her hands adjusting her silly, slightly askew wig, and then sighed. Nibbling at her lip, she gestured toward the closed door of his office. "I'm sorry. I guess I *was* using you, really. I didn't mean for it to go this far. And after all that, they didn't come, anyway."

No, but another five minutes or so and either he or Jill— preferably both—might have!

"Who didn't come?" He stepped closer, unable to resist breathing in the flowery scent of her perfume, mixed with the vanilla lotion she'd always favored.

She finally seemed to snap out of her erotic lethargy, recognizing the intimacy so thick between them. Taking a quick step back, she almost tripped over her own feet. Seth kept his hands on her waist, holding her steady. "You okay?"

"You still make me weak in the knees," she admitted.

"Ditto."

She smiled. He smiled back, simply unable to resist her. "I've missed you like crazy."

This time, she was the one who replied, "Ditto."

Then, as if knowing he awaited her answer, she said,

"There were some reporters and a cameraman down the hall. One of them was Savannah McCain from channel seven. She is such a predator."

He kept silent, not wanting to discuss Savannah McCain with Jill. She was definitely a predator—Seth had learned that the one and only time he'd taken the woman out.

"I thought they were coming here."

Frowning, he shook his head. "That's some pretty screwy logic…you thought it would be good press for us to get caught by a couple of reporters, making out on top of my desk like a pair of horny teenagers?"

She rolled her eyes. "That was *not* the plan."

"I sure hope not. Because, I hate to tell you, Jill, as plans go, that one really sucks."

Plopping down onto his chair, she explained. "The plan was to get Bjorn to take Todd before they saw me with him. Then I could wait in here. When they arrived, they'd walk in on you kissing a dark-haired woman and would leave immediately."

"Yeah, right. You obviously don't know Savannah McCain. She'd have had her cameraman setting up to get the best angle of our make-out session."

That's the way the reporter operated—finding and zoning in on any titillation she could find—but she would also do whatever she could to personally screw Seth. She hadn't taken his decision not to ask her out again very well. In fact, she'd been pretty damned obnoxious about it.

Jill was shaking her head in disbelief. "They wouldn't—"

"For someone who's been as badly burned by the press as you, you give them a lot of credit."

Her jaw stiffened. "I can't imagine anyone wanting to intrude on a private…moment."

He leaned his hip against his desk, looking down at her, resisting the urge to straighten out her wig. He couldn't risk touching her again, not without wanting to haul her back into his arms to continue what they'd so crazily started.

"Honey, if they had recognized you, they would not only have intruded, they'd have been voracious."

"They wouldn't have recognized—"

"That wig of yours is ridiculous." He nodded toward the window. "And your face is right outside the window, smiling into this room. Savannah McCain would have to be blind not to recognize you, and I have the feeling her eyesight is as razor sharp as her tongue."

Jill looked down at her own clenched hands. "Then I guess it's a good thing they didn't come in here."

He laughed. "Definitely a good thing. I don't imagine it would look good for the natural girl to be going at it on a desk in a public building with a guy from her past."

She peeked at him through half-lowered lashes. "And it would have gotten the reporters on your back, wouldn't it? As if you're not already in the middle of this nightmare mystery baby case."

True. Seth definitely didn't want any more of a spotlight shining on him. And not just because of the case and the hospital. No, the biggest concern was the adoption agency. A public scandal would be one more nail in the coffin in which the agency was trying to bury his application. Not that Savannah McCain would care. In fact, since she already had it in for him, she'd probably delight in sabotaging him any way she could. That old saying about a woman scorned…

"It wouldn't have been great for either one of us," he admitted, not wanting to make her feel any worse than she already did. "But it's done. Nothing happened."

As a slow flush rose in her cheeks, he laughed softly.

"Okay, something happened. But only the two of us know about it. Which is how it will stay, Jill, I swear."

Relief flashed in her eyes. "Thank you. I truly didn't mean to use you. Can I confess…"

"What?"

Her lips parted in a warm, tenderly reminiscent smile. "That I'm not sorry I kissed you. Not because of the threat of the reporters…but because of myself? Back at the house…that second kiss…"

"I was an ass."

"Yeah," she said with a nod. "But it reminded me of a *lot* of things."

"Yeah, it reminded me of some things, too."

Long, slow, wet kisses. The way her smooth skin tasted. The way her heart would beat out of control when he paid lavish attention to her beautiful breasts, or when he'd overcome her shyness and introduced her to the body-rocking pleasures of oral sex. The way she screamed and then cried the first time he made her come. *Damn.*

Unable to resist any longer, he leaned down and tucked a tiny tendril of baby-fine blond hair back into the netting of her wig. Erotic memories were shoved safely back, deep inside his brain, where they belonged. "I'm not sorry, either, Jill."

"Before today, it had been a long time."

"Yeah. A very long time."

They exchanged one final, intimate stare before Jill rose to her feet. "I guess I should go." She walked to the door. After peeking out into the corridor, she glanced at him over her shoulder. "Coast is clear. They must have changed their minds."

He couldn't contain his own sigh of relief at the respite from the reporters.

"So, I guess I can head to the parking garage. Bjorn should have gotten Todd safely out of the hospital now, and I can meet up with them at home. Thanks again, Seth."

Though he knew she wanted to leave, his curiosity was

greatly aroused. He finally focused on how anxious she'd been—not to disguise her own identity, but to prevent the press from seeing her with her own child.

"Jill, can you tell me one thing? Why does the world not know you have a baby? Why are you afraid to be seen with Todd?"

"That's a complicated question," she replied, still standing by the door, her hand on the knob.

"No, it's a simple question," he countered. "Just maybe a complicated answer?"

She released the knob and turned to face him. "Right. And not one I really feel comfortable talking about.…"

He swallowed hard, knowing she didn't trust him.

"At least not here," she continued. "Those reporters could still come walking in at any minute."

Since he had nothing to lose, especially because she was about to walk out the door again, this time for who knew how long, Seth's mouth jumped a few steps ahead of his brain. "How about talking later? Have dinner with me."

He wasn't aware he was holding his breath until it escaped his lungs with a whoosh when she nodded.

"Okay. Dinner sounds great." Warmth flashed in her eyes, then she nibbled her lip. "But not tonight. I'm afraid tonight I have some consequences to lay down to a young man who's gotten a little too cocky about running away from adults."

Recognizing the look on her face, Seth didn't envy Todd.

"I think we're due for a staring contest over the big pile of carrots he will refuse to eat," she continued. "I'm going to insist he needs lots of them to improve his eyesight so he can *see* how his actions upset me and the guys."

"Smart thinking," he said with a grin, knowing Todd would swear to have perfect vision when his charming, determined mother was through with him.

"Is tomorrow night okay?"

He nodded. "Perfect, especially since it's Friday. And we'll have something healthy. I bet you never ate that omelette this morning."

She shook her head and smirked. "Grabbed a burger at a drive-through on the way downtown."

He rolled his eyes. Same old Jill.

God, it was good to have her back in his world.

CHAPTER SEVEN

"WHAT'S A DATE?"

Jill paused with her spiky mascara brush an inch from her lashes, watching Todd sidle into her room eating an enormous chocolate chip cookie. "Funny, I don't remember saying you could have dessert already."

"That's funny, 'cause I don't remember *asking* you," he said, looking so completely earnest she forgave him the blatant cheekiness.

"I was being sarcastic, Todd. You should have asked."

He scuffed his toe on the floor, then peeked at her between half-lowered lashes. "I finished my dinner first."

"All your green beans?"

Todd's eyes shifted. Not a good sign. "Uh-huh."

Jill raised a brow, waiting.

"Most of 'em."

"How many?"

"Four, 'cause I'm four," he confessed. "So that should be enough, right? Uncle Tony said it was."

She swiveled in her chair, tapping the tip of her finger against her cheek. "Hmm...I thought you said yesterday at the hospital that you're four and a half."

Todd blinked, then widened his eyes and broke into an excited smile. It brought out those sucker-punching dimples that had sealed her fate to be putty in his hands from the first time he flashed them. "You mean I can use a knife to cut one in half?"

Todd with a sharp utensil. Not a good idea. Three of his

favorite stuffed animals still had the crooked, hand-sewn scars from where he'd performed surgery with a pair of kids Fiskar's last summer. He'd then sobbed until his completely needle-and-thread-challenged mother had repaired them.

"Eat your cookie."

Todd took a few bites, wiped some smeary chocolate off his lips with the back of his sleeve, then plopped on the floor beside her vanity table. "So what's a date?"

Something Mommy hasn't been on since the Clinton administration. She sighed. "A date is sort of like an appointment. An arranged time to do something."

"Like a dentist appointment?" he asked, raising a skeptical brow. "You don't need makeup, Mommy, just to go let that guy poke you in the mouth. Then he'll smear some stuff on your teeth. It's supposed to taste like cherries, but it doesn't. It tastes like dog drool."

She glanced over at Scoot, who was curled up in his favorite spot on her chaise longue. He raised his head and stared mournfully at Todd. Smart pooch.

"Eaten a lot of dog drool lately?"

Todd snickered. "Scoot gives messy kisses."

Yum. "Actually, honey, it's not like a dentist appointment. It's a nicer appointment. Like…a hair or nails appointment."

Todd grabbed his wavy brown hair and grimaced.

"Okay," she tried again. "It's like me talking to Jason's mommy and arranging for you to go over to his house at a certain time to make goopy spiders and roaches in his bug-maker oven." She shuddered, remembering the night she'd found one of those critters under her pillow where Todd had left it to "surprise her." He'd surprised her all right—almost right out the darn window.

"Oh! You have a *play* date." She heard the silent *Duh!* at the end of his sentence.

Hmm…playing with Seth Nannery. That brought up

some distinctly interesting visuals, none of which involved toys or bug-making ovens. She hadn't *played* with a man in a long time. A very long time. And she'd never played with one who made her feel as out-of-her-mind fabulous as Seth had.

She swallowed, trying to thrust away the sultry memories. She and Seth had only ever made love completely that one time. But oh, goodness, there had been many other times when they'd come so close. They'd explored and cajoled, tasted and caressed. Experimenting like two hormonal teenagers who were totally hot for each other but had made the decision to wait until their twenties to have sex. They'd made it…by a few hours.

Enough. This was a friendly, platonic evening so they could catch up on old times. In spite of the wildly passionate kisses they'd shared yesterday, she and Seth were *not* romantically involved. So the only playing they'd be doing tonight would be if he ended up walking her to the door and got caught up in a raucous game of Risk with the guys. Bjorn, Sven and Tony would wage their typical battle over Europe while Jill secretly gobbled up all of Asia and North America. Board games. Not sex games.

"Right," she finally told Todd. "I have a kind of play date to go out to dinner with my friend, Seth Nannery."

"Duck man."

"Why do you call him that?"

Todd shrugged. "'Cause he has a duck on his door with an *X* through it. He told Shana the duck was sitting there just waiting for those guys with the cameras. But I don't know why."

A sitting duck. Ha. Opening a tube of lipstick—not a Mother Nature product, since the cosmetics manufactured by her employer made her break out in hives—Jill leaned closer to her makeup mirror and began applying it.

"So is the duck man my dad?"

Jill jerked so hard, she drew a crimson line from her mouth to her cheekbone. Grabbing for a tissue in a stall for time, she wiped the smear off, watching Todd out of the corner of her eye. He giggled about the lipstick mishap. "No, honey." She reached down to lift Todd into her lap. "He's not your dad."

If things had worked out differently, he might have been....

Todd sighed, well used to the answer. In the past few months, he'd asked the question about a few men. Only the ones he liked, so he hadn't asked about the dentist after his first appointment last spring.

Since he was too young to understand the situation, Jill had been careful with her explanations. How could a four-year-old be expected to understand the truth? "You know I wanted you so much that I decided to keep you all to myself, right, baby?"

"I'm not a baby," he insisted with a ferocious frown.

"Hate to tell ya this, pal, but you are *my* baby, and you always will be." She hunched her shoulders and spoke in a wavering whisper. "Even when I'm a rickety old lady with a cane and white hair and three long black hairs sticking out of my double chin."

He giggled, distracted as she'd hoped he would be.

Distraction tactics wouldn't always work. Someday, when he was older, she'd have to explain everything to him. But for now, she was content telling him the partial truth—that she'd wanted him so much, she'd made the decision to have a baby alone. And that while some families had a daddy and a mommy, there were also lots of families with just a mommy or just a daddy.

Todd didn't like it, but he had conceded the point. Since he was in a child care center with other kids who talked about their families, he knew she was telling the truth. It seemed to be enough, at least until the next time he met a man he liked and began speculating again.

He obviously liked Seth. The realization warmed her for some reason.

"When I meet my real dad, you are gonna tell me, right?" Todd asked with a sigh.

How was she supposed to tell a four-year-old that what he wanted was never going to happen? Medical procedures and sperm donors wouldn't be up for discussion for a few years, at least. But in the meantime… "Doesn't having uncles living in the house at least partially make up for not having a daddy around?"

Todd shrugged. "I guess."

As if sensing she couldn't talk about this anymore, Todd reached his arms around her neck and pulled her cheek down for a squishy, delicious kiss. She nuzzled him back, then finished getting ready.

A few minutes later, dressed in a loose-fitting dress that hid the sharper angles of her too lean body, Jill walked downstairs with Todd. Tony, Sven and Bjorn sat in the living room, watching a pay-per-view wrestling match. Todd raced into the room and dived onto Sven's shoulders over the back of the couch.

"Oh, no, The Rock, he has got me!"

Jill hid a smile as the Swedish youth rolled Todd over his shoulder, scooting over to make room for him on the couch. The top of his little head barely reached either of his blond "uncles"" shoulders.

She'd never imagined when she agreed to house some student nurses that they'd so quickly become part of the family. And she'd certainly never imagined how quickly Todd would become the baby brother to all three of them. "You guys set for tonight?"

Tony stood and walked over to check out her dress. "You

are looking very nice,'' he said, walking around her in a circle. ''Too skinny, my mama would say, but nice.''

''Thanks. I think.''

''Where are you and your friend going tonight?'' Bjorn asked.

''What time will you be returning?'' This from Sven.

''Where does he live so I may go to his house and break his legs if he brings you home in tears?''

Tony liked to pretend he had mafia connections.

''Dinner,'' she told Bjorn. ''Not late,'' she said to Sven. Then she turned to Tony. ''I have no idea where he lives, and you need to stop watching *The Sopranos.*''

He rolled his eyes. ''A television show, ha! You forget, I am Italian. My family back in Sicily—''

''You're from Venice,'' Sven said with a grunt.

''My ancestors—''

''Yah, yah,'' Bjorn said, rolling his eyes as he reached for a handful of popcorn from a massive bowl. ''Sure, they're all from Sicily, except your father—''

''The *conductor,*'' he and Sven finished in unison, making no effort to hide their snorts of laughter.

Tony sniffed, tried to look offended, and failed miserably. Finally he joined in their laughter. ''You mock me. But I will tell you, his conductor's wand—well, a deadlier weapon has never been used by a father.''

Todd's eyes widened. ''He spanked you with it?''

Jill bit her lip, not liking the flash of dismay in her son's eyes. Tony obviously saw it, too. He crouched down in front of Todd. ''No, no, but he used to point at me with it, and threaten to make me play…the viola!''

As Todd giggled, Jill heard the doorbell. ''He's here.''

Sven, Bjorn and Tony all exchanged a knowing look.

''Behave, boys, or I'll let Todd choose the pancake flavor this Sunday.''

''Jelly bean!'' Todd shouted.

As Jill left the room to get the door, she heard the satisfying groans of three young men.

Yep. They'd definitely be on their best behavior.

"THIS IS absolutely not a date," Seth told himself for the twentieth time as he waited on Jill's front porch. In spite of the knowing look his elderly neighbor, Rhoda, had given him when she'd passed him on the stairs on his way out this evening, this was not about romance. It was just a dinner between two old friends. Two old, hot-for-each-other, you-have-the-power-to-rip-my-heart-out friends.

"Maybe this wasn't such a good idea," he muttered.

"Yes, it was."

Hell, he hadn't noticed the door opening. "Hi, Jill."

"Having second thoughts?" she asked as she stepped aside to let him into the house.

He shook his head and followed her, watching the graceful way her body moved. She looked beautiful, wrapped in a soft, gauzy dress the color of the midnight-blue sky. Her long, pale blond hair snaked over her shoulder in a thick, luxurious braid. And for a silent, charged moment, Seth thought about nothing more than pulling the braid apart and separating the strands between his fingers.

"Seth?"

He dragged his eyes off her, forcing a smile. "Sorry."

"You never answered my question. Are you having second thoughts about tonight?"

"No. Definitely not."

No second thoughts. No turning back. No regretting the wasted years, not now when they could be starting something new. Okay, so maybe it was too late for any romantic relationship. Maybe they'd hurt each other too much all those years ago and maybe she'd never trust him again.

But it was at least worth finding out.

"Is one of your boarders watching Todd tonight?"

"All of them," she said with a grin. "Four guys and pay-per-view wrestling. Sometimes this house is so full of testosterone I'm afraid I'm going to start sprouting whiskers and scratching myself."

Yeah, right. Jill was all woman, all ethereal beauty and gentle grace, and so lovely it almost hurt to look at her. She'd affected him yesterday. Tonight—with her whisper-soft dress, her welcoming smile, the twinkle of happiness in her eyes—she absolutely slew him.

"I sometimes feel like I'm living in a frat house," she continued.

"Sounds like old times. With your brothers."

"Yeah," she agreed. "Only now, I *really* get to boss them all around!"

Remembering the way her younger brothers would groan about Jill telling them what to do during their teenage years, he figured she was enjoying the hell out of her current situation.

After a proper introduction to her three foreign exchange students—who took turns making it very clear he'd better bring her home safe and sound—and a quick conversation about nasty green vegetables with Todd, Seth helped Jill with her coat and led her to his car. "So, Todd's comfortable home alone with the 'uncles'?"

"Yes." She probably heard the unasked question. "And I'm comfortable leaving him."

They buckled up and drove away as a misty rain began fogging up the windshield. Alone with her in the confines of his car, Seth found it much too easy to savor every breath, catching a hint of her gently scented skin, hearing the wispy sound her dress made whenever she moved. *Get a grip.*

"I'm sure you have complete trust in them," he finally replied, remembering they'd been discussing her boarders.

"Oh, absolutely. The international nursing exchange program does a complete background check, as does Seattle

Memorial." She laughed softly. "And so did the P.I. I hired."

He didn't blame her a bit. Not when it came to her son's safety.

"It's worked out so well. Particularly with Todd moving over to Round the Clock from Forrester Square Day Care, where he used to go. On the days he has to go in, one of the guys is usually available to take him or bring him home."

Judging by her house, Jill had the money for nannies or a live-in housekeeper. But he didn't even ask why she had Todd enrolled in a day care program. She'd never deprive her child of the chance to interact with other kids, to be a normal little boy going through normal childhood experiences. He'd have expected nothing less of her.

"So, did the carrots do the trick with Todd last night?"

"For now," she said with a sigh. "He swears he will use his stronger, carrot-nourished eyes to 'see' how the naughty things he wants to do might affect other people."

Seth nodded. Jill's tactics might be unusual, but he liked the way she was parenting her son. A creative, imaginative boy like Todd would be less impressed with the loss of his video games than by vivid mental pictures of possible outcomes to his actions.

"You're doing a great job with him, Jill," he admitted as he drove. "I hope I'll be as good a parent as you."

"Thank you," she murmured. Then she turned in her seat to stare at him intently. "Speaking of which, you do know you're in for a rough time, right? It is not easy raising a child alone."

So why are you doing it? He wanted to know, wanted to understand why Jill and her son were alone. Where was Todd's father? Why had he left? And, almost as important, was there any chance he'd be coming back into the picture?

"I know," he finally replied. "But I dare you to tell me it's not worth it."

"Oh, it's worth it. I wouldn't give up a single day I've had with Todd." Then she frowned. "Except, maybe, the day he learned the word *no*. Could have done without that one, let me tell you." Then she groaned. "Or the day he went to Round the Clock and showed all his friends the funny thing Grandpa did with his middle finger when somebody cut him off on the road."

Seth definitely pictured the moment. "Your dad's still a character, huh?"

She nodded. "He hates driving in Seattle. Likes the flat farmland back home."

He heard a soft sigh escape her lips and knew she was thinking of her family. "Do you see them a lot?"

"My parents come out a couple of times a year. And I still go home for the holidays."

Home for the holidays. They were coming up—Halloween in a week, Thanksgiving right around the corner. Seth hadn't given much thought to the holiday season this year, not wanting to picture how different everything would be without his father. He wasn't ready to face that quite yet, particularly with his mom still living in New York with Gina.

He had spent a few Christmases with Gina—his biological mother—in his early years, before she'd let Seth go live with her sister and brother-in-law. They'd definitely been interesting. Not particularly what he'd call warm and family oriented, though. Since Gina played the role of starlet whether performing or not, Christmases had usually involved fancy resorts, reporters, young foreign lovers and parties.

The first time Seth had ever put lights on a tree had been with his new dad—his uncle—who'd adopted him at age eight. They hadn't missed a Christmas since.

Until this year.

He pushed the melancholy thoughts out of his brain and focused on the here and now. As well as the who. If someone had told him a year ago he'd soon be in Seattle, sitting in a car with Jill Jamison, driving out for a friendly dinner, he'd have been looking for the men in the white coats.

When they arrived at the restaurant, a cozy bistro overlooking Lake Union, they were shown to a small, private booth in a back corner, as Seth had requested. "I'm sure you're used to being recognized, but I figured you might want to be unobtrusive. Discreet."

She raised a brow as she sat opposite him and thanked the hostess. "Because I'm out with a man? You don't want to end up on the cover of a tabloid, I take it."

No, he definitely didn't. But that wasn't the reason he'd asked for a secluded table. He wanted Jill to relax, to enjoy an evening when she didn't have to be "on"…not for him, not for the media, not for anyone. He had the feeling she seldom had such opportunities when she left her beautiful, secluded house.

"I don't think I'm tabloid worthy," he said after the waiter took their drink orders and left them alone.

"It wouldn't look good to the adoption agency if you were."

As usual, she'd leaped to the correct conclusion.

"No, I suppose it wouldn't," he admitted. "But if it means getting to see you looking happy and relaxed, it's worth it."

Her smile widened, even as she shook her head in bemusement. "I still can't quite wrap my mind around the idea of you adopting a baby. Raising a child alone."

Though no one was nearby, he leaned closer and lowered his voice, wanting to make sure they weren't overheard. Jill hadn't explained yet why she kept so quiet about her son, but he knew that's the way she wanted it. He had to respect her wishes. "Why not? You're doing a damn good job as a single mom. There are a lot of single dads out there, too."

"I wasn't being sexist," she quickly explained. "It's just you're so young, there's lots of time for you to...have kids."

Conceive kids. That's what she was thinking, that's the word he'd mentally inserted. And he'd be willing to bet that sent her mind tripping right along where his went...down memory lane to that narrow dorm room bed on her twentieth birthday.

He grabbed his drink from the waiter, who'd just returned. While the guy placed Jill's wine in front of her, Seth took two healthy sips of his beer. Afterward, he took a deep breath and tried to remain focused on the pleasant here and now. Not on the erotic there and then.

"I fully intend to...have more kids, I mean. After this first one. I can enjoy fatherhood as an adoptive dad, then as a biological one." His grin widened. "Hell, Jill, you know me. I always want it all."

She brought her glass of wine to her lips, but not before he saw a small, quick frown darken her face. Her lower lip quivered a bit and she blinked rapidly. "I hope you succeed," she murmured. "I hope you get everything you want." She glanced around the room. "Thankfully, no one appears to have recognized me yet, so you don't have to worry about the tabloids hurting your chances."

He couldn't believe she was back to that—thinking it could be bad for him to be seen with her. "I can imagine worse people to be seen in public with than the one and only Natural Girl."

He shook his head, remembering the original reason he'd gone to see her the previous morning. A reason that now seemed just a ridiculous excuse to seek her out. The idea of asking for her help with the adoption had been a crutch to lean on while he worked up the nerve to walk up to her door and ring the bell, knowing she might still hate his guts. Once he'd seen her face, spent some time with her again, he'd realized he no longer needed the excuse.

He liked having her back in his life. Period.

"Yeah, until you spill a drink on yourself and read the next day about how I threw it on you during a lovers' spat."

"I'm not as clumsy as Matt Damon," he said with a wry smile. "Besides, you're the wholesome girl next door, the earth mother. I don't think you could damage my reputation too badly."

She raised a dubious brow. "Yeah, the sweet, wholesome woman who lives with three young studs, had a baby out of wedlock, is allergic to the makeup she peddles and has a son known as Todd the Terrible."

He almost choked on a mouthful of water.

"I think you could find someone better to give you a reference," she finally concluded with a heavy sigh.

Reference. She thought she wasn't good enough to give him a damn reference! "Hey, none of that," he said, taking her hand in his on top of the table.

He glanced down at their joined hands. She rubbed the tip of her finger against his palm in a simple caress loaded with sensation. He almost pulled away. It was downright dangerous to be so affected by another person.

"You want the truth? Here it is." He knew he might look like a real jerk for what he was about to admit, but needed to do it, anyway. For her sake. "I didn't come to you yesterday for a reference. I came to you because I had this crazy idea of talking you into posing as my girlfriend to try to help with the adoption. That's how serious I am about you having a *great* image. So stop knocking yourself."

This time, *she* was the one who nearly choked on her drink. She pulled her hand away, then started to laugh. "Wow, I guess you definitely found out the hard way what a nutty plan that was.'' Her eyes sparkled in genuine amusement. ''No wonder you were so shocked by the guys.''

No, he'd been shocked by the guys because he'd been jealous as hell. But he didn't think she was ready to hear that yet.

''Why nutty?'' He knew she was still putting herself down in spite of her laughter. ''You're a terrific mother.''

''Thank you.''

''And a well-respected professional.''

She rolled her eyes. ''Yeah, right. A professional smiler.''

''Babe, if you could patent that smile of yours, you'd be a millionaire.''

She winced.

''Never mind. I already figured you *are* a millionaire.''

Nibbling the tip of her finger, she gave him a tiny nod.

''You'd have to be, with your address. Isn't Bill Gates one of your neighbors?''

She rolled her eyes. ''Uh…no. We're several million dollars apart in acreage.''

But she still had bucks. For some reason, hearing her confirm what he should have easily figured out before didn't bother Seth. Jill had never much cared about money. And neither had he. There were probably a lot of men who'd be feeling threatened by such a successful woman, especially such a beautiful one. Seth wasn't one of them.

He had enough respect for women—and confidence in himself—to never keep score when it came to things like career or money. He'd been raised with two sisters in a household that stressed respect between the sexes. The lessons his father had taught him had definitely sunk in.

''So, should I start trying to convince you I'm not a gigolo offering to be your love slave if you'll be my sugar mama?''

Her lush lower lip pushed out in an exaggerated pout.

"Aw, gee. I'd gotten my hopes up and everything. I was all ready to be...taken advantage of."

A rush of heat dropped through Seth's body as he focused on her mouth, on the wicked look in her eyes that had answered his joking suggestion with a deliberately sultry one.

He shook his head and lifted his glass. "You're bad."

The waiter returned before she could reply. After they ordered and were again alone, Jill cleared her throat.

"Okay, Seth, you talked me into it. I'll do it."

"Do what?"

She met his stare, her pale blue eyes locking with his own. "I'll pose as your girlfriend and help you with the adoption."

CHAPTER EIGHT

BECAUSE ANOTHER PARTY was seated at the table next to them shortly after Jill agreed to Seth's idea, they didn't discuss it much during dinner. She sensed his shock, which was probably equaled by her own. She hadn't realized she was going to say the words until they'd fallen out of her mouth and tumbled there between them, unable to be taken back.

Are you nuts, Jill Jamison? Pretend to be his girlfriend? Spend intimate time with a man who could get you out of your panties in under five minutes if he made one serious effort?

But later, as they were leaving the restaurant, she acknowledged the idea wasn't so crazy after all. Thinking over some of the things he'd said, some of his plans, made her see at least one possible benefit to the ruse: keeping herself from getting too emotionally involved with Seth again.

"Seth, look, you're a great guy. You'll be a wonderful father. So why shouldn't I help you, if I can, in achieving your goal?"

"It was a stupid plan, Jill," he insisted. "You're busy, you've got enough going on without getting involved in my problems. Your job, your house, your son…"

"None of which means I can't help out an old friend."

The word *friend* stuck a little bit on her tongue. God knew, she'd thought of Seth in a lot of ways over the years, but *friend* wasn't generally in the list of terms she'd used to describe him.

After the kisses they'd shared yesterday, she knew the feelings between them still ran a whole lot deeper than friendship. At least on her part.

But she was an adult—she could put those more primal emotions aside. She could ignore the attraction that still sparked between them, the snapping sensations on her skin every time his hand brushed hers. She could forget the way her whole body swayed toward him when she walked by his side. Her fingers would eventually stop itching to tangle in his hair, and he'd never notice how she kept leaning closer to him, breathing deeply to catch hints of his clean, earthy cologne.

Yes, she could get past her physical reactions and try to be a friend to this man who'd once meant so very much to her. She'd buried her sensual side for several years as she focused on being a mother. No reason she couldn't keep it in check now. Even if just looking at his lips made her remember the way he'd once eaten half a container of whipped cream off her body.

How on earth had she remained a virgin until her twentieth birthday?

Focus.

"I can do this," she insisted.

As a matter of fact, she believed she *had* to do it. By going into this as partners—friends—working toward a common goal, there was no way she could become confused about what was happening between them. She would always know she was playacting, pretending to be involved with Seth to help his chances for adoption. Knowing that from the start should prevent her from getting any stupid ideas. It would prevent foolish, impossible dreams from intruding on what she intended to be a friendly, platonic relationship.

Because they could never be what they'd been to each other in the past. Seth wanted what he'd always wanted.

He'd adopt a child, then later, when he met the right woman, he'd have the two-point-five additional kids.

Jill couldn't be that woman. Not *ever*. She couldn't give him the kids. Todd had been her one shot at motherhood. There would be no more pregnancies, no more babies for her. Once again, like eleven years ago, Seth was talking about dreams that she was not in a position to share.

Last time it had been her job that came between them. This time it was her reproductive organs…or lack thereof.

So, as twisted as the logic might sound, agreeing to pretend to be Seth's lady friend could help her remember she could never be involved with him in reality.

"I will be such an asset," she assured him as he unlocked the car door. "A completely respectable, responsible, all put together, great female influence."

She punched him when he responded by snorting with laughter. "What's so darned funny?"

"You had me up until the all-put-together part," he admitted, playfully rubbing his upper arm where she'd hit him. "Because organized you're not, sweetheart."

Her eyes narrowed. "You watch me, Seth. I'll be so nauseatingly normal, unobtrusive and nurturing, the agency will be begging you to let me help you raise your kid. So what do you say?"

She leaned against the car, facing him, watching the way his light brown hair was touched by gold under the muted glow of the street lamp. His green eyes practically glittered in the darkness as he stared at her, probably trying to see if she really intended to go through with it.

"Do we have a deal?" she prompted.

"You're sure you want to do this, Jill? I mean, you don't have to out of any old leftover loyalty or anything. I'm sure I can get the agency's approval for the adoption even if I'm a single guy."

"Yeah," she muttered in disgust. "But by the time they

admit that, you'll be old enough to be a grandfather, not a dad." Her tone dared him to disagree, but he didn't.

"Well…" he finally said, sounding like he was at least considering her proposal.

"What?"

"I got a call this afternoon from the agency. They're sending a caseworker out to my apartment on Monday evening. If you were there, I could introduce you." He quickly frowned. "But it's not like I want you to outright lie. We won't be coming out and saying we're engaged or anything."

She shook off the little spark that word conjured up. "Nope. We'll just be showing the caseworker that you are a happy-at-home, normal, family kind of man who is capable of a long-term relationship with another person. After all, we have known each other for a long time."

He tsked. "Even though we didn't set eyes on each other for eleven years."

"Details, details." She waved an airy hand. "Anyway, I'll be the maternal, nurturing female friend, there to lend a hand to you now or in the future when you have a screaming six-month-old with colic on your hands."

"Yikes."

"Prepare yourself, buddy. Those colicky six-month-olds are scarier than the thought of wearing spandex after childbirth."

He chuckled as he opened the car door and helped her in, watching while she buckled her seat belt. Then he walked around and got in the other side.

"Okay," he murmured as he joined her. "If you're serious about it, I'd appreciate any help you can give me."

She heard the note of appreciation in Seth's voice. "We were a good team, once," she replied softly. "We'll make you a daddy yet."

Just not the way they'd once dreamed of doing.

She fell silent, watching the lights from the buildings along the shore reflecting off the dark surface of the water.

Things didn't always work out the way people dreamed about them. But having the chance to make Seth's dream come true seemed, in some small way, a chance to help someone she'd once very much cared about. The same way she'd been helped by the doctors, her family, her friends. Heck, even the anonymous sperm donor who'd helped her create Todd.

Other people, including strangers, had given her what she most desired. How fortunate that she'd have the chance to do the same thing, give the same gift, to someone who'd long ago seemed to be the very center of her entire world.

"Speaking of colicky six-month-olds and kids in general," Seth said, seeming to sense her desire for a change of subject, "you never got around to the complicated answer to my simple question from yesterday."

She instantly knew what he was talking about. "Darn, I was kind of hoping you'd forgotten about that."

He shrugged as they drove out of the parking lot. "Hey, if it's none of my business, say so. I was just curious about how you managed to keep Todd's existence so quiet. And *why* you keep it so quiet."

Okay, she could handle this. He wasn't asking for the sticky details—the whos, whats or hows that would have involved yucky, depressing medical stuff, her health, sperm donors and the like. That was definitely not a conversation she wanted to have with Seth—not yet, anyway. Especially not with the way he worried about her. She didn't like the reaction people had when they found out the truth. Seth might hear the *C*-word and turn into an overprotective worrier who would never relax and be himself around her.

"I should think the why would be pretty obvious," she replied softly. "Think about our entire evening, how careful you were to try to shield me from the view of other people in the restaurant. The way the people at the next table stared and whispered when they figured out who I was.''

He nodded. ''You live in the spotlight.''

''Right. And I don't want my son living there with me.''

''Lots of celebrities are raising kids,'' he pointed out.

''True. But how many of them are raising a child *alone,* while working at a job that requires a lot of travel? Do you have any idea how tough that is?''

''I probably understand better than you imagine,'' he murmured. She heard a note of something in Seth's voice that surprised her. Intensity? Wistfulness? She couldn't name it.

''Anyway,'' she continued, ''a lot of public figures with children have a partner to step in to provide some normalcy while one is on location or making appearances. I'm in this all by my lonesome.'' Not wanting Seth to ask about Todd's other parent, she hurried on. ''So, because of that, and for…other reasons…I made the decision to keep my pregnancy and motherhood a secret.''

He didn't ask about the other reasons, so she didn't have to scramble around to try to figure out just how much of her medical history she wanted to share with him. If Seth was like most men, she could throw out the wickedly dangerous two words that would shut up ninety-five percent of the male population: *Pap smear.* But he wasn't like most men. He wouldn't shut up—he'd ask for more details. And who the heck wanted to have a conversation including those two words on a first date?

Cool it. This isn't a date. First or otherwise.

Anyway, date or not, she simply didn't want to go there. Not with Seth. Not right now.

''It's worked for you?'' he asked, sounding genuinely curious and a touch admiring. ''You've managed to have both and to keep them separate?''

''Absolutely. Which is a good thing, since George Wanamaker—he owns Mother Nature—really likes the world to see me as the girl next door…*not* a single mother.''

He lowered his voice. ''But are you happy? Deep down?''

She shrugged. ''Is anybody completely happy?'' She heard a note of regret in her own voice and forced herself to smile. ''Look, I've got a great life. I really should have been born a Gemini because I have two very distinct sides. Part of me is J.J., the cover girl who loves her job, adores flirting with the camera and running from the paparazzi. And I'm also part Jill, the mom, a homebody who likes nothing better than licking the creamy filling out of Oreos with her four-year-old.''

He grimaced. ''Don't tell me you still throw the cookies away.''

''Okay.'' She wouldn't tell him.

He just shook his head.

''So, in answer to your question, yes, I'm happy. It's worked out well. My job can be very stressful.…'' *Particularly lately.* ''And it's been a godsend having a private world that nobody knows about to come back to at night. Todd's my home. Even the guys are part of my private world, a world just for me. I wouldn't do anything to risk that.''

She crossed her arms, shivering slightly in the coolness of the car. Seth obviously noticed and reached for the heater button. ''You okay? Are you cold?''

''No, I'm fine.'' He looked as if he didn't believe her, so she explained. ''I was thinking what I really like is knowing there's *not* a great big target drawn on my son's head. If few people know about him, there's less of a chance of some wacko stalker wanting to get my attention through my baby.''

He visibly stiffened. ''Has anyone ever—''

"I've had my share. What person in the public eye hasn't? Nothing serious."

He shot her a look out of the corner of his eye, demanding that she tell him the truth. Knowing Seth, he wouldn't relent until she gave him some details. She sighed. "Somebody broke into my hotel room in New York once and slashed up my clothes."

"Oh, God…"

"And," she continued, "I had to get a restraining order against one rather unfortunate gentleman who has since, I am told, been incarcerated. But that's about it, other than the odd pornographic fan letter or death threat."

When he muttered a low curse, she added, "None of which typically get past my publicist into my mailbox."

"Don't you ever get sick of it?"

"Some of it. The bad parts. The schedule can be crazy. It's harder now that Todd's older to keep up with the travel and the appearances. Next year, when he starts school, I won't be able to whisk him across the country for a month at a time."

"No," he said softly, "you won't. So it sounds like you're going to have some decisions to make."

Before she could answer, they both heard the ring of a cell phone. "Sorry," he said as he took the call.

Jill remained quiet while he spoke on the phone. Judging by what Seth said, the person was calling about the mysterious baby still in the care of Shana Devlin and Keith Hewitt. Somehow, in the excitement of seeing Seth again, of making the decision to help him with the adoption, she'd nearly forgotten the frantic demands of his job. His shoulders stiffened, and his frown reminded her of just how much was at stake for Seth at Seattle Memorial.

"Everything okay?" she asked after he hung up.

"Yeah. But I'm going to have to go back to the hospital

after I drop you off. I was supposed to meet with the detective on the case yesterday, but he didn't show.''

Jill glanced at the clock on the dashboard of Seth's car and shook her head. "There's no need to drive me all the way home when we're already close to the hospital. Why don't we zip by there first? I don't mind."

"You're sure?"

"Absolutely sure," she replied, not bothering to hide her smile. "To be honest, I haven't been out with another adult on a Friday night in so long, I'd forgotten how nice it can be. I'm not quite ready for it to end."

No, she didn't want the evening to end. She and Seth might have been apart for more than a decade, but in one short evening, she'd remembered why she'd enjoyed being with him. He was easy to talk to, easy to listen to…definitely easy to look at. With him, she felt completely free to be herself. Not the Natural Girl—J.J. Not the big sister slash landlady. Not the mommy. Just Jill, the person.

It had been a long time since she'd felt so free.

"Besides," she continued, "I'm afraid it would totally destroy the guys' image of me if I arrive back home by nine o'clock the very first time they saw me going out with a man."

"So you don't live a swinging model's life, huh?"

She snorted a laugh. "I think they were all terribly let down the week they arrived. The famous model is in bed…*alone*…by ten, can't cook, never wears makeup and spends way more evenings watching Nickelodeon shows than schmoozing with glamorous friends."

"Boy, if I keep you out until eleven, the guys are going to think you're a real party animal, huh?"

She nodded.

"Okay then," he said, turning the car toward the hospital. "A hot swinging night at the hospital it is."

Jill leaned back in her seat, glad the phone call had not

only extended the evening, but distracted Seth from their previous conversation. They'd talked as much as she wanted to about the ups and downs of her unconventional life.

They drove in silence for a few minutes, but it was a comfortable silence between two people who'd always been in sync with each other. How funny that they'd fallen right into the same easy relationship, even if it was colored with the undertones of physical attraction that had never subsided between them.

The attraction hadn't disappeared throughout their evening. Not even after Jill had silently acknowledged that in spite of how much she wanted Seth, she couldn't have him.

Still, she'd been very aware of him. Every move of his body had drawn her eye. The way his lips pursed when he sipped from his glass had made her heart skip more than one beat. His hands on his silverware, his smile, the way his golden brown hair fell over his brow when he glanced down…*everything* about him appealed to her, to the inner Jill—the deeply sensual woman she'd kept buried for such a long time.

And once in a while, when she'd look up too quickly and find him staring at her, she knew he was every bit as aware. Every bit as affected.

It really was too bad she'd already figured out there could be nothing for them in the future, due to his goals and her medical history. Because, deep inside her most secret self, she could admit how much she wanted there to be something for them in the here and now.

Something physical. Something rich and sensual and evocative.

If she were a riskier woman, an unattached, live-in-the-moment kind of woman, she'd grab the here and now, the rich and sensual, and to hell with the future. She wasn't that woman, however. Maybe she could have been, had there not been Todd to consider. But there *was* Todd. There was her real life and her real responsibilities.

Having a hot, reckless affair with a man who could arouse her with a single look across a table in a crowded restaurant didn't fit into her current life. Unfortunately for her.

Hearing Seth chuckle quietly, she took a deep breath and forcibly pulled her mind out of forbidden, erotic territory and back to the reality of their current relationship as friends. "What's so funny?"

"I could have told the guys you're not a night owl. How many times did you fall asleep during a movie before I finally learned never to take you to a late show?"

She raised a brow, thankful for his light teasing. That made it easier to think of him as a buddy, almost as one of the guys, rather than the man who'd introduced her to certain parts of her body she hadn't known existed before he'd touched them. Or the one who'd left her shaking and unbelievably needy when he'd kissed her yesterday.

"How do you know it wasn't the movies that put me to sleep?"

"Jill, you nodded off during *Lethal Weapon*."

"Long movie."

"During the Mel Gibson half-naked part." He remembered her Mel Gibson phase. Later, she'd almost worn out her videotape of *Lethal Weapon*. Particularly the gratuitous bare butt scene.

"Okay, you got me." Nibbling her lip, she admitted, "I guess I'm still an Iowa farm girl at heart. Early to bed, early to rise, and all that good, wholesome, natural girl stuff." She knew she sounded disgusted, but couldn't help it. Just once she'd like to be thought of as the mysterious, exotic, femme fatale. Not the corn-fed beauty from the Midwest.

"Yeah, add that to the diet soda and lo mein at 10:00 a.m., and you definitely add up to Miss All-American."

"We all have our little proclivities," she said with a prim

sniff. "I'd be willing to bet you still dump the occasional raw egg and O.J. in the blender before a bruising game of one-on-one in the park with your buddies?"

He sighed, obviously reminiscing. "I miss those days. Most of my college friends have left Seattle. Nobody to play basketball with except my seventy-year-old neighbor, Rhoda."

She giggled.

"Don't laugh. She's pretty damn good in spite of her cane."

"I don't think I'd be telling too many people you're getting your ass whupped on the basketball court by a cane-wielding geriatric."

"I didn't say she whupped my ass." He glanced over at her, amusement dancing in his eyes. "I can usually take her out with an elbow to the ribs."

She shook her head as she laughed. "We're so warped."

"Yeah, I'm remembering that."

She was, too. The two of them had loved nothing more than getting involved in silly, outrageous conversations in the old days. The memories almost made it easier to understand her own son. She supposed that sweetly tart little piece of fruit hadn't fallen so far from the family tree after all.

"I think Sven and Bjorn played in high school back in Sweden," she finally mused. "If you're interested."

"Ouch. Talk about *bruising* games. Then again, the big ones are pretty slow."

She lowered her face so he wouldn't see her smile. "Sven also tried out for the Olympic track team."

"I think my knee is already begging me to forget about it," he replied with an exaggerated wince. "Maybe I'd better stick to Tinkertoys with Todd. That's more my speed these days."

"Oh, yeah, you're so ancient at thirty-one." She shook her head and pursed her lips. "Besides, I hate to tell you this, but Tinkertoys are way out, buddy. You want to hang with my son, you'd better bone up on superheroes saving the planet."

"I don't think I saved any of my Underoos."

Jill snorted with laughter. "Todd has a whole drawer full of them—underwear and p.j.'s. Maybe I should just let him wear those with some red fabric for a cape."

"I'm crushed that they're not made for old guys like me." He let out an exaggerated sigh and glanced at her over his shoulder. "I've searched everywhere."

"You could probably find some on eBay."

He winced. "Used."

"Gotcha."

"Should I keep quiet about your superhero underwear quest? I don't imagine that'd do your image any good."

He raised a brow and gave her a wickedly knowing look. "Maybe I just date women with superhero fantasies."

She swallowed hard, her mind going exactly where he'd meant it to. Oh, boy, could she relate. The Seth she remembered had definitely seemed to have some body parts made out of steel.

How could this man make her laugh and make her hot and aroused with the same damn words?

As Seth drove, easily navigating the dark, wet streets, Jill watched, lost in thought. In spite of the way their last afternoon in her dorm room had colored her perspective, it was now easy to remember how very much she'd liked being with him. Laughing with him. Becoming hopelessly aroused by him. Never knowing what he'd say or do next, but trusting it to be something wonderful.

He was funny and sexy. Confident and self-deprecating. Smart and nurturing. Cocky and tender.

She'd never known a man as completely comfortable with who he was, with his own masculinity, his own place in the world. She'd sometimes envied Seth that, always knowing where he was going and what he wanted. His ability to go after whatever he desired, while never hesitating in laughing at himself when the occasion warranted it, had been an intoxicating combination for her as a young woman.

She'd never known another man like him. And she hoped her son grew up to be such a man.

"So, are you sure Todd's not going to want to be a nurse now? Those guys of yours are single-handedly going to change the image of male nurses."

"No, I don't think that's even occurred to him yet. He personally thinks giving shots has to be the worst job in the world, since getting them is worse than being hugged and kissed by an old, wrinkly-faced grandfather."

As they passed one of the huge totem poles in the downtown area, she knew they were nearing the hospital. "So, you never told me, why does the detective want to meet with you now? It's pretty late on a Friday night to be working, even for Seattle's finest, isn't it?"

"This case has gotten to be a 24/7 job, apparently." He glanced at her and grinned. "It seems Detective Dorsey was coming to see me yesterday, to give me an update, when he saw you and Todd leaving. I guess his daughter is friendly with Todd down at Round the Clock, and he recognized him right away."

"Detective Jaron Dorsey? He's Tina's dad. According to Todd," she continued, "Tina Dorsey is planning on being his wife. Or a fire truck. She hasn't yet decided which."

He nodded, thinking it over. "Interesting career choices. Which one is Todd rooting for?"

"He says it doesn't matter. If she doesn't want to be his wife, he'll still get to drive around on her all day because he plans to be a fireman."

This time he snorted with laughter and Jill laughed with him as she added, "Unless, of course, he nails the flying thing, in which case he intends to go straight into super-heroing.''

His laughter ended with a genuine, heartfelt smile. ''That kid of yours is something else. You are one lucky woman, Jill.''

Yes, indeed she was. How remarkably astute of Seth to have figured that out so quickly for himself.

She stared at his profile, softly illuminated by the dash-board lights, admiring the strength of his jaw, the sweep of his lashes. God, there was so much to like about this man. Not the least of which was his impeccable judgment about children.

If only he didn't *so* want one of his own…

''Tell me about Tina's dad,'' she said, sending that thought to the depths of her subconscious. She had no business dreaming about Seth changing his mind. ''Why'd he decide not to come to see you yesterday?''

''Jaron knows you don't like reporters, so when he saw you, he steered Savannah McCain away from my office.''

That explained why the ravenous reporter hadn't caught them making out on Seth's desk the day before. ''He must have been the one talking to her and her cameraman down the hall.''

Seth shrugged. As they pulled into the garage, Seth bee-lined for a private parking area for employees of the hospital. ''All I can say is he's got great timing.''

''Oh?''

''Yep. If they'd been a few minutes earlier, or later, you wouldn't have had to jump on me in my office.''

She gasped. ''I didn't jump on you!''

''Face it, Jill, you jumped.'' He shot her a knowing look. ''Not that I'm complaining.''

Embarrassed, she bit her bottom lip. She did not want to start talking to Seth about their wild kiss, because that would only make her want another one. Kissing Seth was like giving in to a craving and eating nacho cheese chips. The more she nibbled, the more she wanted. If she wasn't careful, she could devour an entire bag. Or find herself naked and horizontal with a man she already knew had the power to break her heart. Because she couldn't have him...not for keeps.

Not without costing him the one thing he'd wanted for as long as she'd known the man.

"Well," she said, intentionally changing the subject, "I guess I owe Detective Dorsey one. That was very nice of him. Are detectives allowed to accept thank-you gifts? I think I'll bake him some cookies."

"Hmm...hope he likes Cajun food," he mused as he pulled away from the intersection.

She tilted her head in confusion.

"You know, since everything you cook turns out blackened."

As she stuck her tongue out at him in the darkness, Jill heard his soft laughter.

"It's okay, Jill. I turned out to be a damn good cook."

"Yeah, that's what Tony said. He ate my omelette yesterday after I left to chase you down and punish you for thinking I'd stooped to seducing babies."

He reached for her hand in the darkness, entwining his fingers with hers. "Have I told you again that I'm sorry?"

Staring at their joined hands, she shook her head.

"I'm sorry."

She smiled as Seth got out of the car and came around to open her door. Just how long could a grown woman be expected to resist something as addictive and delicious as nacho chips....

Or first loves?

CHAPTER NINE

JARON COULD HAVE MET with Seth Nannery the next day rather than return to the hospital that night. He didn't doubt he'd be back at Seattle Memorial, even though it would be Saturday. He figured Nannery would, too, given the guy's frenzy to keep the hospital looking helpful and crystal clean to the media.

But alone in the apartment with the kids out at an early Halloween party, he found himself heading back to the E.R. He'd called the hospital PR guru on the way in.

Nannery had been the excuse. The way Annabelle Peters's entire face lit up when he walked in had been the payoff. Since she was working the night shift tonight, and he'd been upstate all day, they hadn't seen each other for hours. She obviously hadn't expected to see him until the next morning.

He ignored the peeking nurses and bustling med students to give her a warm kiss hello. The soft, dreamy look in her eyes told him she didn't mind. "Where are Tina and Ricky?"

"At a party. I know, I know, Halloween's not for another week, but one of their friends is jumping the gun to avoid next weekend's rush, and they badgered me until I said they could go." He gave an exaggerated sigh. "I'm sure they're devouring a ton of orange candy and drinking enough sugary hot apple cider to have them up going to the bathroom twenty times tonight."

She smiled, the kind of warm, loving smile that told him

she saw right through his grumbling. "Uh-huh. And I'm quite sure you didn't go through an entire roll of film before they left, getting those costumes of theirs from every angle?"

Yeah. She definitely saw right through him. "Have I thanked you enough for saving my butt on those? With this rain, the crepe paper idea would have resulted in one soggy pink witch and a sopping red wizard."

A flush of warmth rose in her cheeks. Jaron knew she was thinking about the day they'd worked on the costumes with his kids. That had been a turning point in their relationship.

"I can't wait to see them go trick-or-treating next weekend," she said.

While sharing a quick coffee break in the lounge, Jaron filled her in on the details he'd learned today about the couple involved in the car crash. Annabelle, more than most, had a keen interest in the case. She had, after all, been treating one of the victims when the woman had passed away. Jaron didn't know quite how Annabelle handled that part of her job. Then again, he sometimes had to wonder how he managed to deal with his own.

Family. Home. Tina and Ricky. And now her.

Knowing she had to get back to work, he kissed her goodbye. "I'll stop in before I leave again, okay?"

"Might be busy. A week before Halloween, a Friday night and a full moon."

"Oooh, hot times in the E.R. tonight," he muttered.

She lifted a brow. "And in the police station, I bet."

Yep. They had a lot in common. He was still mulling over how perfect that was while he rode the elevator up to Seth Nannery's office. The head of PR was just unlocking the door, ushering in a tall, slim blonde when Jaron arrived at the PR office.

"Perfect timing," the other man said when he looked up and saw him approaching.

Jaron glanced briefly at the woman.

"There's someone who wants to thank you for your help yesterday," Seth continued.

Curious now, Jaron followed Seth into his darkened office. He waited for him to flip on the light, then saw the woman standing by the desk. He recognized her right away, particularly since her face was spotlighted on a billboard right out the window. "Jill…"

"Hi, Jaron," she said, walking over and extending a hand in greeting. "I really appreciated you rescuing me from that shark from channel seven."

After chatting briefly with Jill about their children, as well as the great staff down at Round the Clock, Jaron began to fill Seth in on the investigation, as he'd promised to do. The spin doctor appeared completely comfortable talking in front of Jill, leading Jaron to suspect the two knew each other very well. Judging by the way the other man couldn't keep his eyes off the blonde, and the way she, in turn, kept finding every excuse she could to touch his arm or lean close to him, they had a *very* friendly relationship.

Or, hell, he could be imagining things. Just because he finally had some romance in his life again, he'd gone soft and sappy, looking for it in everybody else's, too.

"So, you were saying you'd gone up to a town near the Canadian border to follow up on some leads?" Seth prompted.

Jill cleared her throat. "Do you want me to step outside while you talk?"

Seth grabbed her hand. "This is not official. I trust you." He glanced at Jaron, silently telling him the same thing. "Okay with you, Detective?"

Jaron nodded. In her position, Jill Jamison knew a thing or two about privacy and keeping secrets. "Yeah."

Todd's mother smiled slightly as she sat back down. Jaron noticed she didn't let go of Nannery's hand. Maybe his suspicions hadn't been so soft and sappy after all.

Jaron looked at Seth. "Just remember, it's all off the record, at least for now. I'm doing this because I owe you for the way I suspected Annabelle—and the hospital—in the beginning."

"Understood."

"Now, what were you saying?" Jill said.

"Well, you know we tracked the stolen car the couple had been driving to a little town called Glacier, near the Canadian border."

"How did you know it was the same car?" Jill asked. "Wasn't it destroyed in the crash?"

Jaron nodded. "Yeah, it was in bad shape from the impact with the truck." His throat tightened. "And the fire." Jaron closed his eyes briefly, still picturing the violent crash. It amazed him that the baby had survived, completely unharmed. Or that the female in the passenger seat had lived long enough to make it to the E.R., where she'd been treated by Annabelle.

God, life could be so cruel. He knew that more than a lot of people, given the loss of his wife two years ago. Which made it even more incredible that he, Ricky and Tina could have discovered such happiness again…with Annabelle.

"But the crime lab was eventually able to identify the VIN," he finally continued.

He didn't tell her that the lab had had to piece together the number from a couple of locations in the car, since they'd been unable to find even a few square inches undamaged by the fire. Forcing the mental image of the twisted, burning metal—and the faces of the couple in the crash—out of his brain, Jaron said, "That was the first real break we got, other than the medical evidence."

"So, did the original owners of the car help in the investigation?" Seth asked.

Jaron sighed. "They didn't know anything. But once we had information on the theft, and the location, we at least had somewhere else to dig."

"And possible witnesses who could connect the couple—and the baby—to the car?" Seth said, looking speculative.

Jaron continued. "I had someone from my group go up to Glacier to investigate the area. They scoured the town, local businesses, parking lot customers. Nothing." He shook his head, reliving the frustration of the past week or so, when the investigation had appeared stalled.

"So what happened?" Jill asked.

A weary smile widened his lips. "One of those little gifts we never take for granted in law enforcement. My partner and I decided we were getting tired of sitting around with our thumbs up our...well, we were tired of waiting for something to turn up. So we went up to Glacier today to try to shake something loose."

"Any luck?" Seth asked.

Jaron nodded. "Yeah. One of the people we were interviewing from the parking lot mentioned he thought he saw a couple with a baby walking into the lot from the small regional hospital up the street the day the car was stolen. The guy had gone out of town on an extended business trip, so nobody talked to him during the first sweep."

Seth leaned forward in his chair, intensely focused. Obviously the spin doctor knew when the good stuff was about to come out. "Now we get to it."

"You bet," Jaron confirmed.

"It was lucky you found him," Jill said. "So, the hospital—that was where you turned next?"

"Yeah. As it turns out, the car was taken on the very same night three female infants were born or being treated in that hospital."

"Including the baby from the crash?" Jill seemed concerned, not intrusive.

"We don't know yet," Jaron admitted. "One of the babies was checked out by her parents really fast and against medical advice, given her age. They left in a hurry, and were abrupt with some of the staff. Not illegal, just…unusual. We're trying to get physical descriptions of the parents to see if they match the couple killed in the accident."

Or at least what the couple killed had looked like before the accident.

He didn't share that tidbit, either.

Nannery nodded, obviously leaping directly to the same initial conclusion Jaron and his investigative team had reached. "You think they stole the baby right out of the hospital?"

Jaron shrugged, but shook his head. "It makes sense… except there were no missing infants. There were the proper number of babies in the facility both before and after that night. Nobody went home empty-handed."

"But she *wasn't* their baby, according to the DNA, right?" Jill frowned in speculation. "Maybe they'd already kidnapped a newborn, something was wrong, and they came to the hospital for treatment. They panicked, thinking someone would find out she wasn't really theirs, and took off."

Jaron didn't wonder about her detailed knowledge of the case. Everyone in Seattle had been following it. The media had reported the DNA findings—proving the baby hadn't been with her biological parents—days ago.

Before he could reply, he saw Nannery cross his arms and narrow his eyes. "Or maybe two of the babies were switched right there in the hospital."

Jaron nodded slowly. "Bingo. That's exactly what we're thinking. We'll have to rule out error on the hospital's part, of course, but at this point we're working on the theory that the couple killed in the car crash made a deliberate switch.

Judging by the autopsy, the female victim delivered a baby at the same time we estimate baby Chris was born. It nearly all fits.''

"Not entirely." Jill shook her head, looking disbelieving. "Why on earth would someone switch their own baby with someone else's? That makes no sense to me, particularly not as a mother."

Nor to Jaron, as a father. "Like I said…it *nearly* fits."

Because, for the life of him, Jaron couldn't make sense of it, either. What would drive any parents to swap their baby for a stranger's? He'd sooner lose a limb than risk one precious day with his son and daughter.

"Probably, when we find the answer to that question," he said with a deep sigh, "we'll be able to solve this entire case."

Seth cleared his throat, obviously having thought of something. But he didn't speak up. He looked uncomfortable with whatever he'd been about to say, crossing his arms in front of his chest and remaining silent.

Jaron had seen the tactic before. "What is it? You've thought of something."

Todd's mother turned to stare expectantly at Seth, too.

"Well," Nannery replied in a slow, reluctant voice, "I think if you're looking at possible reasons someone might deliberately switch a baby…you should probably start in the hospital's pediatric records."

After one moment, Jaron knew exactly what the other man meant.

No, a normal set of parents wouldn't switch a perfectly healthy baby for a stranger's. Which meant they might not have been dealing with a normal set of parents.

Or they might not have been dealing with a perfectly healthy baby.

THOUGH HE HADN'T known him long, Seth really liked Jaron Dorsey. The detective was forthright and honest. Obviously a tough-edged cop, he also seemed incredibly fair. And it was quite apparent that Dorsey doted on his kids.

He hadn't liked the idea Seth had brought up any more than Seth did. Was it possible the desperate parents had switched their baby for another one for a medical reason? Sounded crazy, but no crazier than thinking someone would swap babies for no reason at all.

Hell. That brought up a whole new set of frightening possibilities. First and foremost being the other baby. Whoever she was, wherever she was, she might well be in need of medical attention. Or she might have a set of grief-stricken parents who had no idea she wasn't even theirs!

The pressure had just increased on the Seattle PD. Jaron looked even more weary when he stood up to leave. After he again reminded them of their need to keep things confidential until the police were ready to reveal more details, he said good-night and left.

Seth and Jill remained in his office, sitting quietly for a moment or two. Jill stared at her own hands, obviously mulling over everything the detective had shared with them. "Seth, why do you think the police should start with the medical records? Don't you think they've already scoured through them for DNA and blood types?"

He merely shrugged, not comfortable pointing out the unpleasant explanation.

"I still can't think of one good reason why any mother would switch her baby with someone else's. Giving up a child for her own good, because you can't raise her, is one thing. But dumping one and taking another…that's just inconceivable." She lowered her voice to a whisper. "Like trading a pair of shoes for another color."

Seth—not yet a parent—thought it unlikely, and pretty sick. Still, it wasn't entirely impossible. After all, he had firsthand experience with mothers who didn't have a whole hell of a lot of maternal instinct.

But Jill didn't know that. Never had, probably never would. He couldn't picture Jill meeting Gina in the future. Including his father's funeral, he himself had only seen her three times in the past four years.

"Hopefully the police will find out, one way or another," Seth said. "If the babies were switched, I hope to God they find out soon so they can get baby Chris back where she belongs." *And make sure the other baby is okay.*

Jill stared at him, apparently noticing his genuine concern over the situation. "This is hard for you, isn't it? Aside from your job, the hospital and everything. The whole issue of abandoned or stolen babies is touchy right now. Because of the adoption."

Closing the blinds, which he'd forgotten to do earlier today when leaving work, he nodded. "Yeah. But I guess it's touchy for anyone who loves kids, isn't it?"

She shivered. "God, I remember being here in the hospital after Todd was born, afraid to let him out of my sight. I didn't want to go to sleep unless my mom or dad was in the room because I was afraid I'd wake up and he'd be gone."

Seth froze, picturing Jill here in this building, going through childbirth, holding Todd for the first time. Nursing him, changing him, falling in love with him from the moment she saw his wrinkled little face. He swallowed hard. "You delivered here?"

She nodded.

Seth then focused on the rest of her comment. "You relied on your mom and dad." He leaned a hip against his desk, crossing his arms in front of his chest in a casual pose so forced he wondered that she didn't call him on it. "So, should I assume Todd's father wasn't around?"

Jill shook her head slowly, a hint of color rising her

cheeks. He recognized the look. She didn't want to talk about Todd's father. "No."

It's none of your business, anyway.

"Sorry, I shouldn't have pried," he said, knowing she wanted him to move on to another subject. "I guess we should go. It's ten-thirty. Those guys of yours are probably ready to send out a search party if this is the latest you've stayed out in a long time."

She giggled, looking relieved he'd let her off the hook.

Maybe one day she'd trust him enough to tell him the whole story. He found himself hoping it wasn't what it looked like—that Jill couldn't talk about Todd's father because it was too painful for her. That would indicate she'd had serious, lasting feelings for the guy. And while Seth had long ago acknowledged her right to get on with her life after they'd split up, he'd never quite worked his mind up to picturing her actually being in love with someone else.

Nope. Didn't want to go there. So he didn't particularly mind letting the subject drop.

Jill stood to leave, but as she did, her purse fell out of her lap, its contents spilling onto the floor. "Whoa," she whispered with a quick gasp. She raised a hand to her brow. "Guess I stood up too fast again."

Seeing her pale face and the way her lashes fluttered as she rapidly blinked her eyes, Seth took her arm. "You okay?"

"Fine," she insisted. "Maybe it's just too late for me to be out. Another hour and I'll turn into a pumpkin." She flashed him a smile. "I'm usually zonked out cold by this time on a Friday night."

He chuckled. "Oh, you fast-living woman you. Let me get your stuff."

She didn't protest, leading him to think she really was feeling unwell. "Are you coming down with something?"

he asked as he gently pushed her back into her chair. "You didn't eat much at dinner."

She shook her head. "No. It's stress, that's all. My schedule's been pretty crazy lately."

He nodded, knowing what that was like. "Sounds like you need to relax. Maybe take some time off."

"Time off? With a four-year-old in the house? Right."

He chuckled as he bent down to retrieve her purse and its spilled contents. Her hairbrush had landed under another chair, and a tube of lipstick had rolled beneath the desk. Seth picked them up, grateful no scary-looking feminine products had scattered in his office. He'd been raised with two sisters. Feminine products still instantly made him think of moody teenage girls, a run on anything chocolate in the house—including semisweet baking squares—and him and his father hiding out in the basement, working on science projects, to wait out the storm.

"Here you go," he said, placing the purse on her lap. He was still crouched right in front of her, his torso nearly touching her knees as she sat in the chair. Their eyes met and locked in the kind of intense concentration that they'd been skirting around all evening.

The kind they'd shared a long time ago.

He thought about smiling, laughing away the moment by teasing her about bringing him to his knees.

He didn't. Somehow he couldn't joke, couldn't laugh, not when he was so close to her, not when his hand remained on her thigh, beside the purse he'd deposited there.

A deep breath and her soft cologne filled his senses. Beneath his fingers, he felt her leg quiver, just a tiny bit, as they both acknowledged the sudden atmosphere of intimacy enveloping them.

He wanted her. On a deep, basic, primal level buried inside him, he considered this woman his and his alone.

Whether separated by several states, a slew of billboards or eleven years.

He'd always wanted her. He probably always would. So it was genuinely impossible to prevent his mind from filling up with memories of being with her, touching her, tasting her.

Right here, right now, he wanted to kiss Jill more than he wanted to wake up to see another sunrise.

She leaned closer, reaching out to brush his hair back off his forehead. Where her fingers touched him, his body reacted with sizzling awareness.

''Thank you,'' she whispered. She didn't pull away, but instead ran her fingers in a light caress across his temple, down his jaw and to his chin. When she oh-so-delicately slid the back of her pinky across his lips, he could no more resist her than the moon could resist the earth's gravity.

Weaving his hands into the loose braid of long, shimmery hair he tugged her toward him. He gave her a moment to pull away, but she leaned closer until their mouths met in a sweet, warm kiss.

She twisted her hands into his shirt, pulling him closer, tilting a little and licking at his lips to tell him what she wanted.

More.

And how she wanted it.

Wet. Hot. Deep and slow.

He obliged, meeting the erotic, welcoming curl of her tongue with his own, noting the luscious way she tasted— like the mocha coffee she'd drunk after dinner. And pure, undiluted Jill, who'd always tasted perfect to him.

His hands were sliding under the hem of her gauzy dress to touch the softness of her legs before his brain could send the command for him to keep his distance. Her silky hose created a delicious, slick sensation against his fingertips, and she moaned, deep in her throat, when he gently caressed the delicate skin at the inside of her knees.

"This wasn't supposed to happen," she murmured against his lips. Dropping her head back, she closed her eyes, offering him the soft skin of her throat to sample. He did so, pressing butterfly-soft kisses along her jawline, then to her pulse point, and finally the spot under her right ear that had always made her quiver.

She still quivered.

"Seth…"

"Sh…"

If they talked about it, if they analyzed it, they'd stop. And he didn't want to stop. Simple as that.

Releasing the fabric of his shirt, she moved her hands higher, until she touched the side of his neck. A simple scrape of her fingertip on his throat had him groaning. It was all he could do to remain sane when she delicately stroked his neck and kneaded the muscle in his shoulder.

"We'll stop soon, 'kay?" she whispered as she leaned closer to press a hot, wet kiss on his throat.

He reacted by pushing the filmy fabric of her dress higher. Inch by inch. Revealing more of her long, lovely legs, which invited his touch and his gaze. "Uh-huh."

It sure didn't feel like she was stopping. Particularly when her fingers began to deftly unfasten the buttons of his shirt, giving her access to his overheated skin. Then she flattened her palms on his chest, nearly sending him right out of his mind as she stroked the muscles there.

"I told myself an hour ago I couldn't do this—couldn't have you," she whispered as she slid closer, until her parted legs curved around both sides of his body and her hair brushed his cheek.

Judging by the hot feel of feminine skin, covered only by her thin stockings and what looked to be a miniscule pair of peach satin panties, he figured she'd changed her mind.

Lucky him.

"I still know I can't have you, Seth. Not in the long run," she mumbled. He almost questioned that, almost shook himself out of the erotically induced fog filling his brain. Then she shrugged one shoulder, somehow allowing her loose dress to fall off and bare her pale skin. And thought evaporated.

"But tonight I'm tempted to forget about the long run. I seem to want to focus on the here and now."

When she arched back, reaching up only to unfasten the top button of her dress, he knew she wanted his mouth on her.

A saint couldn't have resisted the silent invitation.

His breath caught in his throat as he watched her slip the button free, then trail the tip of her index finger down to the hollow of her throat. Lower. He followed with his lips, tasting her, kissing her, savoring every bit of her as she bared her perfect, lovely breasts and leaned back to give him access.

Then he was tasting her, nibbling on the delicate curve, nudging her pale blue bra down and out of the way. He stared for a moment, noting that motherhood had made her fuller, and he hungered for a taste of her.

Unable to resist, he rubbed his lips over her beautifully puckered nipple. She hissed, jerked in reaction and twined her fingers in his hair.

"Do you like it like this, Jill?" he whispered, flicking his tongue out to sample that sensitive, dark peak. "Do you still love being tasted? Here?"

She moaned. "More than you can imagine…it's been forever."

Yeah. Forever since he'd tasted her, held her, suckled her. He did so now, coaxing her nipple into his mouth just the way he knew she liked, covering the other with his palm and listening to her coos of pleasure.

He moved his other hand up her thigh, with agonizing slowness, until he finally reached the top of her stocking and came in contact with warm, vibrant skin. He groaned, stroking her, teasing her. He was overwhelmed by the warmth, the almost electric connection. The shocking intensity and sensuality.

He had it all, right here at his fingertips. And he definitely wanted more. When he slid his hand higher, until his fingers flirted with the lacy elastic side of her panties, her thrilled little whimper told him she wanted more, too.

Thankfully he paused to kick away some boxes on the floor beside the chair…to make room. Because two seconds before he would have pulled her down on top of him, he heard voices outside the door. ''They said he was up here. Would you come on?''

Jill's eyes immediately shot open and Seth yanked himself away. As she fumbled to tug her pretty blue bra back in place, he glanced at the door and noticed it was unlocked.

He had time to mutter, ''Hell,'' before the door opened and a woman's voice intruded. ''Well, I guess the Public Relations Director isn't *working* late on a Friday night after all.''

He didn't have to look to recognize the voice.

Savannah McCain.

CHAPTER TEN

JILL DIDN'T KNOW which upset her more—that she and Seth had been caught in a terribly intimate position by a well-known nosy reporter. Or that the reporter hadn't caught them five minutes later—*after* she'd had a chance to go just a little further with Seth. Considering the hot, achy emptiness between her thighs, and the way her nipples remained tight and exquisitely sensitive, she thought it was the latter.

Five minutes. They could have done a lot in five more minutes. Maybe not everything. Oh, no, not nearly everything she wanted to do with this man.

But a lot.

''Savannah,'' Seth said as he rose from the floor and nodded at the brunette.

The woman stared back and forth between the two of them, her tight smile not disguising her avid curiosity. And a hint of something else—anger? Jill couldn't say, but she had the feeling it was more than a reporter's desire for a scoop that made the woman look so ready to dig for dirt.

Before Savannah said a word, her harried-looking cameraman entered the office. Thankfully, his camera was turned off and pointing toward the floor. Jill intended for it to stay that way.

''Ever hear of knocking on a closed door?'' Seth continued, his voice quiet, but not completely hiding a note of rigidly controlled coolness.

''It's a public building,'' the woman replied easily. ''Besides, I was told you were *working* up here. Not—'' she gestured toward Jill ''—playing.''

Seth shrugged, his unconcern so apparent, only someone who knew him very well would have noticed the pulse beating in his temple or the way he kept his fingers clenched into his palms. ''What can I do for you, Ms. McCain?''

''I was looking for Detective Dorsey in the E.R. and they said he'd come up to see you.''

''He left a few minutes ago.''

She glanced toward Jill and her tone hardened. ''Didn't take long for you to move on to other things, did it?'' Then she paused, almost doing a double take. Her eyes widened. ''Oh, my God, you're J.J., aren't you? The Mother Nature rep?''

Taking a deep breath, Jill nodded as she rose from the chair. She'd forgotten about feeling woozy earlier, since she'd been completely caught up in Seth's arms. So she surprised herself by wobbling a little as she stood up. Seth immediately stepped closer, placing a steadying hand at her elbow. He gave her a concerned look and she shrugged, ignoring the dizzy sensation. After a moment, she gave Seth an appreciative smile, nodded that she was okay, and stepped away to stand on her own.

His expression demanded answers. Jill, who'd written off the light-headedness as stress and fatigue, was beginning to wonder if she shouldn't talk to her doctor and get some answers, too.

Savannah McCain watched the entire exchange without comment.

''Yes, I'm J.J.,'' Jill finally replied. ''We met last year.''

''At the Cancer Society fund-raiser,'' the reporter said. ''My, wouldn't fans of the *wholesome* girl-next-door be surprised to see you like this.'' She glanced over her shoulder toward the cameraman, obviously noticing his equipment was decidedly off. A frown tugged at her brow as she glanced back and forth between Jill and Seth.

To his credit, Seth managed to look incredibly relaxed as he crossed his arms and leaned one hip against his desk. "I just told you Detective Dorsey left," he said. "You might have passed him in the elevator. If you hurry, you can probably still catch him back down in the E.R."

The woman stepped closer to Jill. She obviously had no intention of leaving. "What are you doing here, J.J.? Do you and Seth…know each other?"

"We're old friends," Jill replied, noting the woman's use of Seth's first name.

The other woman looked skeptical. "Old friends. How nice. Funny, I don't typically greet my friends with quite so much enthusiasm."

Jill gave her a pleasant smile. "Oh, do you have any?"

She saw Seth's shoulders shake and knew he was mentally making meowing sounds in her direction. Okay, she'd been totally catty. Tough. Once in a while, the occasion warranted pure cattiness.

The reporter cast one more look at Jill, staring at her from head to toe. Jill dug her fingers into her own palms, smiling placidly, determined not to reach up to check if she'd missed a button on her dress, or to see just what frenzied condition her hair was in. Or whether her lips still showed the reddened evidence of Seth's passionate kisses. Judging by the way her mouth still tingled, she figured that was a great big yes. But she wouldn't give the woman the satisfaction of acting as though she had anything to be ashamed of.

The one time she'd met Savannah McCain, Jill had pegged her as a predator. Any sign of weakness and she'd go for the jugular. Just like she had at the fund-raiser when she'd tried to press Jill for information about her own medical background. It was as if she'd been able to sense that

Jill's commitment to cancer research was more personal than anyone had realized.

Thankfully, Jill's doctors and the hospital had been careful about upholding privacy rules, because she'd found out later that Ms. McCain had done some digging.

Nope. Couldn't give someone like this an opening—she'd go right on the attack.

Obviously realizing she wasn't going to turn Jill into a babbling idiot with the intimidating stare that probably worked on the average person on the street, the woman turned to Seth. "I came looking for an update for the eleven-o'clock broadcast. I'd hoped Detective Dorsey could give us a live interview, since I heard he was here." She cast another knowing look at Jill. "I never imagined you'd be here so late, Mr. Nannery. My, you're very diligent, aren't you?"

Seth never flinched. He didn't acknowledge her swipes by so much as a tightening of his jaw. "If you want to secure Detective Dorsey for an interview, you'd better hurry back downstairs, or you're going to be late for your own newscast."

He cast a pointed look at a clock hanging on the wall beside his desk. Jill watched as indecision washed over the reporter's face. Story? Or dirt?

Finally, the brunette frowned. "I should go." She stared hard at Seth. "I'll pop in to talk to you first thing Monday morning about how you and the hospital are handling things. I imagine you think the end of this investigation is in sight if you feel comfortable enough to use your office for...other private meetings." She turned to the door. "Nice seeing you again, J.J."

Then she was gone.

"She's such a bitch," Jill couldn't help muttering when they were alone again.

Seth chuckled. "Don't hold back. Tell me how you really feel, babe."

Nibbling her lower lip, she gave an apologetic grimace. "I'm sorry, that wasn't nice, was it? But I didn't like the way she looked at us."

"She and I have some personal animosity."

Understanding dawned. "You dated her."

"Once."

"And?"

He shrugged helplessly. "She's such a bitch."

The laughter had returned to Seth's green eyes and Jill took a moment to enjoy the warmth. How Savannah McCain could have stood having him look at her with such complete dispassion, such disregard, she didn't know. Jill wouldn't have been able to stand it. Because the alternative was so very intoxicating. When Seth Nannery looked at her with his tender, admiring, *hungry* gaze, Jill could barely keep a straight thought in her head.

"I guess I should get you home," he said softly, making no move to step closer and resume their passionate interlude.

She hid a sigh. "Yes, you probably should."

Definitely should. Before she got any more crazy ideas about falling on top of him on the floor, on the desk—heck, right on the chair—and finishing what they'd started.

Hadn't she decided less than two hours ago she couldn't have that kind of relationship with Seth? That they had to be friends and nothing else? At the rate they'd been going, they would have been naked and conjoined before the eleven-o'clock news had ended...if they hadn't been interrupted.

So maybe it was just as well they had been.

As he helped her with her coat, then led her out of the office, Seth said, "By the way, Jill, I won't apologize again. I'm not sorry for tonight."

She gave him a helpless shrug in response. "Me, neither."

He must have noticed her hesitation. "But?"

"But that doesn't mean this can happen again. I'm not the free, unencumbered girl you knew, Seth. I have a little boy at home who's my first priority. I can't afford…" *Love. Heartbreak. Euphoria.*

"Can't afford another friend?"

She snorted at the thought. "Friend? Friends don't usually kiss the stuffing out of each other or lick each other's necks."

And other still-tingling body parts.

He answered with a soft laugh. "Let's not analyze this, all right? Let's just see what happens."

"I have to think of Todd," she replied softly. She didn't meet his eyes as she buttoned her coat, then watched him lock his office door.

He tilted her chin up and made her meet his steady gaze. "Todd is a great kid. And I'm dying to get to know him."

He meant it. She could tell that by the look in his eyes. "You're serious?"

"Absolutely."

Knowing she might regret it, she couldn't resist making plans to see him again. Soon. "I told him we'd go to the zoo tomorrow."

A relieved smile brought out those killer dimples and the laugh lines beside his beautiful eyes. "The zoo sounds perfect. A nice, *friendly* outing." He glanced at her hair. "Are we going incognito?"

Fingering a long strand of her own hair, she shrugged. "You partial to redheads?"

"Yeah." He reached out and brushed his hand down her long braid, touching her only there, but somehow loading the simple caress with tenderness and emotion. Then he leaned close and brushed a soft kiss against her temple. "But I like blondes better."

She let out a shivery, helpless little sigh. "Then blonde it is."

WHEN JILL HAD SAID he'd be accompanying a blonde to the zoo the next day, Seth had figured she'd be going as herself. A toned down, nondescriptly dressed, dark-glasses-wearing version of the Natural Girl. He hadn't expected the spiked-haired, heavily made up punk child who greeted him at her house.

The bleached blonde wig was cropped short, stuck out in a hundred directions and should have looked ridiculous. It didn't. Neither did the flamboyantly sexy makeup. Instead, it transformed the sweet, wholesome beauty he knew into a sultry, sassy temptress who batted her heavily made up eyes at him as she opened the door.

"Punk rocker day at the Seattle Zoo?"

"My latest disguise."

"I like it."

"Hi, Duck Man!"

Todd, it appeared, was going to the zoo in disguise, too.

"Is there a *Grease* reunion I haven't heard about yet?" he asked with a grin as he spied the little boy, who was dressed in jeans, a white T-shirt and a tiny black leather jacket. His hair was slicked back and Todd wore a funky pair of sunglasses that most kids wouldn't keep on, but which he appeared to adore. He kept peering over them, then nudging them back up on his nose with the tip of his index finger.

"Why don't you put those on top of your head until we get outside and you need them?" Jill asked.

"I don't have enough hair to hold 'em up," the boy replied, sounding disgruntled. "Or big ears like Grandpa."

"You're saying you want big ears like Grandpa?"

Todd wrinkled his nose, scrunched up his eyes and shook his head. "Not if they come with all that hair growing out of them."

Hiding a smile, Seth shook his head as he crouched down in front of the boy. "Let me show you a trick." Pulling the tiny designer glasses off Todd's face, he folded them and hung one arm in the front of the tight T-shirt. Then, spreading open his leather bomber, Seth showed Todd his own glasses, hanging in just the same way.

"Hey, this works!"

Seth couldn't resist a playful tug on Todd's slickened hair as Jill gave him a smile of appreciation.

"So," he asked her, "where's your leather jacket and tight T-shirt?"

She tugged open her long coat, revealing a sassy, sexy-as-hell tight red sweater that clung to her curves and reminded him of how she'd tasted just about twelve hours before. Below the sweater, she wore a flirty jean miniskirt, and, in concession to the chilly weather, black tights and ankle boots.

"Nobody's gonna mistake you for the Natural Girl, babe," Seth admitted with a laugh, knowing that's exactly what she'd been going for.

"Good." She took his arm.

"Too bad you didn't come to take us to the zoo tomorrow," Todd said. "We always have runch on Sundays."

"Runch?"

"Brunch," Jill explained with a chuckle.

"I like runch," Seth told Todd, unable to resist returning the kid's freckle-faced grin. He and Jill exchanged an amused glance as they watched Todd tugging at the waist of his stiff jeans, adjusting the fit.

"You come tomorrow, then," Todd insisted when he finally gave up on making himself more comfortable.

Seth turned to Jill, not about to paint her into a corner. "Maybe that should be up to your mom."

She and Todd exchanged a look and he noticed the sense of shared mischievousness. Though Jill and her son didn't look much alike physically, they definitely shared those dimples, not to mention a wicked laugh.

He began to wonder what he'd gotten himself into.

"Okay," Jill said as she rebuttoned her coat, grabbed her purse and led him to the door. "We'd love to have you for runch. You bring the maple syrup."

Maple syrup. Sounded okay so far.

Then Jill winked at her son. "We're plenty stocked up on jelly beans."

SETH WAS PLEASANTLY surprised by the jelly bean pancakes. He'd initially thought he'd rather chow down on a peanut butter and banana sandwich—which he'd given up sometime around fourth grade—but he swallowed his doubt and sampled the breakfast entree, unable to disappoint Todd.

The black licorice-flavored ones didn't go well with maple syrup. But the red jelly beans were pretty darn good.

"I'm just like Sam-I-Am!" Todd chortled.

"Dr. Seuss book—*Green Eggs and Ham*," Jill explained. "He was a food adventurer, too. Like Todd."

Seth took another bite of pancake. "I think I'd rather have jelly bean pancakes than green eggs *or* green ham."

Todd apparently agreed. "Me, too. Ya know, I think green eggs are rotten, and that's why nobody wanted to try 'em. And I seen green ham once, on a sandwich I hid behind my bed. I sneaked it up for a snack, only I forgot about it, and it turned all green and fuzzy. I found it 'cause I was looking for my big red fire truck with the longest ladder, not the middle-size fire truck with the shorter ladder...."

Seth could barely keep up. But oh, my God, did he love

trying. Even when he hadn't known Todd was Jill's, he'd been drawn to the precocious little guy.

Jill's boarders also tried a bit of each of Todd's creations, amid much good-natured griping. Bjorn had to work at the hospital, but Sven and Tony kept them entertained, making exaggerated claims of torture whenever Todd piled yet another pancake on their plates.

In all, Sunday's brunch was a laugh-filled, gentle, fun morning…the best he'd had in ages. The sense of warmth and kinship in Jill's big kitchen impressed him. No, she hadn't created her family in the usual way, but there was no question she'd created one nonetheless. Sven and Tony treated her like a big sister, and lovingly teased Todd like a kid brother, putting up with his chatter and whopping stories with a lot of humor and a great deal of patience.

From their good-natured banter, he knew Jill's tenants saw him as a potentially good thing in her life. Judging by some of their jokes, and from what she'd said Friday night, he realized Jill didn't have much of a social calendar. Her days and nights apparently consisted of work in the outside world, and warmth and laughter within the walls of this house. No whirlwind excitement, no exotic travel when her job didn't absolutely demand it.

No romance. Which her tenants apparently wanted to change.

The guys wanted her to be happy, to have something beyond her son and her job. For some reason, they seemed to approve of Seth as a romantic candidate for Jill. It reminded him briefly of the way her four younger brothers had welcomed him into the family all those years ago during a trip back to Jill's home in Iowa.

He noticed Todd and Sven exchanging knowing nods and smiles when he piled a plate full of the pancakes. And when he told Todd they were the best he'd ever tasted, even though he generally preferred peppermint patty pancakes, they'd given each other a thumbs up.

Jill didn't eat any pancakes, so Seth insisted on making her another of his famous omelettes, then watched as she ate every bite. This, too, got him a nod of approval from the young men in her life.

There was definitely some matchmaking going on in the house.

He didn't question that her young friends would be so loyal to her. For all her wit, her quick smile, her indefatigable good humor, she was still so feminine, so fragile, so delicately beautiful it sometimes hurt to look at her.

She didn't seem as tired as she had been last week. But she was still too thin, too rushed and, judging by the way she'd gobbled as much cotton candy and popcorn as her son at the zoo the day before, not eating right. Something he wanted to remedy. If she would let him.

"So the zoo was good, ya?" Sven asked as he downed yet another huge glass of orange juice. Seth wondered whether Jill—and the hospital—had the budget to feed these guys.

"Great!" Todd replied. "'Cept when we had to leave real fast 'cause of the man with the camera."

Seth and Jill looked at each other. Todd had apparently realized why they'd hurried him out of the zoo after promising he could visit the monkeys one more time.

A man with a camera had indeed been paying a lot of attention to them. He didn't snap away like a paparazzi would have, but he always seemed to be around.

Probably it had been a coincidence, and he'd just been an avid animal lover. Still, he'd made them both uncomfortable, particularly after Savannah McCain's nasty little innuendo-filled report from the Friday night news. Her cameraman hadn't videotaped them in Seth's office, but the reporter had made a few comments about being surprised to find the hospital PR director in his office, late on a Friday night, with a famous model. She'd mentioned Jill by her well-known public persona, J.J.

Could have been worse, he supposed. The camera could have been rolling. And if the photographer had they arrived a few seconds sooner, he'd have gotten a nice shot of Seth nibbling on Jill's perfectly shaped breast. He didn't suppose the caseworker they were going to be meeting at his place the next night would have liked that very much.

Neither, of course, would the hospital administration.

But, wow, had it been worth it.

Turning to the sink, he thrust off the hot memory and poured himself a glass of cold water. A big one. As he sipped it, trying to return his attention to the raucous conversation going on at the table, he glanced over and caught Jill staring at him. She didn't smile. She didn't look away. Instead she slowly raised a hand to her face, delicately brushing a long, soft strand of hair off her cheek, her every move a study in grace and femininity.

So much for friendly and cordial. Right now Seth had tripped right back a good thirty-six hours or so and felt his heart pounding and his body aching to finish what they'd started. To touch her. Hold her. To strip off her clothes and let that long curtain of hair be the only thing touching her body other than Seth's hands. His mouth. And every other part of him.

He drained the glass and looked away, not trusting himself to continue staring at her, wondering how the others in the room could miss the fact that he was drowning here. Drowning in a well of desire deepened by eleven years of wondering.

"So, Uncle Seth, are you sure you don't wanna come with me, Uncle Sven and Uncle Tony to see *Digitalis versus Monoman?*"

Seeing Todd's hopeful expression, Seth hid a smile as he

shook his head. He hadn't expected to be dubbed "uncle" but found himself liking the title. Besides, Todd definitely had a way of bringing attention to himself—and away from his mother, whom Seth didn't trust himself to think about again right now. "Sorry, big guy, I promised your mom a walk on the beach."

Todd rolled his eyes. "Bo-o-o-ring."

"Not so boring," Tony said with a suggestive wag of his eyebrows, which was mimicked by Sven. "When you are bigger, maybe I will explain."

It sounded as if the two men expected Seth and Jill to spend a romantic afternoon together. He wondered if they'd intentionally planned the movie outing, trying to give Jill and him a chance to be alone.

For a couple of young, freewheeling guys, they seemed to have a pretty strong romantic streak. Seth almost chuckled, knowing the two mountains in human form probably wouldn't appreciate being thought of as softies.

Romance hadn't been on Seth's mind when he'd agreed to take a long afternoon walk outside. Fresh air and good company were all the incentive he needed. It was a beautiful day. Sunny and crisp, not a cloud in the sky, the kind of day Seattle often enjoyed in spite of its reputation for never-ending rain.

Jill looked as if she could use a relaxing day outdoors. And she didn't want to push her luck by going out in public with Todd two days in a row, particularly with the worries over the nosy photographer. So, as tempting as it was to go watch robotic cartoon superheroes battle it out in far-off galaxies, Seth really preferred to spend a quiet day with Jill.

Here.

Alone.

Maybe…

No. There would be nothing like what happened Friday night. Despite his own flash of weakness, which he wondered if she'd noticed, he wouldn't make a move on Jill today. No matter what the two European nurses might think was going to happen when they walked out the door, dragging Todd with them, Seth intended a strictly hands-off, lips-off policy.

Jill had retreated back behind her warm, gracious smile. The two of them hadn't so much as touched since Friday night. She'd told him she couldn't afford entanglements, and her friendly but impersonal attitude since then made him believe she meant it.

He wasn't going to push her. Friday night had happened. They didn't regret it, but Jill wasn't ready for an encore. It had been a fluke. Another of those tributes to memory. It hadn't meant a thing and wouldn't be repeated.

At least not until she wanted it to.

And then, of course, once she said the word, Seth planned to make love to her until neither one of them could stand up.

A WALK on the beach with Seth had sounded like such a simple excursion. A gentle, unthreatening, cordial outing. When she walked with Todd and the guys, there was a lot of laughter, some skimming of stones, the occasional splashing and racing up and down the rocky sand.

But from the moment she and Seth watched Todd and his protective baby-sitters drive off for their movie outing, Jill had realized she'd put herself in a very dangerous situation. As they set off, side by side, she was aware of every movement of his lean body beside hers. She noted each deeply inhaled breath, and watched the way the breeze brought a hint of redness to his cheeks. The sunlight illuminated dozens of sparkling strands of gold in his thick brown hair, drawing her eye again and again. She was so overwhelmed by her desire to bury her fingers in it that she could barely focus on anything else.

She'd been an utter fool to think they could ever have a non-physical relationship. Right now, *all* she could think about was the physical. As a matter of fact, she'd been thinking about it since the minute he'd walked through her door yesterday morning. He'd practically eaten her up with his eyes before disguising his appreciation for her zoo ensemble with a quick laugh and his dry wit.

With Todd between them, holding their hands—so quick to pick his feet up off the ground and be "swung" every third step—she'd been able to put the flash of intense awareness out of her mind. It had returned today in the strangest of places: her full, boisterous kitchen.

Watching Seth reach for another of those hideous pancakes, seeing him so easily befriend not only Todd but her two friends, she'd again been reminded of everything she liked about him. Memories of the liking had much too easily segued to memories of the lusting.

She sensed he felt the same way, though he hid it well. But there had been one moment that morning when his thoughts had been revealed. One brief flash of something intense and personal had sparked a fire low in her belly and made her heart skip a beat.

Their eyes had met to share an amused look over the heads of Todd and the guys, who were eating their ridiculous main course and devouring two pounds of bacon. Seth had stared, and she'd known what he was thinking. She'd stared…letting him see that her thoughts mirrored his own.

Then he'd looked away, smiling at her little boy with genuine tenderness, and she'd simply melted.

He was hot and sexy. Tender and loving. Considerate and nurturing. Funny and charming.

Her first love. Her *only* love.

She'd never gotten over him. She somehow doubted she ever would. She'd been raised by parents who believed in one true love. Their silent, physical example had provided a lesson that sunk into her heart, her very soul. It had rooted and blossomed, and somewhere along the way, she'd decided she could accept no less for herself.

That conviction had made Seth's absence from her life for the past eleven years nearly unbearable. And made a future without him utterly inconceivable.

So…she could remain his friend, do the best she could with what she'd allow herself to have. Since she couldn't be what he wanted, couldn't give him his heart's desire—a baby—she could try for a long-term friendship.

Or she could take a chance on the here and now, build up another store of memories to last her for the next long stretch of her life, which she'd eventually have to live without him.

Jill the mother—Jill the wholesome, Natural Girl from the Midwest—whispered to play it safe. Friendship was better than heartbreak and loneliness.

Jill the free spirit, who'd lived through many of the ups and downs life had to offer, said to grab what she could get and trust fate to make things turn out right. Or at least make her strong enough to survive when he was gone again.

Seth held her arm as they walked down the rocky slope leading to the lake, wearing an appreciative look that said how much he enjoyed being outside on such a beautiful day.

Seeing Seth's genuine smile made her weak in the knees. Always had. Probably always would. It brought to mind other things. Too many things. Like the smile he'd always worn after they kissed. The sultry, heavy-lidded stare of appreciation he'd been unable to disguise the first time she'd been naked in front of him. The laughter they'd shared, even in the most intimate of moments.

"You're sure you want to walk?" he asked. Jill had been silent since they'd climbed down the rocky hillside to the shore of the lake.

She flushed, averting her eyes, wondering what he'd think

if he could read her less than wholesome thoughts. "Oh, yes. This is perfect, really. Much better than bad animation and a loud soundtrack with voices that don't match the movement of the mouths on the screen."

It seemed the most natural thing in the world for him to take her hand as they walked, for their fingers to curl together in warmth and companionship. But every ounce of her attention focused on that hand, on every millimeter of skin to skin contact.

Cool it, Jill.

Why could she not focus on the lovely day, the clear blue sky, the wind whipping off the lake? Why was she aware only of how strong and warm his body felt next to hers? How could she be so hot and needy—physically aroused, damn it—merely because that deliciously rough palm of his was scraping against her own?

She shivered.

"Cold?"

No. Definitely not cold. She was growing warmer by the minute, knowing they were alone, completely alone, for the first time since he'd taken her home Friday night. The night they'd kissed so passionately in his office.

"I'm fine, thanks," she mumbled.

He put his arm around her shoulder anyway and she nearly groaned. Sweet, protective Seth, sharing his body heat. She wondered what he'd think if he knew what she really wanted him to share with her. Headboard-rocking, soul-shattering, scream-inducing sex.

It's decision time. Yes, or no?

It had been such a long time. Not just since she'd been with Seth, but since she'd been with anyone. Jill had never been one to go for casual sex. She had too much of that good, Iowa farm girl mentality to fall into bed at the drop of a hat.

Yes, there had been one or two brief relationships when

she was first starting out in modeling, mostly because she was trying to find herself after losing Seth. Since then, however…nothing of any substance.

She'd gotten used to it. Her career had been her focus, followed by her health concerns. Then, of course, came Todd. Motherhood had been an around the clock commitment, and there'd been no time for dating or, heaven forbid, sex.

Besides, for some reason, though she'd only made love with him once, she'd compared her few other lovers with Seth and found them lacking. She'd never craved that kind of intimacy with anyone else but him.

She craved it now, though. The empty, achy place inside her rumbled to life at the flash of images rushing through her mind.

Jill didn't expect him to share his heart, and certainly not his future. She knew she couldn't have those. And she'd thought she was okay with that, with a friendly, platonic relationship.

That's what they'd been going for yesterday, during their wonderful trip to the zoo, and again today, during the laughter-filled brunch at the house. Somehow, though, between the laughter, behind the smiles, she'd been growing more and more drawn to him. Not just emotionally, but physically. Sexually.

A few days back in this man's company and she'd begun to remember that she'd once been a very sensual woman. Not just a mother. Not just a sweet, wholesome model. But a woman who needed the physical pleasure Seth Nannery had once given her.

Their kisses Friday had started something burning. Their laughter, shared moments, tenderness and humor had fueled that fire. Now they were alone. His arm was over her shoulders, his body pressed against hers, their hips touching, their legs moving in an easy, unaffected synchronization.

And suddenly her decision was made. *Yes.*

"Seth, if you don't kiss me again soon I think I'm gonna explode," she finally admitted in a hoarse, broken whisper.

He froze. Turned. Stared at her. "What did you say?"

"I said, kiss me. Please. Remind me again of what we had so I'll know I didn't imagine it."

When he didn't immediately comply, she wondered if he'd lost interest, if seeing her in the role of mother and big sister for the past two days had killed those feelings forever. Ever blunt, she asked him, "You don't want me anymore?"

Something warm and intimate lit his eyes. "I want you." Then his gaze traveled lower, down her body. He was looking at her with hunger and pure, undiluted heat. His voice deepened, grew thick. "I want you more than ever."

She almost sighed.

"I just didn't think *you* were prepared for anything beyond friendship."

Friendship? Yes, she wanted that, especially with him. But she also wanted intimacy and eroticism again. Pounding sex and sweet, tender lovemaking. And loads and loads of orgasms, which she'd done without for so very long.

She nibbled the corner of her lip, glancing at him through half-lowered lashes. "Seth, do you think friends can have sex?"

He waited until curiosity made her stare up at him. Then he stared searchingly into her eyes, probably gauging how deeply she wanted what she was asking for. Jill held nothing back, knowing her lips were parted and hungry, her eyes ravenous and her entire body swaying toward him, partly in invitation, partly in silent demand. Mostly in uncontrollable want.

"Sure, Jill." His voice was smooth. "Friends can have sex."

She wondered if he heard her heart pound even louder.

"But *we* can't."

A tiny cry escaped her lips before she could prevent it.

Then he smiled that smile, flashed those dimples, tempted her beyond all rational thought. "We're not friends, babe," he explained with infinite tenderness and certainty. "We're lovers. We always have been."

She swallowed hard, trying to focus on his words, not on the pounding, throbbing feel of the hot blood rushing through her veins.

He lazily ran his fingers through her hair, brushing a wisp off her temple, and leaned closer to whisper, "So we can't have sex. You and I, Jill, we can only make love."

CHAPTER ELEVEN

JILL COULDN'T prevent an anticipatory smile from crossing her lips. Not sex. They'd make love. The look in Seth's eyes promised it would be unforgettable. They'd finally have the chance to pursue the tender, erotic adventure they'd been denied eleven years ago. But a voice of caution in her brain made her add, "Can we still take this as it comes? Not read anything more into it other than we damn well deserve to finish what we started so many years ago?"

He nodded slowly. "Yeah. We're definitely gonna finish what we started." Then he bent to kiss her and doubt evaporated. Thought disappeared. There was only sweet, hot passion.

Seth's lips and tongue tasted her, sipping of her mouth as if she were an intoxicatingly sweet drink and he was parched from thirst. She slid her arms around his neck. Tilting her head, she moaned as their tongues met and tangled in a sort of hungry yet lazily sensuous dance.

His hands dropped to her waist. Cupped her hips. Then slid lower, curving over her bottom so he could pull her tighter against his body. His very aroused body.

"Oh, Seth," she whimpered, again flooded with need.

She wanted him. Wanted that part of him. Deep inside her. Then he ran one hand up her back, brushing soft, teasing caresses over her spine. She shivered, silently ordering him to linger, to touch her more thoroughly. More erotically.

Instead he continued to tease her, rubbing here, brushing the tips of his fingers there, until she was nearly out of her mind with want. Finally, he touched her neck, ran the tip of one finger along her jaw, then slipped his hand in her hair.

"Mmm," she moaned as he cupped her head. She shifted again so they could continue their long, endless kiss, which offered so much, hinted at such pleasure, both sought and promised the consummation of a long dormant need.

Finally, he pulled away slightly and stared down at her. Jill wondered if she looked as completely hungry as he did, because that was definitely how she felt. "Let's go back to the house," he whispered. "It's not exactly private out here."

She didn't say a word. Instead, she grabbed his hand and tugged him after her to hurry back up the beach. He started to laugh as their quick walk became a jog, then a frantic sprint. They were panting for breath by the time they scaled the hill and reached her back balcony.

He pressed up behind her and nuzzled her neck while she fumbled for the keys. "Anxious, are we?"

She leaned back, closing her eyes, focusing on the feel of his mouth on her nape. Leaning back against him, she let her bottom linger suggestively against his noticeable arousal. She almost cried out at the erotic intimacy of the position. "I'm dying," she finally replied. "If you step away from me, I think I might fall. My legs are weak."

"From our race on the beach?" he mumbled as he delicately nibbled on her earlobe, slipping a hand around to her tummy and pulling her tighter against him.

She shook her head. "From you." She pressed harder, teasing him, wanting him as out of control and insane as she felt.

He made a guttural sound and lowered his hand. Close. Very close to where she ached to be touched. "Mmm, I could take you right here, right now, and not care what the neighbors think."

She winked. "I don't have any close neighbors."

He chuckled. "You're very wicked."

She tilted her head up to catch his mouth in another hot, frenzied kiss, more turned on than she'd have imagined by his naughty suggestion. She really didn't have any close neighbors.

"Open the damn door, Jill," he muttered when they finally drew apart to suck in a breath.

She dug in her pocket again, yanking the key ring out and promptly dropping it onto the deck. As she turned around to see where the keys had landed, Seth crouched down to retrieve them.

Sensual, delightful thoughts crowded her brain as she looked down at him. She shivered, making a tiny helpless sound as the sensitive spot between her legs swelled even harder.

Seth stared at her body. He was eye level with her hip, mere inches from her shaking thighs. She watched him wage a silent battle against doing what she knew they were both picturing. He could so easily bury his face in her stomach. Unzip her slacks. Taste her until she came apart right against his beautiful mouth. As she had so many times before when they'd been lovers in all but the most technical sense of the word.

He chose that moment to look up, meeting her eyes. He'd obviously noticed her reaction—the weakness in her legs, the way she swayed toward him without conscious thought. The musky, feminine warmth she couldn't disguise.

He smiled. A sultry smile promising her he'd make her erotic fantasy come true. Soon. Very soon.

"Inside," he whispered softly as he rose to his feet. She grabbed the keys he extended, but couldn't resist pulling him close for another mind-blowing kiss. Lifting one leg, she wrapped it around his jean-clad calves and tugged him closer so that hard, throbbing part of him came where she wanted him most.

"Inside, *now,* Jill," he mumbled against her lips, "or I swear I won't care if your closest neighbors are digging out their binoculars."

She twisted, jamming the key into the lock. Turning the knob, she practically fell into the house—into the brightly lit sunroom. He was right there with her, kicking the door shut behind them. It had barely closed before she grabbed for his leather jacket and pushed it off his shoulders.

Seeing the long-sleeved, button-down shirt, she frowned. She had no patience for buttons. So she started to yank and pull, until finally his shirt was open, his gloriously hard, masculine chest bare for her to touch with her hands and her hungry gaze.

He was simply magnificent. The young, whipcord-lean youth she'd known had matured into one fine, full-grown, muscular man. He didn't have the body of someone who worked in an office all day, and she nearly purred, thankful Seth was the athletic type. His enjoyment of physical activity had definitely paid off. She wanted to bite her way from his flat abs all the way up to his biceps. Then back down again. Lower. Everywhere.

"You...I..." She continued to ogle him. "Oh, you look sooo good."

He pointed to her sweater. "That. Off. Now."

She nodded and gave him a mock salute. Grinning, she tugged the fluffy pink sweater up and over her head, almost cursing her long hair when it tangled with the fabric.

Seth didn't wait. Before she realized what he was doing, she felt his mouth on her midriff, his lips moving over every curve and hollow, then lower, pressing a hot, moist kiss onto her belly. She disentangled herself and threw the top to the floor, looking down and seeing him kneeling in front of her as he had out on the deck.

"This is what I wanted to do outside," he mumbled against the curve of her waist. "And you wanted it, too."

She closed her eyes. "It's a start."

"You remember…"

She moaned. "Uh-huh."

"Let's…"

"Definitely."

Then his hands were at the waist of her khaki slacks. He unfastened them, pushing them down with slow deliberation, his heavy-lidded eyes darkening. He undressed her until she wore nothing but a pair of flimsy, silk pink panties that matched a tiny, lacy bra.

Stepping back, he looked at her, awestruck. "You're so beautiful."

She pointed to his jeans. "You. Those. Off. Now." He grinned and reached for his belt, the muscles in his shoulders and arms flexing beneath the smooth, tanned skin.

Was there possibly a sexier sight on earth, she wondered, than a gorgeous, hungry man unfastening his pants with a look of knowing anticipation in his eyes before making love? If so, she'd never witnessed it.

She stared, much as he had, while he stripped off his clothes—all of them. Jill gasped and grabbed the arm of the closest chair for balance, knowing part of him would soon be buried inside her.

"I know you want to make love," she said. "In every way possible. And we will, okay?" She reached up to unhook her bra. "But first, Seth, please…just *take* me." The bra fell away, baring her breasts to his avid stare. "Take me now."

He reached for her and took her into his arms, sending a flood of delight rushing through her at the skin-to-skin contact. Then they dropped to the floor, Seth beneath her, pulling her on top of him. "Why don't *you* take whatever you want," he offered with a wicked smile. "Anything you want. Any way you want it."

"I want you inside me. Immediately, if not sooner."

She closed her eyes, picturing the possibilities, growing even more aroused. Seth seemed to do the same. She felt him grow harder—if that was possible—against the thin, flimsy lace of her panties."

As if he couldn't go another moment without tasting her, he leaned up to nibble her breast. Blowing on one distended nipple until she writhed against him, he finally sucked it deeply into his mouth. Sensation shot from there right down her body to where she already throbbed against him.

With his mouth on her breast, his hand tangled in her hair, and his glorious manhood cupped so intimately between her legs, Jill found the erotic part of herself she'd lost so long ago. A warm explosion of delight rocked through her, and she cried out, tensing at first, then calming to allow the wave of pleasure to wash through her.

When she opened her eyes, she saw Seth staring up at her, his expression both incredibly tender, yet hungry enough to gobble her up. "Jill?"

"Okay, I think I'm done," she whispered with a laugh. "I didn't expect that so soon."

He tugged her down, cupping her head, tangling the fingers of his other hand into her hair. Just before catching her lips in a hot, wet kiss, he whispered, "Honey, you are *far* from done."

The sultry promise aroused her all over again as they kissed and stroked each other into a mindless frenzy.

He helped her push the panties out of the way, almost tearing them in their frenzy to be separated by nothing but whatever daylight could squeeze between them. She rose to her knees, straddling his lean hips, and slid up and down against the hungriest part of him, so he could feel for himself how very much he'd aroused her.

He groaned. Jill watched the cords of muscle in his neck tighten as he arched his head back and closed his eyes, so obviously holding on to the last ounce of his control with everything he had. Then he opened them, frowning with frustration. "Damn, I didn't think to grab protection...."

She shook her head. "It's not a problem."

His visible relief almost made her laugh. Their eyes met, communicating silently as they both realized they were finally going to be intimately connected again after so long.

She gave him a tender smile, then finally lowered herself onto him. Joining him. Taking him. Being filled by him as she'd never been filled by anyone else in her entire life.

Which, at this moment, she was very glad about.

"I've missed you like hell," he whispered as he pulled her down again, kissing her deeply as they both savored the connection of their bodies.

"Ditto," she replied with a throaty sigh of pleasure.

She moved, stroking him deep within, silently saying all the things she hadn't said to him in the past. And he answered in the same manner, loving her in every way but verbally. Until finally he rolled her onto her back and took them both to the height of ecstasy again.

SETH WATCHED Jill's breathing begin to slow and the flush fade from her lovely face. His own heart still raced a bit as they lay entangled on the carpeted floor of her sunroom.

No matter how many times he'd told himself over the years that his time with Jill couldn't possibly have been as good as he'd remembered it, he knew now it had been. The best sexual experience he'd had in his life—second only to today's.

He'd been with other woman over the years, but none had ever touched his soul while touching his body.

He brushed a long strand of hair off her face and smiled as she turned to kiss his palm. "You okay?"

"Very much okay."

Rolling onto his back, he pulled her with him until she curled against him, her head on his shoulder. "Just how long is that movie, anyway?"

Giggling, she replied, "Long enough for us to take a shower. A *long* shower."

A myriad of sultry possibilities made a shower seem absolutely imperative. He smiled lazily. "You're insatiable."

"Can you handle it?"

"Oh, yeah, I can definitely handle it."

And he so looked forward to handling it.

Though he didn't want to think of anything except what they'd just done—and what else they were going to do this afternoon in her big, beautiful, empty house, he had to clarify something. "I'm really sorry about almost forgetting the whole birth control issue." Not digging for any details, he still wanted to be sure she was okay handling that side of their newly intimate relationship. "You said it was okay. I take it you're…on something?"

She didn't answer right away and wouldn't meet his eyes. Her body, which had been warm and pliant a moment before, stiffened slightly. Not wanting anything to come between them, not now, when they were just starting something new and fragile, he tipped her chin up and made her look at him. "Jill, honey, what's the matter?" He swallowed, then relied on every bit of his spin doctor training to let a lie cross his lips. "Babe, you're a beautiful woman. I don't think you've been celibate all these years. If you're on the pill…"

"I'm not on the pill."

At least she was talking. "Okay."

"And I haven't, uh…" She cleared her throat and nibbled her lip. "There haven't been very many relationships in my life, Seth. None at all for several years."

He couldn't prevent his tiny sigh of relief. A few. He

could deal with that. Not that it was any of his damn business, and he knew it. "No problem."

Her eyes shifted again. Their conversation obviously hadn't reached the important part yet.

"What is it you want to tell me but don't want to tell me?" he asked. "And don't try to deny it. I know that look. The wide-eyed innocence combined with you chewing a hole in your bottom lip means you have something on your mind."

She laughed softly. "You know me too well."

He ran a lazy hand over her shoulder, stroking her, silently asking her to trust him, encouraging her to continue.

"Seth, the reason I said we didn't need to worry about birth control isn't because I'm already using something. It's because it's not an issue for me."

Not following, he merely watched, and waited for her to continue. Finally, she looked up at him with genuine emotion shining in her beautiful blue eyes. "I don't use birth control because I don't need it," she whispered. "Todd was my one and only shot at motherhood." She visibly swallowed, but pressed on. "Seth, I can never have another baby."

Though Jill's eyes weren't glassy, and her stare remained unwavering, Seth heard the catch in her voice.

Then he focused on what she'd said and his heart constricted a little in his chest. She could never have another baby? *Never?*

"You mean you're physically unable?"

She nodded.

"But how? Why?"

"I had some medical problems a few years ago. Before I had Todd. I had one shot and I went for it. Afterward, I had to make a choice and I made it." Her voice sounded sad, but she did not sound regretful. "Anyway, more babies are impossible for me, Seth. Completely impossible."

Completely impossible. Beautiful, heartbreakingly sweet Jill, the wonderful mother who so adored her son, could never have another child. He wanted to howl on her behalf at the injustice.

He pulled her closer, wrapping his arms around her back, caressing the delicate waist, the vulnerable neck. "I'm so sorry." Feeling a suspicious wetness against his chest, he didn't press her for details. Instead, he speculated aloud, "That's why you had Todd. That's why you're raising him alone."

It made sense. He didn't need to know all the details to begin to piece together the scenario. "You found out something was wrong, put off treatment to have a baby, then dealt with your own health after he was born."

She almost sat up, her surprise on her face. "How'd you figure that out?"

He pulled her back down. "You're too good, too decent a person to deny your son a relationship with his father. So obviously there was no father around by the time he was born. This was a…business arrangement of some type, wasn't it?"

He knew he was right. Jill had been alone during her pregnancy and Todd's babyhood. He didn't question how he knew, he just knew.

"Yes," she whispered. "I went to the reproductive version of a perfume counter, picked out a sample I liked, tried it on for size and got a positive pregnancy test a few weeks later."

He almost laughed, as she'd obviously intended. "Sperm donation."

"Yep."

One of the most beautiful women in the world, certainly the most beautiful he'd ever known, and she'd conceived a baby via sperm donation. Sometimes life was so bizarre.

"So," he said, knowing she could hear the intensity in

his voice as he lowered his tone. "Tell me the rest of it. Tell me everything, Jill, starting on the day I was stupid enough to walk out of your dorm room and let you get away."

And she did.

Speaking slowly, quietly, she told him about a disturbing find during an annual gynecological test when she was in her early twenties. Followed by more frequent tests, more of the same findings.

His heart almost stopped when she said the word *cancer*.

She quickly clarified. "Precancerous cells, Seth. I did not have cervical cancer. *Ever*."

Thank God.

She went on to tell him about the first of several minor procedures to try to determine how serious the problem was. Then, finally, she detailed one pivotal conversation with her doctor, who'd urged her to remove the real threat of cancer in the future by removing part of her reproductive self right away.

"Did he know how much you always wanted children?"

Jill shook her head. "Probably not. He said it would be possible, after the procedure, for me to carry a baby to term. Unfortunately, not having much of a cervix would mean surgery and a high-risk pregnancy." She gave a forced-sounding chuckle. "Like trying to keep a wine bottle from leaking when you don't have the cork."

Again the smart-aleck, trying to lighten the subject. He squeezed her shoulders. "What happened?"

"I told him I needed to wait a year so I could to at least try to have a baby."

"And you had Todd."

"Call me Miss Fertility—the first try and I was knocked up. Had my sweet baby boy by C-section. Three months later, the doctor did his thing and I've had clean Pap tests ever since."

Seth wondered about something she'd said. "So technically you can conceive a baby, you just can't carry one?"

Her eyes grew cloudy, and he wondered if he'd said the wrong thing. Truly, it was only curiosity that made him ask, but she seemed almost hurt by the question.

"Not since I've had Todd," she admitted. "After Todd's birth, after the doctor performed the procedure, he discouraged me from another pregnancy. Trying to have another child—even if he took steps to try to ensure I could carry it to term—would cause tremendous strain and could easily rupture the— Oh, man, this is such a strange conversation to be having lying here naked with you!"

He shook his head and pressed a reassuring kiss on her lips. "No, it's a perfectly natural conversation. Jill, I was raised with two sisters. I have heard about a few parts of the female plumbing system. I know what you're saying."

And he did. Another pregnancy and she could end up with a ruptured uterus. Very dangerous. Potentially fatal.

Unfathomable.

His heart literally skipped two beats as pure terror washed over him. To lose Jill…

"I realized then what I had to do," she admitted. "The maternal instinct to try to have another baby anyway might eventually overcome my good sense and desire to live to a ripe old age. I might someday grow complacent, thinking I could ignore what the doctors said."

Yeah, knowing Jill had eventually wanted a big family, he could see her making that kind of choice.

"Anyway, I could never risk doing something that could leave my son an orphan, all alone in this world."

He knew what she was going to say even before she said it.

"So, at the doctor's urging, I took permanent steps to make sure I'd never conceive another baby. Back to the hospital went Jill. Another lovely round of surgery, and my childbearing days were done.''

His heart broke a little more for her, lying here in his arms, sounding so brave and trying to make him laugh when he knew a part of her had to have died on that day.

"I'm so sorry, Jill. So *very* sorry I wasn't there for you when all this happened.''

"I wasn't very pleasant to be around,'' she replied with a helpless sniff.''

"I don't care. I would have been beside you every step of the way. What a damned fool I was.''

Because if he hadn't let her go, if he hadn't pushed her into making an impossible choice on her twentieth birthday, at least Jill would have had someone to lean on, to help make these awful decisions. And maybe, just maybe, Todd would be his child, instead of the son of some nameless, faceless stranger.

"Okay, enough of this,'' she insisted.

"One more thing.''

She sighed heavily. "You're so pushy.''

"Yeah, that's one of the things you like best about me, isn't it?'' he asked, knowing damn well it wasn't.

She snickered. "What else do you want to know?''

Hoping not to let her see how terrified he was, he quietly asked, "How are you now, Jill?''

She slid up onto his body, resting her chin on her own cupped hands so her breath touched the hair on his chest. When she wriggled against him, appearing so innocent, as if merely making herself comfortable, she succeeded in distracting him for a second. He forced himself to ignore his body's renewed interest. "No, you're not going to get away without answering. You're thin and tired looking. I've seen you when you've been light-headed. Are you okay?''

Please God, let her be okay.

She reached up to cup his cheek with one hand and met

his eyes, unflinching. "I'm absolutely fine, Seth. I promise you. I have never missed an appointment with my gynecologist—and my last one was only two months ago. Every test since the surgery has been one hundred percent clear. I have never had, do not and hopefully never will have cancer of any type."

He let relief wash over him for a long moment, nodding his head and closing his eyes to send up a silent thanks. "Okay, you keep those appointments," he finally replied when he felt able to speak again. "But what about your fatigue? Your dizzy spells? When's the last time you had just a regular all-around physical?"

"You mean one that doesn't involve stirrups and complete, abject mortification?"

He couldn't prevent a laugh. "Yeah."

She rolled her eyes. "I'm way over doctors, Seth. Believe me, I've had enough for any two lifetimes. But I do make sure to see the ones who count."

He persisted. "So it's been a long time."

"I guess." She looked grouchy. Lowering her lashes, she licked her lips. "It's been a long time since a lot of things."

His groin instantly stirred in interest as she began to move against him with deliberate provocation. He knew what things she was talking about and couldn't help asking, "A *really* long time?"

She scrunched her eyes shut, as if embarrassed. "We're talking years here. So much for the freewheeling model, huh?" She peeked at him through half-lowered lashes and grinned. "And you can bet I have a lot I want to do to make up for lost time, Seth."

"Oh, absolutely," he said with a growl of anticipation. But as she bent to kiss him, he couldn't resist adding, "Jill? Promise me tomorrow you'll call the doctor and schedule a checkup."

When she seemed about to protest, he slowly thrust up

against her, silently reminding her that the more they argued, the longer it would be before they could continue catching up on everything else they'd missed.

She arched toward him and moaned, low and sultry. Oh, yeah, Jill definitely wanted to proceed. "Okay. Tomorrow. Now, enough talk. That movie was only two hours long."

CHAPTER TWELVE

SEATTLE MEMORIAL continued to boil and rumble Monday morning, so Seth didn't have a minute to check in with Jill.

As he could have predicted, Savannah McCain's spite was instrumental in getting Seth's day off to a bad start. He'd been called in for a meeting with the administration because of her obnoxious, innuendo-filled report from Friday night.

The meeting had gone okay, probably more because the hospital wanted to maintain Jill's goodwill than his own. Any celebrity who brought her child to Round the Clock had to be handled with care. He was just thankful Savannah's cameraman hadn't been filming. That would've made things stickier.

Seth apologized, but also reminded his boss that he'd come in at ten o'clock at night, in the middle of a date, because of his dedication to the hospital. By the end of the meeting, the administrator had even managed a sincere-sounding thank-you for the job Seth had been doing with the mystery baby situation.

Just when he thought his day would turn out all right, Savannah, the piranha in human form, showed up digging for even more dirt. Seth answered any questions related to the hospital and the mystery baby, and completely ignored her on the whole J.J. issue. At last, thankfully, her pager went off and she got the hell out of his office.

Right after lunch, he left to attend a seminar on hospital litigation at a downtown conference center. It was a great chance to turn off his pager and get away from the whole mess for a while. He was blessedly unreachable to most of the world. The hospital knew his cell number and so did Jill. Anyone else who wanted to reach him could damn well wait.

He found it difficult to focus on the workshop because his thoughts kept returning to Jill. Not just what they'd shared—three times—the previous day in her house. But everything she'd told him. Everything she'd been through.

God, she was strong. Strong and determined and lovely. And now that he had her back in his life, he knew for sure why he'd never moved on with anyone else. It had always been Jill or no one. No matter how much he'd wanted a family, wanted kids of his own and the perfect Brady Bunch lifestyle he'd fantasized about as a kid who'd been dragged around the world by his flamboyant mother, in his heart, it had always been Jill.

He loved her. He had since the time he'd seen her generously pulling her coat off her own fragile shoulders to offer it to a homeless woman on the street during their first date. He loved her generous spirit and her great sense of humor and her courage and her integrity. Her wicked grin. Everything about her.

And now, finally, after eleven years, he sensed they could have the future they should have had all along, even if it wasn't quite the way he'd always pictured it.

Once he'd gotten home the previous night and thought long and hard about what Jill had been through, the realization had hit him. A future with Jill would mean no biological children.

He'd waited for a sense of loss or emptiness. There was a moment of regret, then he'd focused on Jill. Having her back in his life. Building a new kind of family, much as she had. With Todd, the child he hoped to adopt, and who knew how many more. More students from Europe, maybe an infant from overseas. Or maybe not. Maybe just him and Jill and Todd.

That would be fine with him. Having lived the past eleven years of his life without her, he knew he could live with anything—as long as she was by his side.

JILL'S DAY was going along swimmingly, everything neat and according to plan. She and Todd had spent a lot of "alone" time, she'd done her hair and her nails, picked out the perfect outfit that screamed "motherly" for the meeting with the adoption caseworker that night. She'd also kept her promise to Seth and made an appointment for a full physical. The doctor's office had a cancellation the very next day and promised to fit her in.

Everything was fine. Then, at around two, things fell apart with a single phone call. "J.J., can you comment on the story in today's *We See Seattle*? The paper just hit the stands, and we'd love a comment."

A reporter. Great. How completely annoying that she would have to change her phone number, yet again, because some nosy reporter had tracked her latest one down.

The question he'd asked finally sunk in. Story? *We See Seattle*? The free local scandal sheet was published weekly by a small company here in town that had aspirations to someday be noticed by the readers who lived for the national tabloids and their smut. "What story?"

"The story about your new lover and his secret relationship with another woman. Is it true you're having an affair with the PR director of Seattle Memorial? And do you know if he's married to the other woman? Is she the mother of his child?"

Wife? Child? What the hell? "I don't know about any story."

The reporter laughed, sounding a little sympathetic and a little oily at the same time. "Uh, you should probably check it out. It's showing up on newsstands as we speak. There are some rather interesting photographs that you'll probably wish hadn't gone public.''

Photographs? No. Not of their trip to the zoo. Oh, please, God, please don't let some slimeball reporter have sold pictures of her baby to the media.

Not giving it a second thought, she hung up the phone, yelled for Todd and grabbed her keys and coat. A quick drive down the hill to the closest convenience store and she was able to spot the bin for the weekly rag. It had been freshly stocked and practically overflowed with papers. She hopped out of the car, grabbed as many copies as she could hold, and jumped back in. Todd watched wide-eyed, for once not saying a word, as if he could sense Jill's upset.

Finally, knowing Todd was concerned, she forced herself to take a deep, calming breath. She ignored the papers, thrusting them onto a corner kitchen counter as soon as they arrived home, and focused only on him until naptime. Then and only then did she return to the quiet kitchen and look at the top copy of *We See Seattle*.

She soon wished she hadn't.

SETH MADE IT HOME only a few minutes before the adoption caseworker was set to arrive Monday evening. There had been no time to go back to the hospital. Since no one had called, he wasn't concerned. He hadn't realized how much he'd needed an afternoon away from his office, his pager and the rigors of his job until he'd been trapped in a workshop where he could just listen and learn rather than stress and react.

Thankfully, he'd cleaned up his apartment the night before and taken out the recycling so the worker wouldn't see a beer bottle or two and make any negative assumptions. He'd also taken a box of condoms out of the bathroom medicine cabinet and brought them to work, leaving them in his desk. God knew he hadn't needed them in a while, but there was always a chance the worker would do some snooping, looking for reasons to find fault.

Hoping Jill would already have arrived, he scanned the parking lot for her bright orange VW bug. Not here. But he didn't doubt she soon would be. Jill knew how important tonight was for him; she wouldn't be late.

Hurrying inside, he put on a pot of coffee. "Damn, what if Mrs. Thomason only drinks decaf?" he mumbled, wondering if he should just put the coffee away and offer something else.

Spying a flashing red light on his answering machine, he punched the play button and looked through the fridge to see what else he had to offer. When the voice of the caseworker, Myra Thomason, came on, saying she'd had an emergency arise and would not be able to come this evening, he didn't know whether to feel relief or disappointment.

He wanted to get this over with. But he knew he was pretty distracted—and had been since his conversation with Jill yesterday. Well, more than just the conversation! He'd been distracted by the memories of the incredibly pleasurable things they'd shared on the floor of her sunroom. And in her shower. And again in her bed.

He didn't know how he'd lived without her for so long. Or how he'd lived without the kind of sensual, yet deeply emotional connection they'd shared.

The machine continued to play past the first message, indicating there had been more calls, but before he could listen to them, he heard someone knocking. Tapping the off button, he left the kitchen and opened the door.

"Hey," he said, seeing Jill standing there. "I'm sorry. I just checked my messages. The caseworker's not coming after all."

Instead of looking relieved, Jill turned a shade more pale.

Her already bright eyes welled with tears. "It's because of me. It's my fault. Everything's ruined, Seth, and it's my fault."

Instead of asking her what on earth she was talking about, instinct made him grab her and pull her into his arms. He cupped her head, tenderly running his fingers through her hair, and held her tight. Her arms slid around his neck to hold him as she mumbled against his neck, "That lousy photographer. We *were* being followed, Seth. Saturday. And again yesterday."

Followed? Photographer? He definitely didn't like the sound of this. Leading her inside, he shut the door behind them and sat her down in the living room. "Wait a second, let me get you a glass of water, okay?"

He did so, hurrying back with a cold drink, watching as she sipped from it. The color gradually returned to her cheeks and she took a few deep breaths. "Okay," he said. "Tell me what happened."

She hoisted a large bag, which she'd dropped beside the door when she'd come in. Dumping its contents out onto the coffee table, she nibbled her lip. "I stopped at a couple of stores and grabbed every copy I could. My back seat is full of them."

Finally, knowing he'd better see for himself, he picked up one of the newspapers. *We See Seattle.* He'd noticed the gossip rag a few times but had never actually picked one up. So he had no way of knowing whether or not the paper always put such glaring photos of couples sharing provocatively intimate embraces on the cover.

It took a second for him to recognize the couple. "Holy shit."

She gave a harsh laugh. "Yeah."

He and Jill were prominently featured front and center on page one, kissing passionately. Obviously, someone with a powerful lens had been spying on them yesterday. The sneaky bastard had captured the moment on her deck when Seth had been behind her, and she'd turned her face up for a deep, wet kiss. Her fingers cupped his cheek, his hand was visibly low on her body, and they were so close together it was impossible to tell their clothes apart. The picture screamed eroticism. Intense, unbridled desire, which was, of course, exactly what they'd been feeling when the photo had been taken.

"Okay. We had a Peeping Tom," he muttered, feeling pretty damn violated but not wanting Jill to see just how upset he was. Not for himself…but for her.

"There's more. Lots more. I can't believe you didn't get harassed by the press all afternoon, too."

"I was at a seminar and couldn't be reached," he mumbled, feeling very grateful for that fact.

"I wish I'd been out of reach, too."

Hearing the mournful tone in her voice, he squeezed her hand. Then he flipped to the bottom half of the front page, saw more pictures of them kissing—on the beach as well as on the deck. He finally went back and read the headlines. "The Natural Girl a Home Wrecker?"

Home wrecker? Whose home had she supposedly wrecked?

He read on, hardly recognizing the couple described in the story. He grunted in disgust. "So I'm the new heartbreaker of Seattle Memorial, leaving a trail of women in my path, and I've now hooked up with the infamous Natural Girl, J.J., who's a natural-born seductress?"

She rolled her eyes. "It gets better. Wait until you see the picture of you with the poor, cheated-on mother of your child."

He had no idea what she was talking about—not until he turned the page to continue the story. And saw the pictures of him, a disguised Jill and Todd.

"Damn."

"They didn't recognize me, since they identified me as some poor, betrayed woman of yours. They think you were with your family at the zoo Saturday, and me, the home-wrecking tramp, on Sunday."

"So, if they didn't know it was you…"

She immediately nodded. "Right. It was *you* they were following. I think someone was out to cause trouble for you and used me to do it."

He bit off a curse, muttering, "Savannah."

"That would be my first guess. She probably called some sleazy freelance photographer in the middle of the night Friday."

Yeah. He figured it the same way.

She sighed heavily. "Jeez, Seth, you must really leave an impression if the woman decided to try to ruin you because you didn't take her out again."

"I just don't think she's used to being told no." He dropped the paper and put an arm around her shoulders. "This is a rag, Jill. Nobody reads it, nobody believes it. Nothing but innuendo. We were kissing, fully clothed. Big deal. As for the rest, it's so easily disproved it's ridiculous."

She sighed. "Yeah, easy to disprove. We just have to publicly admit it was me and my son with you at the zoo."

He finally recognized the catch-22. Jill did not want to expose Todd to life in the public eye. And for the stupid, nearly-impossible-to-believe reason that he hadn't asked Savannah McCain out on a second date, Jill would be faced with doing just that if they denounced the story.

"We'll ignore it."

She shook her head, still burrowed against him. "We can't. This kind of publicity could kill you with the adoption agency."

Hell, he hadn't even thought about that. But she was right. He didn't imagine the agency would look with favor on a single man—with job and residential instability in his recent past, and now a philanderer in the public eye—as a strong candidate for fatherhood.

Jill looked devastated. As if she'd been at fault. He pulled her tighter. "Jill, it doesn't matter. You and I can easily straighten this out with the caseworker when she reschedules. I can prove I've never been married and that Todd's not mine. We don't have to dignify this garbage with any kind of public response."

Her lower lip trembled slightly, but she did attempt a smile. "You think that would work?"

"I absolutely think it will work. You watch, the agency will understand. And nobody will pay a bit of attention to this. It'll be forgotten within a few days, as if it never happened."

She didn't look entirely as if she believed him, but appeared willing to give it a shot. Drying her moist eyes, she sipped her water, then put her glass down. Pushing him back on the couch, she curled up against him until they reclined there, spooned together, as comfortably intimate as a pair of longtime lovers.

"So," she murmured, "we have the evening open, right? Anything special you want to do?"

He nudged her until she lay on her back, then moved over her and gave her a wolfish smile. "I can think of one or two things."

He lowered his mouth to press a warm, intimate kiss to her lips, drinking her in, letting his body soak up the pleasure of tasting Jill. She moaned deeply, and he followed the sound, tasting the long column of her neck, placing a kiss in the hollow of her throat.

Reaching for the top button of her blouse, he slid it free, then tasted each inch of her skin as it was revealed. Soon he was sampling the lovely upper curve of her breast, feeling the thudding of her heart against his cheek.

"I wasn't able to think of anything but this all night last night," she mumbled, her voice thick and throaty.

"This?" he asked as he nudged her lacy bra out of the way and flicked his tongue out to taste her sweetly puckered nipple.

She hissed in response, her entire body jerking up against his. Her fingers tangled in his hair, holding him where he was, silently telling him what she wanted.

He very happily gave it to her. This time, he pushed the bra completely out of the way so he could suck deeply on her perfect breast. He reached up to cup the other in his hand, groaning as her legs curled around his and her body curved up to meet him. Though separated by their clothing, they touched in the most elemental of places, and Seth savored the anticipation of being inside her again.

Soon. Very soon.

But as he reached down to tug her blouse free of her pants, his brain registered voices in the hall. Before he had a chance to do a thing, the door to his apartment opened, and two people walked in. Rhoda, his elderly neighbor, was accompanied by the very last person he'd ever expect to show up at his door.

"Oh, my God." Jill quickly disentangled herself and sat up, rebuttoning her blouse as she did so.

Seth did the same, staring at the two women in the doorway, who were looking at them with wide-eyed interest. "Ever hear of knocking?"

"I did knock, twenty minutes ago, but you weren't here. This lovely lady downstairs came to my aid, gave me a cup of delightful chamomile tea, then graciously agreed to use her spare key to let me wait for you in your apartment."

"Oh, my God," Jill whispered, "That's Gina Chastain."

Seth sighed. Yeah. Gina Chastain. Queen of the slasher flicks in the sixties. More recently the resident diva of a popular daytime soap opera.

Seth sighed. "I don't suppose it would have occurred to you to call first."

Gina entered the room, dropping her expensive fur coat on a chair and smiling brightly. "I did call. From the airport, the very minute I landed. I left a message. Didn't you get it?"

He shook his head. "I mean, you might have called a little more than an hour before you were set to arrive."

She shrugged in complete unconcern. "Now, my darling boy, are you going to greet me with a kiss?" She glanced at Jill, who still looked like a woman who'd been very seriously kissed within the past minute or two. "And introduce me to your friend?"

Seth rose to his feet, running a weary hand over his brow and through his hair. Jill stood up, too, still staring at Gina. Rhoda watched wide-eyed, probably shocked to not only have a B-movie star turned soap diva standing beside her, but also a well-known cosmetics model in the room. Her curious look demanded answers and Seth nearly groaned.

Bad timing. Definitely bad timing, considering he'd had Jill right back where he wanted her—in his arms—when they were so soundly interrupted.

As Gina turned to thank Rhoda, in her typically extravagant, overly dramatic way, Jill whispered, "You know Gina Chastain?"

Seth nodded, resigned. He hadn't expected to have to deal with this situation on top of everything else today. But there was no help for it. If he didn't tell Jill himself, the truth would almost certainly come from Gina. "Yeah. Aunt Gina's a member of the family."

Jill's jaw dropped. "Gina Chastain, from *Deceit and Desire,* is your aunt?"

He shook his head. "Sort of."

Gina waved goodbye to a still gawking Rhoda, shut the door behind her, and turned to watch Seth and Jill.

Seth merely shook his head, trying to figure out how to answer. "Putting it biologically," he finally said, seeing by the sparkle in Gina's eyes that she was enjoying the hell out of catching Seth in a rather...provocative position, "she's my mother."

SETH'S REAL MOTHER was stunning. Petite, with rich, sable-brown hair untouched by a strand of gray. She looked a good decade younger than the fifty or so Jill imagined she must be. Her unlined face, with perfect, flawless skin, was even lovelier than it had been in the second-rate movies Gina had starred in when Jill was a kid.

But she still expected to seriously dislike the woman. Even though Gina gave Jill an exuberant hug, kissing both cheeks the way Tony did, Jill had started to remember things. Things Seth had told her, things he hadn't. Hints, bits and pieces about his childhood, which she'd stored away in her brain, began to come together and make sense.

Seth had been adopted by his aunt and uncle, he'd said. But not until he was eight years old.

He'd hinted at an unconventional childhood. She couldn't imagine anything as unconventional as being reared by a mother who'd once been famous for two things: her ability to scream for a solid forty-five seconds without taking a breath. And her extremely large breasts, which were usually exposed by the murdering maniac about to make hamburger out of her with a chain saw.

Seth's words on that fateful day in her dorm room had etched themselves in her memory. She thought of the haunted, hurt look on his face when he'd asked her to choose between her career and their future. Between modeling...and him.

His mother had made that same choice once upon a time. And twice, Seth had been left to feel that he was second best.

"Oh, God," she whispered. Suddenly feeling sick, she made an excuse and hurried to Seth's bathroom, leaving him trapped in Gina's long, clinging embrace.

Locking the door behind her, she stared at her own reflection in the mirror. She splashed cool water on her face, watching the droplets mingle with the tears she couldn't blink away. "I'm so sorry, Seth," she whispered aloud.

If she closed her eyes, even now, she could still see his face that day they'd broken up. He'd been so young, so deeply hurt, rejected and saddened. If only he'd told her, she'd have made him see she was not choosing stardom over the life they'd planned together.

She'd wanted both. But because of his experience with his mother, Seth hadn't believed it was possible to have both. One would suffer, he'd said, and he wouldn't let his kids come second. Because, God, that's exactly what had happened to him.

His mother had kept him around for a while, then dumped him on other family members more than twenty years ago.

That would be right around the time, if Jill wasn't mistaken, when Gina Chastain had regained her fading popularity by switching from B-thriller films to the small screen. Her vixenish character, Delilah Rapapport, with her numerous affairs, dozen husbands and convoluted rise from stripper to brilliant tycoon, had been the focus of *Deceit and Desire* for more than two decades.

Never had Jill seen a mention of any child when Gina Chastain's name had appeared in the press. So she'd kept her secret well…though, Jill suspected, not for the same reasons Jill had tried to keep Todd out of the spotlight. No, judging by the way Seth had reacted eleven years ago to Jill's chance at modeling, Gina had always put her son second to her work.

How could Seth manage to retain a relationship with the

woman? Jill didn't know that she could have been as for-giving.

As she returned to the living room, she thought it re-markable to find Gina Chastain crying and Seth hugging her, physically comforting the woman who'd given him away at the age of eight—when he'd been old enough to understand exactly what was happening.

Then she paused. Why should she be surprised? Seth was just being the loving, thoughtful man she knew him to be.

Her heart melted. Here was a man to build a life with. To grow old with. To love and be loved by in return. Hadn't she known that all along?

No wonder he'd always owned her heart.

Always.

He looked up and met her gaze. Jill nodded that she was okay, and he returned his focus to Gina.

"Can you believe it?" Gina wailed. "Killed in a train crash?"

Jill's breath caught in her throat. Dear Lord, had Seth lost someone else? So soon after the death of his adoptive fa-ther? "What's wrong?"

Gina stepped away from Seth, lowering herself with a great deal of drama, and an equal amount of grace, to the sofa.

"I need a drink."

Giving Jill a look that promised an explanation, Seth went into the kitchen. He returned carrying a bottle of beer. Gina eyed it doubtfully, then obviously decided beggars couldn't be choosers. Bringing the bottle to her lips, she drained three-quarters of it before pausing for a breath. Then she finished off the rest, finally murmuring, "Thank you. A fifth of scotch would have been better, but that was pretty damn good."

Jill nearly smiled, forgetting her dislike long enough to

enjoy the woman's down-to-earth bluntness, particularly as it came from a most elegant exterior package.

Then she remembered what Seth and Gina had been discussing. A train crash. *Awful.* "Is there something I can do? Or would you two prefer to be alone?"

Gina shook her head and reached out her hand. Grabbing Jill's, she pulled her to sit on the couch, too. "There's nothing you can do. Nothing anyone can do." She paused, her eyes widening for effect. Jill recognized the pose from any number of scenes from *Deceit and Desire.*

"Delilah's dead," the woman pronounced. Jill mentally inserted the stark, heavy music the show used during the most dramatic moments, right before they cut to commercial.

"She's dead!" Gina repeated when Jill didn't respond.

Delilah? The character? Jill sighed, both relieved and a little curious about why Gina was putting up such a fuss. Delilah had "died" at least five times over the years. After every death she'd been brought back in some twisted, convoluted story line, or she'd simply fallen through the gaping plothole the writers had left open for her.

"Come on, Gina," Seth said with a chuckle. "It's a soap opera. Nobody's ever really dead on a soap opera."

Gina dropped back against the arm of the couch, her arm across her brow as she moaned. "No, you don't understand. It was a train wreck. A horrible train wreck."

Considering some of the things Jill had seen on her favorite daytime dramas, including aliens from space and people surviving boat explosions, plane crashes and attacks from vampires, she didn't see the big deal.

Apparently Seth didn't, either. "So, the writers are playing games. I bet you just haven't gotten the latest script yet. I'm sure it'll say the whole town of Port Valley is overjoyed to learn Delilah had missed the train to enjoy one last rendezvous with her twenty-year-old Latin lover-slash-gardener.''

"He's Italian," she muttered. "And he's the chauffeur."

Seth ignored her. "Before that happens, of course, Delilah will hear of her rumored demise and decide it's simply too delicious to come forward. She'll plot to turn up at her own funeral, determined to punish anyone who doesn't show up or look mournful enough."

Gina looked hopeful for one moment, as they all considered the plot plausibility. In soap terms, it was perfectly reasonable. Then Gina threw her hands over her face and moaned, long and loud. "She was decapitated."

Jill gulped.

"Do you understand? Headless!"

"That's not good," Jill murmured.

"Maybe she was just rumored to be decapitated," Seth mused.

Gina wasn't to be consoled. "Her head rolled into a storm drain. They showed the firemen sobbing as they waited for the water company to send someone out to remove the grate."

Yuck. "They don't, uh, show that part, do they?" Jill whispered.

Distracted, Gina leaned closer. "Actually, I was really hoping they would. I decided if I was going out, I should go out the way I started in this business, in a bloody, nightmarish mess. I wanted them to pan the drain, the spotlights catching the glittery reflection of my five-carat diamond earrings. Then a close-up, the rain making Delilah's makeup slide off her face, ending with two giant drops of water moving over her eyes and down her cheeks, like giant tears of goodbye."

Sounded pretty moving. Not that Jill was into watching crying, disembodies heads, but she could understand Gina's desire to go out bloody and emotional. As the soap star said, it seemed appropriate, considering her first film had shown her cut into a hundred pieces by a mutant ax maniac.

"But no," Gina snapped. "They said the censors would never stand for it, so all you see is five shirtless, hunky firemen crying their hearts out."

"Shirtless?" Seth asked.

Gina looked at him like he was dense. "Of course! They took off their shirts to try to put out the fire."

Jill saw him wage a mental war on whether he wanted to question the intelligence of that plot device. Apparently, he decided not to. As for herself, Jill understood it completely. Shirtless, hunky firefighters and soaps belonged together as much as shirtless, hunky men belonged in romance novels. No-brainer.

"So what was your big, final scene?" Jill asked, unable to contain her curiosity. She had to admit, she admired Gina's ability to tell a story.

"They put huge fake stitches on my neck to film the funeral scenes," Gina said as she got up and stalked into the kitchen. They heard the clanking of glass, then the refrigerator door slammed. When she returned, she was chugging another beer. As she lowered it from her lips, she scowled. "I looked like the bride of freakin' Frankenstein."

Jill almost laughed again at the definitely unrefined brashness. As the diva Delilah, Gina Chastain didn't generally talk about the "freakin'" anything.

Seth raised a brow. "You mean they had an open casket for a decapitated train crash victim?"

Gina sniffed, obviously hearing Seth's amusement. Jill bit the inside of her cheek, determined not to laugh, too. Then she tried to be sympathetic. "Maybe they're going to do some supernatural story line? Return you from the dead, bring in a body-swapping element?"

Gina rolled her eyes. "What do you think this is, late-night TV? *Deceit And Desire* is a traditional, conservative show. Delilah is dead, buried, with absolutely not one bloody chance of being brought back, not even for a sweeps month.'' She stuck her bottom lip out in a pout. ''I didn't even get to do the ghost scenes, floating around leaving white feathers so my family would know I went to heaven.''

Considering some of Delilah's dirty deeds, Jill wasn't so sure the character would have ended up with white feathers and wings. Burning embers and pitchforks would probably have been more in character. But she didn't want to make Gina feel any worse.

''They tossed me the script, filmed the whole story line, from sex in a train bunk to head in a storm drain, within a week. They waved me out the door without so much as a going-away party.'' Gina glared. ''Those bitches in wardrobe probably all held one the minute they heard.''

Jill got it. Delilah was dead. Really dead. And that meant… ''So, you're out of a job?''

Gina's baby-blue eyes—rumored to have been written about by some Italian poet who'd committed suicide when she'd rejected him—welled up with tears. ''Yes. Fired. Thrown out like old baggage. As if I didn't make that show what it is today. Three Emmys. I have three Emmys! And I would have had four if it hadn't been for Susan Lucci.''

Seth, who'd taken a seat in a chair across from Gina, leaned back and crossed his arms. ''Why'd they fire you, Gina?''

The woman flushed, suddenly looking less confident. Jill recognized the truth of their relationship—Seth was the grown-up of the pair, no question about it.

He probably always had been.

Her heart hitched a bit, reminding her not to like the woman. That, however, was becoming more difficult, because in spite of her diva qualities, Gina seemed to be one funny, outrageous broad. Just the type of woman Jill admired.

Gina tried to evade the question. "So, have you two known each other long?" Her gaze shifted as she cast an interested stare toward the pile of newspapers, complete with glaring photos. "You obviously know each other *well.*"

Seth wouldn't be distracted. "Gina. Why were you fired?"

"Oh, for goodness' sake," she snapped. "So my agent got a little cocky. The new producers of the show are young and needed to be shown who was boss."

Looked like they'd shown her who was boss...and it wasn't their spoiled star.

"You made a lot of demands," Seth said. "And they didn't want to meet them."

Gina huffed and rolled her eyes.

"More money?"

"Well, of course."

"Lots more?" he pressed. Then he answered himself. "Of course lots more. I'm willing to bet that in spite of your salary, you don't have a pot to..." He shook his head. "What else?"

Gina played dumb.

"Come on, what else did you demand, Gina?"

"I bet Erika Slezak got a condo in the Caribbean," she muttered, crossing her arms in front of her chest and shaking her head. "I bet they bought her a limo, too. And why on earth shouldn't they give me four months off a year? Heavens, I can film little scenes to plug in here and there, so the viewers would only notice me gone for a month or two."

Four months vacation? Car? Condo? Plus big bucks? Jill nearly gave a tiny wolf whistle. Nice perks, if you could get them. Unfortunately, it appeared Gina couldn't.

"Now it's making sense," Seth said with a sigh.

Either Gina suddenly felt sheepish or she was a better

actress than Jill expected. A truly regretful look tugged at
her brow and her bottom lip quivered the slightest bit. She
seemed genuinely sad, a little lost, and closer to her actual
age than she had since she walked through the door. As Jill
watched, Seth reached over and took the older woman's
hand. He squeezed it, gave her a heartbreakingly tender
smile, and Gina finally smiled back.

"Thank goodness your mother was with me in New York
for these past several weeks," she whispered. "She really
got me through."

His mother. Confused for a second, Jill realized the other
woman meant Seth's adoptive mother—Gina's sister, probably. Jill had met her once, when Seth's parents came out
to Seattle for a visit, and she'd very much liked the older
woman.

Gina continued. "I think it was good for her, too, you
know? We really helped each other when we most needed
it."

"I'm glad," Seth said. "Where is she, by the way?"

"Back in Ohio. She says she'll come out to see you
soon."

Seth nodded, looking pleased. For all his patience with
the woman who had given birth to him, there was no question who was the mother of his heart.

"Well," Gina finally said, rising to her feet, "I'm fam-
ished. Where shall we go for dinner? My treat!"

Seth gave Jill a look that said Gina's moment of misery
was over—at least for now. Her bright smile seemed as
genuine as her tears had moments before.

A woman of quick-changing emotions, Seth's mother.

"Gina, you don't have a job," Seth reminded her.

"Okay, *your* treat. And we can plan our campaign."

Now she was getting to it, Jill realized. She had the feeling Gina Chastain hadn't shown up on Seth's doorstep by
chance or whim. She wanted something from him.

"Campaign?" Seth asked. Jill heard the note of amused resignation in his voice.

Gina smiled brilliantly. "Of course, dear boy. You're the best media man I know. Who better to help me figure out how to come out of this mess looking like I walked away from the show because of the fabulous, wonderful new opportunities heading my way? I just know you'll think of something brilliant."

"Yeah, I kinda figured that's why you showed up," Seth said, not looking at all hurt or surprised. He didn't appear to mind that Gina had whirled into his life because she needed something from him, not because she wanted to see him.

Then again, he was probably used to it.

He turned to Jill. "You up for dinner with the infamous Gina Chastain?"

Funny, Jill had planned to heartily dislike the actress. And she couldn't say she wasn't a bit offended on Seth's behalf because of the reason the woman had come to Seattle. But Jill couldn't resist the other woman's bright smile and gregarious charm. She had charisma to spare and could coax a smile out of anyone.

In that respect, Gina Chastain was a lot like her son.

"Okay," she replied. "But let's go somewhere quiet and discreet, okay? I think we could all use a night out of the spotlight."

Gina clapped her hands together and smiled. "Perfect." Stepping between Jill and Seth, she hooked one arm through each of theirs and led them both to the door. "Quiet and discreet it shall be!"

CHAPTER THIRTEEN

SETH WASN'T SURE Gina knew the meaning of the words *quiet* or *discreet,* which probably should have been obvious to Jill from the moment they'd been introduced. As they arrived at a small, elegant café just a few blocks from the hospital, Gina immediately went into star mode. She popped sunglasses on her nose, walked in as if she owned the place and didn't acknowledge anyone who wasn't male, young and attractive.

Then she started—very sweetly, very nicely—bitching.

Their first table had too much glare from the street lamp right outside. Their second was too close to the kitchen. Couldn't they please bring her water without any lemon pulp and really, was it too much to ask for gorgonzola cheese for the salad, rather than blue?

She pretended she didn't want to be recognized, when of course, being noticed was exactly what she wanted.

Jill looked both amused and resigned. She seemed aware—as Seth was—that Gina needed a few moments to bask in some serious adulation from her fans. The woman had had a tough week. Decapitated *and* fired. And, if he knew Gina Chastain, teetering on the brink of financial disaster, too. Wasn't she always?

So, though both he and Jill had had their fair share of unwanted attention and speculation today, they both let Gina get away with reveling in her star glory. Not that she wouldn't bounce back from this. Gina *always* bounced back. From everything.

She hadn't changed, nor did Seth expect she ever would. Gina Chastain was the center of her own universe. Other people merely revolved around her...including her own flesh and blood.

He'd gotten used to it. By the time he was old enough to figure her out, he'd actually been able to forgive and befriend her, too. She was much better at being his friend—and aunt—than she'd been at being his mother.

Actually, though he didn't know if anyone could understand, he really had been relieved to be out of Gina's orbit when she'd let him live with her sister and brother-in-law. Seth had even been the one who requested they make things legal via adoption. He'd wanted a mom, dad and siblings. Not an aunt, uncle and cousins.

Seth had to give Gina credit for doing what was best for him. It had hurt her. He'd seen the reproach in her eyes when he insisted that she let his aunt and uncle become his legal parents. Still, she'd done it anyway. One of her few unselfish acts.

But, selfish or not, Gina was...Gina. Deep down, Seth loved her, though she drove him crazy on occasion. She was vivacious and fun. Charming and bawdy. Extravagant and generous to a fault, which was why she was usually broke.

Life with Gina was an adventure, that was certain. She'd dragged him throughout Europe while she worked in low-budget foreign films during his early years. He'd seen places most kids never even read about, met people who'd shown him just what a big, varied place the world was.

He didn't regret those years. And he'd long since forgiven Gina for choosing that world, and those people, over him. Hell, she'd been practically a kid herself—just seventeen when she'd gotten pregnant. They'd helped raise each other. The truth was, Seth had matured first. At age eight, *he* was the one who decided he was never going to accomplish anything in his life if he didn't stay in one place and go to a

real school for any length of time. It took him pulling out
a kid's book and proving to Gina that he couldn't read past
the first page to get her to admit it, too.

She'd never been really big on education, his mother.

"Maybe this wasn't such a great idea," he muttered to
Jill as a third patron of the restaurant came over and stammered a request for an autograph.

"Are you kidding?" she whispered back. "God, do you
know how fabulous it is for me to *not* be recognized? She
can eclipse me with the glory that is Gina Chastain any old
day!"

He hadn't thought of that before. Jill was just so good at
her job, so naturally flirtatious and at ease in front of a
camera, and so warm and gracious to the public. But no one
wanted to be in the spotlight all the time. Well, no one
except Gina. Jill, however, was nothing like Gina. She
needed and appreciated some off time. Even when Todd
wasn't with her to be protected, Jill seemed happy being
somewhat anonymous during a public outing.

Seth knew he had no business even thinking it, but he
couldn't help wondering if Jill still loved her job as much
as she had in the beginning. There had been several moments in the past few days when she'd seemed happy to be
away from all that. Out from under the microscope, a real
woman instead of the Natural Girl.

Would she consider leaving it? Would she miss it if she
did?

It didn't matter. He'd learned his lesson. He'd never let
something as stupid as a job come between them again. He
was just damn lucky to have her back in his life. Whatever
job she wanted to do, he'd still be thankful to have what he
could with her and Todd.

And maybe, just maybe, what he could have would be
the family he'd always planned to have with Jill Jamison.
He smiled as he sipped his drink. Taking her hand under

the table, he merely shrugged when she raised a questioning brow.

Before he could explain, Jill emitted a sharp, shocked gasp. Following her stare, he couldn't help a flash of relief when he saw it wasn't Savannah McCain with a microphone and a cameraman in tow. He just couldn't deal with that situation tonight. Instead, a portly, gray-haired gentleman approached their table, all his attention focused on Jill.

"Who is it?" Seth whispered.

"George Wanamaker," she replied, her voice as soft as his, but also sounding weary and resigned. "He owns Mother Nature cosmetics. I would imagine he's seen the pictures in today's tabloid, judging by the disapproving look on his face."

Great. Her boss was obviously coming over to give his company spokesperson some serious hell. Seth pushed his chair back from the table, determined not to allow the man to ruin the evening. Jill was smiling…laughing, damn it. They could deal with the press and the rumors tomorrow, and he was fully prepared to tell George Wanamaker exactly that.

Before he could say a word, however, Gina rose to her feet and clapped her hands together. "Why, George, you handsome old thing. I was hoping I'd see you during my trip here to Seattle." Her genuinely pleased smile dared him to resist her. Seth recognized the look.

The man glanced at Gina and his jaw dropped open. A crimson flush rose in his cheeks, and he actually stammered. "Miss Chastain."

"Mother Nature cosmetics was a big sponsor of Gina's show," Jill whispered as they both watched Gina reduce the blustery, confident tycoon to a blushing, starstruck man.

"You must join us," Gina insisted, waving at an empty chair. "I'm here visiting my darling nephew, Seth. He, Jill and I were just talking about how awful it is to live under the horrid microscope of the press. The distortions, the lies—it's simply unbearable.''

Wanamaker glanced over at Jill, this time without the tight expression. He still looked a little dazed, an older, widowed man unaccustomed to being on the receiving end of the charm of a woman like Gina Chastain.

Seth's eyes met Gina's and he lifted his glass to her in silent thanks. She nodded, acknowledging that yes, she had intentionally sidetracked Wanamaker's attention from his slightly scandalous spokesperson.

He had to hand it to Gina. She might be a flighty glamour queen to the rest of the world, but she was an absolute tigress when it came to protecting anyone she deemed ''hers.''

Once George Wanamaker lost his disapproving expression and regained his sense of humor under the unrelenting flirtation of Gina Chastain, their evening was actually very pleasant. Not that Seth wouldn't rather be back at his place, continuing what he and Jill had started right before they'd been interrupted by Gina's arrival. Jill's occasional glances and the way she touched his thigh under the table made him think she felt the same way.

Still, the food was good, the company better. Though Jill didn't eat much, merely picking at her dinner, she did at least laugh a lot. She seemed to genuinely appreciate George Wanamaker's assurances that the press would leave her alone once they got onto a new target.

''Don't you worry about it,'' he murmured. ''You're just under the microscope because Seth here has been in the press so much over this baby case at the hospital.''

''Baby case?'' Gina asked with a raised brow.

Seth quickly told Gina the story and her frown deepened. ''How terribly sad. Have they had any more luck in identifying her yet? What about her real parents?''

Because they'd promised Jaron not to reveal any of the

details he'd given them Friday night, Seth and Jill didn't pass on any additional information. "I'm sure they'll find something out soon," he murmured.

"And once they do, the press will back off both of you," George said, sounding completely certain. "Which is good, because we've got some big things coming up, Jill. Very big things." He looked around and lowered his voice. "We don't want any negative publicity."

She raised a curious brow.

George smiled but didn't say a word.

Gina, who always loved ferreting out secrets, leaned across the table and put her hand on his sleeve. The man jerked a little, and his fingers curled under his palms. Seth struggled to hide a laugh, knowing George was a total goner. Once Gina decided to try to coax someone into spilling all, she was as relentless as a kid begging for candy.

Wanamaker didn't have a chance.

JILL'S SMILE FADED and her laughter dried in her mouth when her boss finally told them all his big secret. Mother Nature was going global. No longer content to be the leader in organic women's skin care products in North America, George and his stockholders had agreed to a merger with a major cosmetics company in France. They'd launch an entire new line aimed at the European consumer.

"The Natural Girl will become the American Girl," he confided with a smile, obviously figuring Jill would be thrilled at the news. "The sunny, smiling blonde with the wholesome beauty women the world over will want to emulate."

She sipped her water.

"This is marvelously exciting," Gina gushed.

Jill watched Gina slide her arm a bit closer to George's, appearing fascinated. Good thing George was paying the vivacious woman such unflinching attention. Otherwise he might have noticed the less than enthusiastic response of his star model.

Going global. European tours, appearances, a new series of commercials. New products for the hair. Fragrances. Lotions. All these things both here and abroad. There would be exciting opportunities to meet and mingle with the beautiful set in exotic countries along the Mediterranean, and a new world of fans.

If she'd been ten years younger, still a fresh-faced, energetic college kid and not a loving mother, it might have sounded wonderful. Now it mostly sounded exhausting.

Somehow, Seth's and Todd's faces were all she could see when she closed her eyes and tried to visualize what George was offering. Maybe that was because she already felt weary and stressed just thinking about it. Uprooting her son; reordering her life. Not being in one place long enough to sink some roots, to have a normal existence. She was tired just thinking about it. Tired and already very, very lonely.

"Now, we will be announcing the plans later this week," George continued. "But we would like to keep them under wraps until Friday, when my marketing people have one final meeting with one of the major department stores in London."

Jill nodded, sipping her water again. When she trusted herself not to allow her eyes to fill with tears, she managed to sneak a glance at Seth to see how he was taking this news.

He was listening politely, looking undisturbed, unfazed by George's announcement. Either he didn't yet understand the ramifications—including extensive travel and possibly relocation to another country for Jill and Todd—or else he understood but didn't really care.

He has to care. The only way Seth wouldn't have any problem with this would be if he truly considered their relationship a short fling. Just a chance to finish what they'd started a long time ago, a brief stopping point before they once again moved in opposite directions.

Could he really believe that? Her heart tightened in her chest and she clenched her fingers on her lap, hiding her sudden unease. Well, why not? Hadn't that been just what she'd been convincing herself they'd have during their walk on the beach? She'd decided there could be no future between them because of her inability to give him what he most wanted. And she'd known full well what she was getting into, risking another broken heart by grabbing whatever kind of relationship she could have with Seth for as long as she could have it.

Maybe he'd been doing the same thing.

He hadn't told her he loved her. She thought he did. God, the way he held her when they made love, the way he looked at her, the way he whispered her name. All of those things made her believe Seth had fallen in love with her again. Or, like her, that he'd never escaped those feelings to begin with.

But he hadn't said the words. He hadn't made promises or asked for vows or commitments. Now, at this moment, he was doing a damn good job of looking like a man who really didn't mind that she was about to jet-set right out of his life again. Maybe because he already had a set image of what he wanted, what he'd soon have. An adopted son or daughter, a steady, happy existence here in Seattle. Without her.

Life without her would also be a life without wigs and disguises. Without sleazy photographers and tabloid papers. Without slobbery dogs and mischievous four-year-olds who loved to tell whoppers. Without foreign male nurses underfoot or a burned-out supermodel who could barely balance her checkbook and could never…*never*…give him the children he'd been waiting for all his adult life.

So, yeah, maybe he'd gone into yesterday's renewal of

their physical relationship with the same initial expectations she had. Maybe he'd decided on a short-term goal to grab some great memories before they had to split apart again, this time for good.

Only, unlike Seth, Jill had already realized what a stupid, insane idea that had been. Because it had been only twenty-four hours, and already she couldn't bear the thought of losing him. All her ideas of living for the moment and taking what she could didn't mean a damn thing. She'd gone and let her heart remember that Seth Nannery always had been and always would be the only man for her.

"Will you excuse me for a moment?" Jill asked, suddenly needing to be alone. She needed to splash some cool water on her face. More than that, she needed to get away, to do something to prevent herself from bursting into tears or into shouts.

Part of her wanted to cry. Part of her wanted to tell George Wanamaker she'd already given him a third of her life and he simply couldn't make one more demand on her.

The biggest part of her suddenly wanted to ask Seth where she stood, where they were going and what he wanted. Mostly she wanted to ask him if they had a future together.

Because right now, she simply had no idea where she stood.

Thinking only of hurrying to the ladies' room before the tears hiding behind her lashes spilled down her cheeks, Jill quickly rose to her feet. As had happened with more and more frequency lately, her vision blurred over for a second, and a rush of dizziness swept through her. She grabbed at the table to steady herself, barely noticing Seth immediately standing to take her arm.

But oh, she definitely noticed the full glass of red wine Gina had been drinking. She noticed the way it wobbled when she grabbed at the table, and sent a silent prayer that it wasn't doing what it looked like it was doing—tipping over onto its side.

It was, though.

Watching in horror, she could only moan as a bloodred path of very fine Merlot spread across the pristine white linen tablecloth. Directly into Gina Chastain's silk-clad lap.

ON TUESDAY, Seth wondered all morning how Jill's doctor's appointment was going. Since the previous night, when she'd been light-headed again, having to grab at the table with enough force to send a glass of wine spilling over into Gina's lap, he'd been able to think of nothing else.

God, please let her be okay. Please let it be stress and fatigue, poor eating habits. Don't let her be sick.

He hadn't realized until this morning just how much her confession about her medical history had scared him. Losing his father last spring had been devastating. He was in no way ready to consider losing someone else he loved.

And, oh, yeah, he loved her. Always had, always would. Period. End of story.

How they'd make this work out with her new job opportunity, he really couldn't say. George Wanamaker's news about their global expansion and what it would mean for Jill's career had both thrilled him for her and torn him up inside. She'd be gone, traveling a lot, living a busy, hectic life with little time to focus on home and family.

So be it. He was not the stupid kid he'd once been. He would not make the same mistake—wouldn't force her into a corner and ask her to choose between one or the other.

If she wanted both—and he believed deep in his heart that she truly did—then both she would have. Hell, he was damn good at what he did. He could leave Seattle Memorial, start a consulting business, spend more time with Todd to take up some of the slack while Jill traveled.

For a while, maybe they could travel together, be a trio

seeing the world. Or better yet, a quartet with the child he planned to adopt. They'd spend time building their family, then Seth would focus on giving their kids a stable home life while Jill did what she had to do.

He could deal with anything, as long as she came home to them.

As long as she was healthy, happy and always came home to them...

He glanced at the clock. Her appointment was at nine. It was now nearly noon, and he was ready to start calling her cell phone. "Where are you?" he whispered.

One good thing—at least Jill herself had begun to realize something was wrong. She hadn't tried to laugh off last night's dizziness, and hadn't protested when Seth insisted on driving her home. He'd insisted he could get her car back to her house later. With George Wanamaker's help, he'd done exactly that.

Wanamaker. There was another interesting situation. Seth allowed himself to smile over Gina's interest in Jill's boss. She'd been pretty obvious about it. And considering she hadn't come back to Seth's place last night after dinner, or answered the phone in her hotel room first thing this morning, he figured she and George had had a *very* good time.

Same old Gina. Nothing like a wealthy, attractive man to distract her from a trifling trouble like losing a job.

Though he didn't know Wanamaker very well, he appeared to be able to handle Gina. Sure, George had been a little uncomfortable at first, being the focus of her flirtation. But the strong-minded businessman had soon been giving as good as he got. Jill and Seth had shared a few amused glances, recognizing that Gina might not be wrapping this particular man around her pinky quite as soon as she usually did.

When his door opened, Seth immediately rose to his feet.

Unfortunately, it wasn't Jill's beautiful face he saw. He hid a sigh of disappointment. "Hey, Jaron."

"Nannery," the other man said with a nod. "You were expecting someone else? Is this a bad time?"

Seth shook his head and gestured toward an empty chair. "Not at all. Please, come in."

Jaron did, giving him an amused smile. "For a womanizing ladies' man, you look pretty tense and uptight."

Jaron had seen the article. Who hadn't? Since Seth had arrived this morning, he'd received a lot of grins from co-workers. He'd also noticed some flirtatious, speculative stares from some of the women and outright envy from a few men.

At least the hospital administrator had also recognized Jill and Todd. Since Jill was apparently a very generous contributor to the hospital, that brief phone call had been relatively painless.

"Had a good weekend, I see?" Jaron prodded with a grin.

Seth rolled his eyes. "Don't start."

Jaron sat down and shrugged. "Photographer must have been a blind idiot not to recognize Jill in that stupid spiked wig."

"Yeah, well, maybe he did. But the headlines wouldn't have been as spicy if they'd read Superstar Model Spends Quiet Day At The Zoo With Her Son And An Old College Friend."

Jaron raised a brow. "Friend?"

Seth didn't answer that one. He knew *friend* wasn't the right word, but didn't suppose Jaron would be interested in hearing about soul mates. Seeing the weariness on Jaron's face, he sensed the detective had information to share. "Do you have any more you're free to tell me about the case?"

The detective nodded. "We've used the stolen car and other clues to learn the identity of the couple killed in the crash. Their names were Jim and Patty Lehr."

Feeling a stab of pity for the couple who died that tragic night, Seth couldn't help asking, "Any explanation as to why they'd do such a thing?"

Jaron's lips tightened. "We're working on that. We also now know baby Chris's real identity." The detective gave him a weak smile as he relayed some good news for a change. "We've determined that we're not dealing with a medical crisis here."

No medical crisis. Thank God. "So the other baby, the one who might have been switched with baby Chris, wasn't sick?"

"Nope. We've had specialists scour all the medical data on Chris and the other baby."

Seth remembered some of what Jaron had told him before. "I thought there were three girls at the hospital that night."

Jaron nodded, looking surprised—and pleased—that Seth had been paying such close attention Friday night. "We ruled one of the babies out. She's of Asian descent through her father. We found the family right away and conducted a quick blood test—routine procedure. The DNA will make it conclusive, but we've pretty much eliminated her as the switched infant."

"Great. What about the third little girl?"

Jaron sighed. "That's where it gets sticky. We know who she is…and thanks to the medical records and tests conducted in the hospital right after her birth, we know she's healthy."

"But?"

Jaron stood and walked over to the window, raising a blind to glance outside. His shoulders hunched and he looked weary. "We can't find her."

Seth shared the man's flash of frustration. "Why not? If you know who the parents are, it should be easy to track them down."

Jaron dropped the blind and turned to look at Seth. "We have the mother's name—Layla Marino—but no address. So far public records turn up nothing." He shook his head in frustration. "The woman's a ghost."

A ghost who possibly didn't know she was nurturing the wrong baby. Or did she? "You're sure she—"

"What?"

Seth didn't want to make the detective's job any more difficult, but knowing Jaron was a damn good cop, he felt pretty sure he'd already thought of this possibility himself. "Have you considered that this Layla person is the one who engineered the switch? Maybe the couple killed in the crash had no idea they were traveling with a child who wasn't their own."

Again a light of respect shone in the detective's eyes. "Yeah, we've considered that. I doubt it, only because of some of the things Annabelle has said about how the dead woman talked before she died. She seemed to be calling out for her baby—but not the baby brought to the hospital with her that night."

Seth didn't know whether to feel relieved or not. If this Layla Marino was not the person who'd switched the babies, that meant she was out there somewhere, raising and loving a child who wasn't hers. Meanwhile her real daughter, Chris, was in the care of strangers, away from her mother and family.

It was like something out of one of Gina's far-fetched soap opera stories. But this was all too true...and was damned tragic.

"Thanks for stopping by to update me," Seth said as Jaron turned to leave the office. He stood and walked the detective to the door, extending his hand.

Jaron shook it and nodded. "You're welcome."

As Jaron walked through the door, Seth added, "And good luck. I hope someone finds this Layla Marino and reunites her with her daughter very soon."

CHAPTER FOURTEEN

ON WEDNESDAY, Jill kissed Todd goodbye as he walked out the door with Tony, heading for Round the Clock. She'd be going to Seattle Memorial herself in a short while, but with the ever present media, she didn't want to risk bringing her son to the child care center in person. With her luck, Savannah McCain and her lackey photographer would be staking the place out, ready to pounce and ask a million questions.

That's what she'd done yesterday when Jill had gone to see Seth after her doctor's appointment. Jill had made sure the reporter got the message...no comment now. No comment *ever*. If channel seven wanted one more word out of J.J.'s mouth, it would be to any other reporter on their beat. In spite of Savannah's false friendliness, Jill had no doubt the woman was the one who'd sicced the tabloid media on her and Seth.

Seth had filled her in on his very brief relationship with the woman, as well as a lot of other details about his life. It seemed that her confessions about her medical background had helped him open up to what it was like being the son of someone like Gina Chastain.

"Seth," she murmured, smiling as she got ready to go back into her doctor's office to get the results of her blood tests. He'd been so incredibly worried—she'd seen that the minute she entered his office yesterday after her appointment. And he hadn't seemed reassured when she'd sworn her doctor didn't believe anything serious was wrong. Until they knew for sure what the problem was, Seth was going to be concerned.

It was probably just as well she hadn't told him some of the things her doctor had mentioned as possibilities. "No." She closed her eyes briefly, determined not to worry about anything until she knew where she stood. That was exactly what she'd repeated to Seth yesterday at lunch, and again while lying in his arms in her own bed last night.

They'd eaten a big dinner as a family, then the guys had taken off for a night on the town, and she and Seth had put Todd to bed. God, how her heart had constricted in her chest as she'd watched Seth animate the world of Sam-I-Am by reading Todd his favorite bedtime story.

Then, later in the dark, quiet house, how her heart had expanded and thudded, overwhelming her with emotion when they'd made love in her room. Saturday had been about raw passion and eroticism. Last night had been strictly about the tender fulfillment of the heart's deepest desire. He'd kissed her endlessly, worshiped her body from head to toe with his hands, his mouth, with every part of himself. That heated, body-rocking fulfillment she'd only ever been able to find in his arms had been there for her again. And again. Until she was sure every ounce of physical pleasure had been wrung from her and she was incapable of any more.

He'd hated to leave, and she'd hated to see him go, particularly since they hadn't even begun to discuss the latest situation with Jill's job. Seth still hadn't made a single comment about it, not asking her to stay, not questioning when she'd leave. Nothing.

Her brain said that meant he didn't care. That he was building up memories and enjoying what they had while he could, knowing it would be short term. Because, really, how could it be anything else? How could they make a long-distance relationship—her son, his job, an adoption—work while living under the microscope of a merciless media and Jill traveling the globe on this new modeling adventure?

No, logically, her mind told her they couldn't.

But that didn't stop her heart from hoping she was wrong.

"IT'S HYPOGLYCEMIA."

Seth shot to his feet the moment Jill stepped into his office late Wednesday morning, seeing by the bright smile on her face that this was good news.

"Spell it out for me," he insisted, walking over to push the door shut and pull her into his arms. She curled against him, wrapping her arms around his waist, burrowing against his chest until he could feel the beating of her heart through her thin, rust-colored sweater.

"Spell it out?" she finally murmured. "I can barely spell the word." Then she laughed. "But it's not a major deal, Seth."

He stepped back, staring into her shining blue eyes, seeing no hint of concern there. Only pure, undiluted happiness mixed with a dash of relief. "Okay, my brain has started functioning again," he mumbled, taking a deep breath as he acknowledged that his heart was finally returning to its normal rhythm. "Hypoglycemia—isn't that usually associated with diabetes?"

She nodded. "Usually." When he frowned, she hurriedly added, "But not always, and not in my case. It's rare, but it happens. I have non-diabetes related hypoglycemia. In laymen's terms, I have low blood sugar. The doctor mentioned it as a possibility yesterday when we talked about my symptoms…weakness, drowsiness, dizziness. Headaches, paleness, all that stuff that you've been so worried about."

He rolled his eyes. "Yeah. All that stuff you called stress and wanted to ignore."

She didn't respond to his subtle *I told you so,* never one to readily admit defeat. He nearly grinned. Typical Jill.

"Anyway, the symptoms fit, but he was skeptical because there was no history of diabetes in my family, nor has there been any sign of it in my medical history. Still, the blood-work—which he had the lab rush for me because of my medical problems in the past—couldn't lie. It's definitely hypoglycemia."

He hugged her again. Stroking her hair, he tangled his fingers in it and leaned down to kiss her forehead, her temple, her earlobe. "Oh, God, I'm so glad."

"You and me both."

He pulled her down to sit on his lap in one of the chairs across from his desk. "So what do we do now? How do you treat it? Medication or anything like that?"

She put her lower lip out in a tiny pout.

"Jill?"

She sighed heavily. "I have to meet with a dietician."

He bit the inside of his cheek to hide a laugh, knowing where this was headed.

"Low carbs. Oh, God, how am I gonna live without lo mein for breakfast?"

"A complete change in diet?" he speculated.

She nodded, looking very disgruntled. "Small frequent meals and snacks, lots of grains, vegetables and fruits. Low carbs."

She sounded as if she'd been told to eat a plate full of roaches and Seth couldn't hold back a laugh.

Finally, she dropped her head forward and shook it until her hair curtained her face. "And, ugh…regular *exercise!*"

So relieved he could barely contain it, Seth pulled her close to press a hot, openmouthed kiss on her lips. "I'll keep you working out," he whispered as she turned on his lap to face him, her fingers curled in his hair.

"Hmm," she whispered. "If it's anything like last night, I think I'd be up for exercise seven days a week."

He nibbled her lips, licking, tasting, teasing her tongue until she wriggled so close to him, he had to surge up against her in response.

"Yeah, last night was good for endurance. Long and slow. Lots of reps," he whispered, hearing her little whimpers as she grew more excited. "But we definitely need to kick up your heart rate. Get more aggressive with the cardio workout."

She nearly purred. "My heart is pounding so hard right now, I feel quite sure you're up to the challenge. Wanna be my personal trainer?"

He wanted to be her personal *everything*.

They kissed again, deeply, erotically, but still with such tenderness and warmth. Seth knew she felt like he did—that they were both sharing not only the passionate response they always brought out in each other, but a genuine sense of relief over Jill's news from the doctor.

"Okay, we almost got into a lot of trouble for doing this here in your office Friday night," Jill finally whispered as she pulled her lips away. "I think I better go now or you're not going to get much work done today."

Seth gave her one more kiss, then sighed, knowing she was right. She slipped off his lap and stood, straightening her clothes. Her smile promised they'd get back to this later.

Definitely.

Before he could demand to know when and where—or invite her back to his place for a leisurely, healthy lunch, followed by an erotically delicious dessert—his phone rang. Giving her an apologetic look, he answered it, immediately recognizing the voice of the case worker from the adoption agency. "Mr. Nannery, I'm afraid I have to cancel again. I won't be able to make this evening's appointment, either."

Damn. The woman had called yesterday and rescheduled

their missed appointment for tonight. At the time, he'd almost thanked her for canceling on Monday—he couldn't imagine what she would have thought of Gina's grandiose arrival.

But two cancellations in one week didn't bode well.

He sighed. "All right, Mrs. Thomason. I understand that things come up. I was looking forward to your home visit, though, because I'm anxious to get the approval. I know the waiting list will add a lot of time to the process."

The woman didn't immediately respond with another offered date. Seth pressed her. "Is there something wrong?"

"I have to admit, my superiors have some…concerns."

He walked around his desk, ducking under the phone cord until he reached his chair. Jill watched him, nibbling on the corner of her lip, apparently realizing who he was talking to.

"What kind of concerns?"

"Well, the media attention hasn't escaped our notice."

He sighed, mentally cursing *We See Seattle*. "I would like to schedule a meeting with you to explain that article in Monday's paper. It is not what it seems. Not at all."

The woman again hesitated. "Mr. Nannery, I'm sure you can explain. But we can't help feeling that the timing is poor on this issue right now. With today's incident, we simply don't know if you can give this matter your full, undivided attention."

"Today's incident?" He wanted to question her, but hesitated to do so with Jill in the room. She already wore a deep frown, hearing just his part of the conversation. If something else had happened, he wanted to know about it and figure out how to deal with it. All she needed to be concentrating on right now was getting better.

"Please, Mrs. Thomason," he urged, knowing he could make the woman understand if he and Jill could sit down with her and talk to her face-to-face. "Let's schedule a time when I can come into your office and fill you in on what's happening…and why it's happening."

She hesitated for just a second, and Seth held his breath. Finally, she made a sound of assent, her tone gentling. "All right. I'll try to work something out."

Thanking her, he hung up to find Jill staring at him expectantly. He quickly explained.

As soon as he finished, he noticed how pale her face suddenly looked. "What did she mean by today's incident?"

"I don't know." But he very much wanted to find out.

SETH LOOKED CALM and in control, but Jill knew him well enough to recognize the tightness of his smile and the stiffness of his shoulders beneath his shirt.

He was worried. Frankly, so was she. Her worst fears seemed to be coming true. If the caseworker was suddenly canceling appointments, it had to have something to do with Seth's relationship with Jill, and the unflattering media attention. "I'm so sorry, Seth. Let me know the minute you hear from her and we'll go in and straighten this out. I can bring the wig, Todd's birth certificate…medical records…whatever."

He shook his head, looking sorry he'd told her. "Hey, don't worry about it. This is going to be fine." Leaving his chair, he walked around to stand beside her again. He gave her a tender, sweet kiss that promised things would be all right, making her forget everything but the feel of his lips, the smoothness of his tongue, and the taste of every breath they shared.

Jill came close to wrapping her arms around his neck and losing herself in his embrace. But one second before she would have done so, she heard voices in the corridor outside his door. She had just enough time to step back before the knob turned and the door swung in.

Savannah McCain strode into the office as if she owned the place. "I thought I might find you here." She leveled a tight smile at Jill.

The reporter beckoned to someone in the hall, and her cameraman entered. He looked sheepish, but this time he did have his camera up and rolling.

"Get out, Ms. McCain," Seth snapped. "And the next time you want to come into my office, you damn well better knock."

She didn't so much as bat an eyelash at his tone. "Oh, the hospital's PR director is no longer meeting with the press?"

"Make an appointment."

She smiled. "I'm not here to see you, anyway." Then she stepped closer and pulled a microphone to her mouth. "J.J., would you care to comment on today's headlines?"

She and Seth exchanged a worried look. "What headlines?"

Savannah had anticipated the question. She handed Jill a copy of a slimy, nationally known tabloid. Jill glanced at it, horrified to see the headline: The Natural Girl A Bar Drunk?

As if the stark words weren't bad enough, there were accompanying photos. A picture of a woozy-looking Jill and a shrieking, wine-stained Gina Chastain graced the cover in full four-color glory. Seth was easily recognizable beside them. A small box of bold type text proclaimed, "J.J., the Natural Girl, gets in wine-tossing brawl with soap diva Gina Chastain. Could they be fighting over the hunky spin doctor from Seattle Memorial?"

Below that was another picture, this one with Jill's hand on her brow, her eyes half-closed. Seth appeared to be physically supporting her. The caption below was even more damning. "Friends speculate on famous model's obvious fatigue and weight loss. Is the Natural Girl using some unnatural drugs?"

"You've got to be kidding me," she said, hearing her own voice break with pure dismay.

Good Lord, the tabloids were painting her as a home-wrecking drug addict, with Seth right there beside her, dragged into the sordidness because of Jill's fame. The fame he'd once, as a child, fought so hard to escape by asking his own mother to give him up for adoption to his aunt and uncle.

Her head began to spin and her stomach to heave. She grabbed the back of the chair, this time dizzy not from low blood sugar levels, but from pure, undiluted dismay.

"So, any comment, J.J.?" Savannah McCain watched wide-eyed, avaricious, waiting for something juicy to broadcast about one of Seattle's famous residents. And wouldn't she just love it if Jill got one of her dizzy spells and staggered right into the camera? What a lovely story that would make for the noon news.

Seth stepped between them, looking nothing like the tender, loving man she knew. Jill had never seen a more beautiful sight than this angry, avenging god who towered over the reporter, his fury so visible the woman took a quick step back.

He got right into Savannah's face. "I should think, Ms. McCain, that you, a supposedly legitimate reporter for one of Seattle's finest television stations, wouldn't stoop to the tabloid tactics of some of your less reputable brethren in the media." He clenched his jaw, and Jill saw him fist his hands at his sides as he worked to control his anger. "Channel seven is a highly respected affiliate," he continued, "and I simply cannot fathom why one of their star reporters would not only read such complete and utter garbage, but be so unprofessional as to actually confront the subject of such libel."

Savannah's mouth opened, as if she intended to reply, but Seth cut her off. This time, though he continued to speak to her, he looked directly into the camera. Jill had no doubt it was Savannah's superiors—her producer, the executives at channel seven—to whom he was addressing his remarks.

"In this time of great trial, when the attention of all people with a smattering of heart or conscience should be focused on the quest to reunite an infant with her real parents, it astounds me that some members of the media are more interested in personal vendettas. That they can create ridiculous tabloid scandals for their own greed or vanity, completely uncaring that one of the most popular, generous, well-loved citizens of the city of Seattle is being ripped apart by a media rag completely lacking in integrity and disregarded by every legitimate reporter in this country."

If Jill wasn't feeling so utterly dismayed, she might have smiled. Man, Seth could spin.

Then he turned again to focus directly on Savannah. He stepped closer until they were nearly nose to nose. Though he lowered his voice, his disgust still rang out loud and clear. "Now, get your goddamn camera and your microphone out of my office or I'm going to send your producer a copy of the messages you left on my answering machine last month when you were so *unhappy* that I didn't want to see you again."

The woman's face paled. Jill wondered if Seth would—or could—make good on his threat. He did have an old-fashioned, tape-playing answering machine. She'd seen it in his apartment Monday. So she supposed it was possible he still had some evidence of Savannah McCain's personal stake in all this.

Or he could be bluffing.

Savannah seemed uncertain for a second. Jill held her breath until the other woman finally backed down. Nodding at her cameraman, she turned and stalked out of the office without another word. The cameraman followed...but not until he'd given Seth a nod and very blatant grin. Jill imagined this was one taped interview he wouldn't mind sending to his bosses back at the channel seven studios.

As soon as they'd gone, Jill sagged against the desk and dropped the newspaper from her fingers. It fluttered to the floor, pages sliding out, displaying more photos of Jill, Seth and Gina during their friendly dinner Monday night.

Seth stared at them. "Bastards."

He was still tense, coiled and tight and angrier than she'd ever seen him in his life. On her behalf, she had no doubt.

She reached out and touched his shoulder, kneading the tight muscles there. "Thank you."

Instead of replying, he hauled her into his arms and held her close. "I'm so sorry. I don't have any doubt that this whole thing is because of me."

Jill doubted it. Maybe Savannah had started out intending to mess with Seth a little bit, as revenge. But things had gone well beyond that now. A national tabloid was involved. Photographers were obviously following them, and more of their paparazzi buddies would follow right along. She knew from experience that the story would appear in every other national tabloid when next week's issues were released. Historically, they all followed suit and covered a story until it was so far removed from the truth, no one even remembered what had triggered it in the first place.

"Well," she murmured as she stepped away and looked down, unable to meet his eyes. "Now we know what the caseworker meant by 'today's incident.'"

He frowned. "We'll explain everything...."

Explain everything to the judgmental people at the adoption agency. She gave a bitter laugh, visualizing how that meeting would go. Sure, the caseworkers would say. In spite of having sleazy photographers ready to accuse Seth of being a philanderer, and his famous girlfriend of being a drug addict, the agency officials were convinced Seth could provide a secure, happy life for the child he want to adopt.

Not in this lifetime. They'd never believe it. And Seth would once again lose out on the family he'd been seeking since he was a lonely, sad little eight-year-old who asked his mother to give him away to someone else.

Her heart grew heavier in her chest and her eyes stung with the tears she somehow couldn't let fall.

It hurt to be so close to having what she truly wanted, only to see, oh, so clearly, that it would never be hers.

Seth ran a hand through his hair in a familiar gesture as comforting as it was heart-breaking. Anger and confusion rolled off him in waves. His concern for her couldn't eliminate his disappointment, she knew that. Seth was an intelligent man…he'd probably already reached the same conclusion she had. This was never going to work. Just like eleven years ago, something would have to give.

She knew what it was.

Rapidly blinking to keep any suspicious moisture away from her cheeks, she forced a gruff chuckle. "Look, Seth, I think the best thing is for me to just go. George wants me to attend the London meeting Friday, anyway. It'll be big and splashy, you'll be a half a world away." She crossed her arms, willing him not to see how much she hated the thought of doing what she planned to do. "Believe me, as cute as you are, I'm the one the paparazzi will be following."

He turned and stared at her. "You're leaving." It wasn't a question.

She nodded, wondering which would devastate her more—to see hurt in his eyes? Or relief.

To her surprise, she saw neither. He merely smiled a gentle, understanding smile and stepped closer. Their bodies nearly touched, though Jill could too easily picture an entire ocean between them. Tucking an errant strand of hair behind her ear, he ran his fingers along her jawline, then tilted her chin up until she looked at him.

''I'll be waiting for you when you get back.''

She tilted her head, confused, not knowing what he was offering, what he was hinting at. Would he be waiting as her friend? Her lover? What?

He didn't explain. Nor did he ask her not to go. He didn't give her ultimatums or make demands. Either Seth had changed…or he simply recognized that her plan was for the best. Part of her wanted to demand that he tell her which it was. A wiser part of her made her keep her lips closed, knowing if he told her it was over, if he said the words aloud, she'd never be able to make it out of this room without breaking down.

God, it would be hard enough to board a plane and fly away from the soul-nurturing life she had here with Todd…and now with Seth. She didn't want to go to London, didn't want to reenter the world of paparazzi and commercials and endless, exhausting appearances, photo shoots, interviews. Mostly, she didn't want to leave her house and her baby. And her love.

There was, however, no other choice.

Before he could say anything else, the door to Seth's office opened again. Jill instantly recognized the hospital administrator, who shot her a concerned look. ''I'm sorry, Miss Jamison, but there are photographers lined up out front. The word is out that you're here.''

''You'd better go,'' Seth said. Then he turned to the administrator. ''I'll go down to the front steps and give a noon statement to the real press. The vultures will stick close by, figuring Jill is in the area.'' He glanced at her again, offering her a supportive smile. ''You can slip out the doctors' exit into the garage and be gone before I finish spinning my spin.''

She had no doubt he was right. Because that's what he did best. He could make anyone believe things were possible.

Even when they were not.

CHAPTER FIFTEEN

HE DIDN'T SEE HER again that day. Seth called Jill Wednesday afternoon to make sure she got home okay, and she assured him she had. They didn't talk about her plans much, beyond her telling him she was catching a flight to London around noon the next day. Her birthday.

The guys would look after Todd until Friday, when her parents would arrive from Iowa. She expected to be gone at least ten days. And when she got back…

When she got back, he'd be waiting. Period.

She might not realize it yet. They'd barely begun to scratch the surface of their renewed relationship. They hadn't had time to make plans, to share their emotions as they'd shared their physical feelings. So maybe Jill didn't believe it yet, didn't quite trust that he meant what he said when he told her he'd be here waiting when she got back.

He planned to show her. To make this crazy, wild ride they were on become a real, stable life. For him, for her, for Todd.

There was no time to convince her now, no way to make her believe they could build a future together. So he simply trusted in her unspoken feelings for him, and his for her. When she got back, he'd show her that he wasn't going anywhere, even if she tried to push him away—as she was doing now.

Oh, he knew she thought it was for his own good. Jill was so protective, so nurturing. No way would she stick around if she thought she was hurting him. But soon she'd understand that nothing could hurt him as much as losing her again. *Nothing*.

Late Thursday morning, he called her one last time, reaching her on her cell phone. He could hear the airport noise in the background and knew she'd be boarding her flight in a few minutes. "Hey," he said, "I just wanted to wish you a safe trip. Have fun in London."

"Thanks."

"Todd is all squared away?"

"Yep. Looking forward to a visit from Grandma and Grandpa." She sighed heavily. "I miss him already."

"He'll be fine. Do you mind if I check in on him?"

"Are you kidding? I'd love it. But…"

"But?"

Her voice dropped to a near whisper. "You don't have to feel obligated or anything."

Obligated. Right. "Jill…"

She cut him off with a whisper. "My plane's boarding."

Finally, knowing she was about to take off and unable to leave things so tenuous between them, he said, "Happy birthday, Jill." Then he lowered his voice, willing her to believe him. "I love you. And I *will* be waiting for you when you get back."

She didn't cut the connection, but remained silent for a moment. He sensed she was crying. "You can't…this won't work."

He laughed softly, so certain things would be all right that he felt no concern, no panic. "Of course it'll work. We've waited too long to not *make* it work, any way we have to."

She remained silent, obviously thinking over his words.

"You go, do what you have to do for as long as you have to do it." Then he smiled, knowing she could hear the love and certainty in his voice. "Just come back to us."

JILL CUT the connection on her cell phone and walked toward the gate. Her carry-on was heavy on her arm. A pair of dark glasses shielded her tear-reddened eyes.

She was boarding a plane, leaving the most wonderful part of her life behind. *Happy stinking birthday to me.*

How heartbreakingly appropriate to come full circle like this. Eleven years ago…another birthday, another turning point in her life. Another choice to make, another path to follow. This time, though, she didn't have the convenient excuse of an ultimatum. Seth hadn't asked a thing of her, hadn't made demands or given her any self-righteous way to justify what she was doing. This was completely her decision. Completely her choice.

Seth acted as though today was not a turning point, that they could make things work when she got back. Jill knew better. Getting on this plane and flying to London was the first step in cutting Seth out of her life for good. For *his* own good.

She was being selfless. Noble. But she'd never felt worse in all her thirty-one years.

"Miss, may I see your identification, please?" the woman at the gate asked her. Nearby, security workers glanced over, ever vigilant, scanning the crowd of international travelers.

Jill reached into her bag for her wallet. It was hidden beneath an issue of *We See Seattle*. She didn't know what demon had made her bring it to begin with, or why she'd been torturing herself by reading the article while she waited, alone, in the airport. As if unable to help herself, she glanced at the photos of her, Seth and Todd at the zoo. Looking so happy, so much a family. So completely beautiful.

"Miss? Your boarding pass?"

She stared at the woman, then looked back at the photo.

Not giving it one more moment's thought, she turned and walked away from the gate.

SETH RAN INTO Sven in the cafeteria Thursday afternoon and learned Todd was here, at Round the Clock. Hearing that all three of the guys had to work until late in the evening, he offered to take Todd back to Jill's. Sven immediately agreed. Meeting Seth at the child care center just after five to check Todd out, he gave Seth a key to the house and Todd a high five goodbye.

Todd talked the entire way home about his day at Round the Clock. He could barely remain in his seat as he discussed the Halloween party planned for the next day, and the costume his mommy had finished sewing for him the night before. Seth ate up every energetic word.

When he could get a word in edgewise, he said, "Anyone ever tell you you're one talkative guy?"

Todd nodded, sending that thick, errant lock of light brown hair of his dangling over his brow. He pushed it away impatiently. "My grandpa says I'm perk...precocious and loquacious," he said, mangling the pronunciation. "That means I'm smart and I talk too much."

Seth grinned. "You know something, that pretty much sums up the kind of kid I was, Todd."

After making them both some dinner, Seth gave in to Todd's pleas for a quick game of Chutes and Ladders. He quickly learned there was no such thing. "Todd, does anyone ever win this game? Or do we keep on getting close to the end, then sliding down the chute until one of us gets sick of it and quits?"

Todd snorted. "That's what Mommy does."

"I'm with Mommy. I give up."

"So I win." The boy raised a brow, daring Seth to disagree. Seth didn't even try. Todd looked very satisfied.

"Is that how you win all your games?"

"Yup."

"Good angle, kid."

Sending Todd up to get a few books to read before bed,

Seth flipped on the TV to catch the end of the local evening news. As soon as the boy returned, arms loaded with a stack of books, he hit the mute button and pulled Todd onto his lap.

Todd instantly reached for the top book.

"Sam-I-Am?"

Making himself comfortable against Seth's chest, Todd nodded. "And can you do the voices again?"

Yeah. He could do the voices. Seth suddenly realized he could do this, be a dad to this great kid every night for the rest of his life and be a very happy man. As long as Jill was coming home to be Todd's mother. And Seth's life partner.

"Voices," he replied, feigning a bad Clint Eastwood accent. "Go ahead. Make my day. Eat those green eggs and ham."

Todd giggled as Seth began to read. Before he got two pages into the story, however, they both heard the front door opening. Figuring one of Jill's boarders had gotten off early, Seth barely glanced up as someone entered.

"Mommy!" Todd launched himself off Seth's lap and raced across the room, dive-bombing Jill until she nearly fell onto the floor. "You're home from London already? Gosh, that was such a fast airplane. Did you take the space shuttle?"

While she hugged and greeted her son, Seth absorbed that she was here, real and solid, looking healthy and full of life. Her face literally glowed, her eyes sparkling with happiness.

"You didn't leave," he said softly when she finally walked over to greet him, Todd glued to her hip.

She shook her head. "The idea of coming back to find you waiting for me was just so appealing, I didn't want to put it off for ten days."

They stared at each other for one long, heady moment. Seth smiled, a slow, understanding smile. She wanted to make it work. She trusted their feelings enough to go with her heart instead of her brain. He could do no less. "We can travel to London together next week if you want," he suggested. "I've been thinking about it…. There's no reason I can't be my own boss, start a consulting company. Loosen up my schedule so we can travel together." He glanced down at Todd and grinned at the boy's wide-eyed anticipation. "All of us. As a family."

Jill nibbled her lip. "Uh, that's not an issue anymore. I'm not going to London. I'm not going to be the American Girl for Mother Nature's big, splashy European debut."

He froze. "What? Tell me you didn't give up your job…."

She shook her head. "Not exactly." Lifting Todd to sit on the back of the sofa, she grinned at them both. "But you know, the more I thought about it, the more I realized European women know quite a lot about beauty. Mother Nature's Natural Girl doesn't have a thing on some of those lovely, elegant women George Wanamaker wants to market to."

She glanced over Seth's shoulder, seeing something that made her smile. "It's time for the Natural Girl to grow up. With the target audience over there, the company needs someone to show what it means to become more beautiful with age. Someone to illustrate the sexiness and glamour of the older woman."

She nodded toward the television. Not yet understanding what she meant, Seth slowly turned and looked at the muted picture on the screen. Jill stood there, speaking into a microphone, surrounded by reporters. Flanking her on one side were the hospital administrator and a man Seth recognized as a doctor from Seattle Memorial. On the other side stood George Wanamaker and…*"Gina?"*

She chuckled. "Your mother is the perfect one to launch this campaign. They adore her over there. Did you know she's got an Italian fan club with thirty-thousand members?''

No, he hadn't known that. But he'd be willing to bet George Wanamaker did. He still couldn't take it all in. "How?"

She picked up the remote control and turned up the volume. "I called George from the airport. Gina, uh… happened…to be with him. The two of them have gotten very cozy, haven't they?"

Seth just continued to stare at the TV, watching Jill address the reporters. "You called a press conference?"

"It was very simple," she replied, plopping down on the sofa, keeping a gentle, balancing hand on Todd's leg. She patted the seat next to her, inviting Seth to sit down, too. "I met with George and Gina over lunch. We agreed that I'll continue here in the U.S., at least for another year or so until I figure out what I wanna be when I grow up."

He chuckled, taking her hand in his and squeezing it.

"Then I zipped back here to pick up a few things and call the hospital. We all met back at Seattle Memorial at five-thirty. Probably just missed you."

Yeah. She had. "Why? What was the purpose—"

"We knew the media was gathered there. And the hospital was looking for some good publicity for a change. My doctor thought the easiest way to dispel this drug rumor would be for me to admit what was really making me look thin and sick." She smiled, as if pleased with how things had turned out. "I agreed to work with the local diabetes foundation and my doctor agreed to let me have lo mein for breakfast a couple of times a year."

After she'd guarded her privacy so well for so long, he really couldn't believe she'd simply put her entire life out there for the media to dissect.

"You missed the part where we discussed my cancer scare. The hospital administrator mentioned my fund-raising efforts on behalf of cancer research." She nibbled her lip. "I stressed the importance of regular checkups after a return to good health."

He turned his attention back to the TV screen, watching as Jill pulled out the spiky blond wig she'd worn to the zoo last Saturday. They both fell silent, listening to her tell the press why she'd felt the need to disguise her identity when out in public with her own child, whom she'd conceived during her cancer scare five years earlier.

"God, Jill, you exposed yourself to them completely." His throat tightened.

"Yeah, and believe it or not," she replied, looking surprised herself, "I was shocked by the expressions of support and understanding from a lot of the reporters. They said they totally understood me wanting to keep my son out of the public eye. I guess there really is an unwritten agreement between celebrities and the media about trying to keep innocent kids out of the picture."

She flipped the TV off, though the previously recorded press conference continued. "Then George came on, expressing his company's admiration for their Natural Girl, and announcing their own donation to the hospital's research programs. Of course, he also introduced Gina, touting her as their big new European spokesperson."

"Bet she loved that."

She nodded. "Yep. She thanked George, then mentioned how wonderful it had been to work with me, someone who's so important to her *nephew,* explaining away those hideous photos from dinner the other night." Jill chuckled. "She didn't out you as her son."

No big surprise. He somehow knew Gina wouldn't want the world to know she was old enough to have a thirty-one-year-old son. "Do I want to know how I came into this whole situation?"

"Well," she explained, "I dug out an old picture of us

together, back in college. I explained that yes, you are the man in my life, and that no, it's nobody's goddamned business if we feel like kissing on my back porch."

He chuckled, knowing she wouldn't have put it in quite those terms.

Todd, meanwhile, stared at them wide-eyed. Seth wasn't sure if he was shocked by hearing his mother curse or by—

"You were *kissing?*" the boy asked in a near yell.

Question answered. Seth laughed. "Yeah. And get ready, buddy, because we're about to do it again."

Todd clapped his hands over his eyes, not watching as Seth drew Jill into his arms, kissing her with every bit of love and emotion of which he was capable. She tasted warm and sweet. Like home. Like forever.

When they drew apart, she whispered, "I love you. I've loved you for as long as I can remember."

"I love you, too," Seth replied. "And I always have."

They kissed again. Slowly, tenderly. Then she whispered, "I want the life we talked about when we were kids, Seth. I know it's later than we planned, and obviously we can't go about it the way we always thought we would. But I've got my career. Now I want the rest…you, children, a family, a real home."

Still not quite believing how much his life had changed in the past eight days, Seth could only nod and pull her back into his arms. He kissed her forehead, her temple, hiding a smile as he watched Todd peeking at them between spread fingers.

"I think today's press conference should help with the adoption agency."

He shrugged. "Even if it doesn't, I've got what I always wanted, Jill. You and Todd will be my family. Yeah, there's adoption, there's foster parenting, there's needy kids in Africa, there's surrogate mothers. Whatever. If it happens, it happens. If not, as long as I've got you two—" he leaned over to scruff up Todd's hair, knowing the bright kid understood every word they were saying "—I'll be the happiest man alive."

She tilted her head back, staring into his eyes as if determining whether he really meant it. "Truly? No spin?"

Laughing, he drew her tightly into his arms again, pulling Todd down on top of them until all three embraced in one warm, encompassing hug.

"No spin, babe. It's the three of us from here on out."

EPILOGUE

THEY WERE MARRIED twelve days later, on a windy, secluded stretch of beach flooded with brilliant sunlight that made the waves of the lake sparkle like liquid gold. Gina served as maid of honor, Todd as best man.

They spoke their own vows. They made their own silent promises. When they were pronounced husband and wife, they shared one long, knowing look of happiness, acknowledging the end of more than eleven years of wanting.

"You ready to go home, Mrs. Nannery?" he asked. The entire wedding party was looking a little blue around the lips on the cold, early November day.

She nodded and took his arm as they walked up the rocky slope to her house. Everyone else followed. Jill's parents and brothers. Seth's mothers—*both* of them—and his sisters. As well as a few intimate friends—George, plus Seth's elderly neighbor Rhoda, who hadn't seemed to mind being helped down the hill by Tony, Sven and Bjorn.

Reaching the deck, they heard the phone ringing as Seth unlocked the back door. Jill hurried inside to answer, figuring someone was calling with more good wishes. Seth and the others entered behind her, helping themselves to hot coffee and the spread of food a caterer had brought out this morning.

When she heard the woman's voice on the phone, she couldn't stop a sudden rush of excitement. "Seth!"

He immediately looked up, and she beckoned him over. "It's Mrs. Thomason."

One week ago, Seth's application to be an adoptive parent had been approved—with the single modification that Jill was his coapplicant. They'd been told the waiting list for a newborn, or for any child under the age of two, was extremely long. But when Seth and Jill had confirmed they would be happy to welcome an older child into their home, they'd been warned things could happen quickly. *Very* quickly.

"Yes, of course," Seth said into the phone. "Absolutely." He glanced at Jill and smiled. "We're definitely ready."

Seth continued to stare at Jill, his eyes full of love, happiness and excitement. Her heart literally skipped a beat.

Could it really be happening? Could everything she'd ever dreamed of having, and thought she'd be denied, simply be given to her in the space of a few weeks?

Everyone else grew quiet, seeming to sense the anticipation in the air as Seth finished the call. After he hung up, Todd was the first to approach him. He tugged on Seth's jacket to get his attention. "Was that the store that sells the kids?"

Laughing, Seth crouched down in front of the boy, though his eyes never left Jill's. Her heart was pounding like crazy in her chest, but she didn't ask what the adoption worker had said.

"Yeah," Seth told Todd. The two of them exchanged a slow smile. "How would you feel about having someone else to help us decorate our Christmas tree in a couple of weeks?"

Todd gave a thumbs-up. "Yes!"

Seth continued to speak to their boy. "You know, Todd, being a big brother is a huge responsibility, especially when you've got a baby sister to look after."

A sister. A girl. Jill started to cry, so overwhelmed with happiness, she couldn't help it.

"She's two and a half years old," Seth told a very intently listening Todd, as well as every other smiling person in the room. "And her name's Chelsie."

He slowly rose to his feet and reached out to cup Jill's cheek. She stopped even trying to wipe away her tears, letting them fall unheeded until they ran onto his fingers. She tilted her head, rubbing her skin against his, taking every bit of warmth, love and emotion he silently offered.

"Chelsie," she murmured.

Seth nodded. Then he lifted their little boy into his arms and held him on his hip. "Mrs. Thomason says Chelsie can't wait to meet her big brother, Todd." He leaned forward to press a kiss on Jill's lips, whispering, "And her mom and dad."

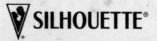

Escape into...

INTRIGUE™

Breathtaking romantic suspense.

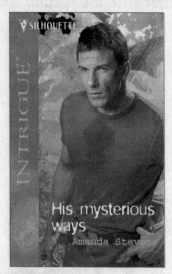

Romantic suspense with a well-developed mystery. The couple always get their happy ending, and the mystery is resolved, thanks to the central couple.

Four new titles are available every month on subscription from the

READER SERVICE™

Escape into...

SPECIAL EDITION™

Life, love and family.

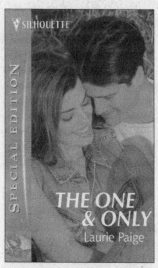

Special Edition are romances between attractive men and women. Family is central to the plot. The novels are warm upbeat dramas grounded in reality with a guaranteed happy ending.

Six new titles are available every month on subscription from the

READER SERVICE™

Escape into...

Sensation™

Passionate and thrilling romantic adventures

Sensation are sexy, exciting, dramatic and thrilling romances, featuring dangerous men and women strong enough to handle them.

Six new titles are available every month on subscription from the

READER SERVICE™